EMMA'S HUMILIATION

'Stop!' came a high pitched voice.

Horrified, Emma opened her eyes. My God! There, standing in the doorway and watching her reflection in the mirror, was Ali Efendi, his cane of office in his hand and his eyes blazing with anger.

'So are you ready now, eh?'

'Ready for what?' asked Emma falteringly, her eyes on the long whippy cane as, blushing, she took her hand away from her beauty bud and shamefacedly adjusted her caftan. She felt just like a naughty little girl, caught stealing sweets. Surely he didn't mean that he was going to beat her for misbehaving? She was the Prince's guest, staying in the guest house, not one of his harem concubines – not yet, at least.

A NEXUS CLASSIC

EMMA'S HUMILIATION

Hilary James

This book is a work of fiction.
In real life, make sure you practise safe, sane and
consensual sex.

This Nexus Classic edition 2004

First published in 1997 by
Nexus
Thames Wharf Studios
Rainville Road
London W6 9HA

www.nexus-books.co.uk

ISBN 0 352 33910 1

Typeset by TW Typesetting, Plymouth, Devon

Printed and bound by Clays Ltd, St Ives PLC

Contents

This, the fifth book in the Emma series, continues the erotic adventures of a young married woman in the world of lesbian love and domination. This time Ursula, Emma's terrifyingly ruthless Mistress, demands that she show complete obedience to a number of strict Masters, including an Arab Prince.

Prologue

(Taken from the end of *Emma's Submission*)

'Emma? Well ... She earns me a lot of money and Doctor Anna has made rather special plans for her, as soon as her husband goes off abroad again for one of his long trips away. But I suppose we could compromise. Let's see ... How long would you want her for? Why don't you simply see her on your visits to Europe? Anyway we can discuss that further on the way to the airport. I'm going off abroad myself shortly for a few days – though I haven't told Emma. Now let's get your baggage down into the car.'

Emma scuttled away, back to her room, her mind in a turmoil. They had been talking about using her as if she had no mind of her own – as if she was a mere slave. It was very exciting not knowing what was going to happen to her next, but this was too much!

She hardly knew which was a more frightening prospect: Doctor Anna or Her Excellency? Oh, what did the future now hold in store?

Suddenly the telephone rang. It was her private line – the one she used in the privacy of her bedroom to make her humiliating reports to Sabhu and Ursula. Hardly anyone knew the number. Who could it be? Hesitantly she picked up the handset.

'Emma?' boomed a man's voice.

'Yes,' she said nervously, looking at the door. Ursula would be furious if she learnt that she was taking a call from a man.

1

'Where the hell have you been? I've been trying to get hold of you for weeks!' boomed Henry's distinctive voice.

Henry! It was Henry, her former lover, before he went off and got married. Henry! The only man who had ever thrilled and dominated her in the same exciting way as Ursula. She felt a sudden tingling sensation running through her body.

'I suppose you've been off with that bloody bitch Ursula! Has she got her claws into you again? Locked you up in a chastity belt has she?'

How did he know? Henry always seemed to guess everything. 'Yes,' she whispered.

'Yes, what?' boomed the voice again. 'You call me sir – and don't forget it'

'Yes sir!' whispered Emma, giving a frightened look at the still open door. But the tingling feeling was growing stronger. Oh Henry! Why did you disappear? she thought.

'That's better,' came Henry's voice. 'Now listen carefully. I'm in a hurry. Meet me at my club in London for lunch next Tuesday. One o'clock sharp!'

'But –' Emma began to wail.

'No ifs or buts, just be there. And look pretty. Don't wear anything under your dress unless you're still locked in that bitch's chastity belt! See you Tuesday!'

The phone went dead.

Emma heard footsteps coming down the corridor. Ursula! Guiltily she hastily put down the phone, her mind more in a torment than ever. But the exciting tingling feeling was almost overwhelming.

'Now, Emma, come and say goodbye to your Mistress,' she heard Ursula call out.

Her mind in a whirl, Emma rushed out into the corridor and, with a sob, flung herself into her Mistress's arms.

'Oh you are being an affectionate little girl, Emma.

Are you going to miss your Mistress very much? Well, I'll see you in London as usual next week and meanwhile don't forget to make all your daily reports to Sabhu. And remember, no flirting with any man, or else!'

Oh my God, Emma was thinking, now what am I to do?

1

Emma

Emma was sitting alone on a large sofa in the ladies'
drawing room of Henry's club, sipping a gin and tonic.

Outwardly, she looked a sophisticated young woman,
smartly dressed, well groomed and very pretty, with a
slim, petite figure and lovely honey-coloured hair
brushed back in a stylish bouffant way. She had a
vivacious and self-confident air. Only her soft eyes
might have betrayed her secret and deeply felt masochis-
tic yearning to be utterly dominated and controlled – by
a man or a woman.

She appeared to be idly flicking through the latest
Harpers and Queen. Indeed she recognised many of the
people in it. She herself came from a well-known Irish
family and her husband John, dull scientist though he
appeared to be, was well-connected in the county in
which they lived. With her lively personality and out-
going ways, Emma had quickly made a hit there.

In fact, however, she was scarcely looking at the
magazine for her mind was in a turmoil of excitement
and anticipation as she waited for Henry to arrive.
Indeed the idea of meeting him after all these months of
being locked up in one of Ursula's cages – months in
which Henry himself had actually got married – was so
exciting that she had arrived an hour early to make sure
that she really had escaped, albeit temporarily, from the
clutches of Ursula.

She had thought she had done so when John had

4

recently returned from another of his long trips abroad. Ursula, of course, had then had to send her home. Thrilled, she had imagined that she would be free again. But Ursula had cleverly got Doctor Anna to send John a note saying that Emma had been seriously ill and was still too weak to carry out her conjugal duties. Instead, she would have to sleep in her own bedroom. This had enabled Ursula to keep Emma – still humiliatingly locked up in her chastity belt and under her control – apart from her husband, even whilst they were actually living under the same roof.

Moreover, the doctor had also said that Emma was too weak to run the house, and this had provided Ursula with the excuse to send a woman called Mrs Maunder, to act as housekeeper – and to keep an eye on Emma.

But that was not all, for only the previous week Ursula had brazenly brought a rich lady client, Her Excellency, the wife of an African dictator, to come and stay for a weekend in the country – and to enjoy Emma under the nose of her unsuspecting husband.

Oh, it had all been so embarrassing . . .

Oh, where was Henry? Why couldn't he arrive early like her? Would he ever have any idea of what she had gone through to get here at all?

First of all, she had had to lie to Mrs Maunder, saying that she was simply going out to lunch with a girlfriend.

Then she had been forced to repeat the lie on the telephone to a suspicious Sabhu, the terrifying Haitian whom Ursula employed to supervise and train her girls. She had waited until it was time to make her humiliating routine morning report to him and then, trying to sound casual, had just slipped it in at the end.

Like Ursula's other girls, Emma both hated and feared Sabhu – and the long dressage whip which he would use on them all at the slightest provocation.

'Mr Sabhu's such a nice gentleman,' Mrs Maunder would say.

But for Emma and the other girls there was nothing nice about this burly Caribbean giant with his cold, frightening, bloodshot eyes, nor about the contemptuous way he treated the European girls in his charge, nor the hugely embarrassing way in which he supervised and controlled their most intimate moments. Moreover, it was also hugely embarrassingly being trained, very explicitly, and by a man, to please Ursula's lady clients – especially by this brutal and uneducated Haitian.

What made it all the more worrying was that, in order to pay for her ticket to London, Emma had secretly had to use the travelling money that Sabhu had given her for her next weekly visit to Ursula's house in two days time. How was she now going to pay to go to London again later in the week? Should she simply ring Ursula and say that she had mislaid her travelling money and ask her to authorise Mrs Maunder to give her some more? Would Ursula smell a rat?

Certainly, there would be the most unholy row if Ursula ever suspected she had used the money to meet Henry! Lovers, or indeed contact with any male other than the dreaded Sabhu, were now forbidden fruit to Emma.

Ursula liked to take advantage of the fact that John, as a scientist, never seemed to have much money, despite having inherited a lovely Queen Anne house. She would therefore keep Emma short of money so that she was dependent on her fluctuating generosity, and so was always anxious to please her.

Indeed, Ursula had taken possession of Emma's cheque book and credit cards, saying that, as she paid the housekeeper and all household bills, especially when John was away, Emma would not need any money. And, even when she herself went away, she always checked Emma's bank statements when she got back.

6

To make it even worse, Ursula also liked to make sure that Emma had very little ready cash in her handbag. Just a little pocket money and travelling money. She had to account for every penny of it in a little cash book which either Ursula or Sabhu would examine and sign when she went up to London for her humiliating weekly trip.

Their idea, of course, was to make sure that she did not spend her money on fattening sweets or chocolates, and so upset the strict diet of yoghurt and fruit that Sabhu had kept her on whilst she had been in his cages, and which Mrs Maunder had instructions to keep her on at home.

Ursula's clients might themselves often be rather large ladies, but they certainly wanted slim young women for their pleasure!

2

Henry

Emma jumped. Her heart pounded with excitement. There, at last, coming towards her across the large room was her erstwhile lover, Henry! Tall and dressed in a well-cut, dark double-breasted suit, a dark blue spotted tie and well-polished black shoes with gold buckles, he was looking as handsome as ever.

Then, to her horror, Emma saw he was deep in conversation with a tall attractive woman. Henry, the man she was now supposed to be meeting, was with another woman! Was she his new wife?

Without a flicker of recognition from Henry, they walked past her and sat down on a large sofa just behind her.

Emma held her breath. What was it that Henry had said in his letter? *Be in the ladies drawing room at noon sharp and wait. Do not show any sign of recognition when I arrive. Just wait for instructions.*

For days she had been longing for this rendezvous. It had been so long since they had last met. Those awful months under Ursula's strict control – a control that was usually delegated to Sabhu, the terrifying Haitian keeper of Ursula's girls.

Now at last Henry was here, even though he was now married! Here she was, too, she thought, secretly meeting him – and yet she was still under Ursula's control. Moreover, highly embarrassingly, she was still locked into Ursula's flexible, and yet very effective, chastity belt, or Bikini-belt, as it was euphemistically called! She could not, she knew, get even a little finger through the plastic grille over her beauty lips, nor underneath it.

She knew well, of course, that Ursula did not insist on Emma and each of her other girls being locked into such a chastity belt merely to keep them frustrated. The belts had been cunningly designed not only as chastity belts but also as purity belts, specifically to meet the requirements of Ursula and her dominant lesbian friends. They all had a strong distaste for the mere idea of their girls becoming aroused or playing with themselves without permission – especially when they were pleasing them.

They wanted a girl always to be kept pure and virginal, and they certainly did not want the girl herself getting pleasure when exciting and stimulating her Mistress, no matter how much she was longing to share her Mistress's enjoyment.

A young nun devotes her life and her thoughts to bowing down and chastely worshipping, on her knees, the figure of Christ. So, too, Ursula insisted on her girls devoting themselves, whether they liked it or not, to worshipping her, also on their knees, but with their mouths applied to her beauty lips or nipples. She liked to have her girls trained to worship her as a kind and wonderful goddess, whose love they were constantly striving to earn, even though they knew deep down that they were unworthy of it.

Being locked into a purity belt, as Ursula regarded the Bikini-belts, was, Emma knew, an essential part of this complicated mental process.

But at least, Emma thought with a laugh, the purity belts were not only designed to control a girl spiritually. They were also very practical: she could spend a penny through the plastic grille over her beauty lips. Moreover, by pulling back the serrated edges of the two little plastic plates that formed a separate circle over her rear,

9

she could also, albeit rather humiliatingly, expose her little orifice and obey a call of nature.

The small plates were spring-loaded so that when released they snapped closed again. She remembered with embarrassment how Sabhu had taught her to hold one of them back with one hand whilst blushingly washing herself and the plates clean with the other hand – in the Turkish fashion, he had said with a callous laugh. Oh, how she hated him!

Indeed, she had learnt that she could safely be left locked into the belt, and thus kept both frustrated and pure, for days on end – even when away from Ursula and that horrible Sabhu. Although the belt fitted tightly over her body, it was cleverly designed to move with her body and did not rub.

Almost as embarrassing as the belt, which was padlocked round her loins, was the matching thick leather collar, studded like a dog's collar, which was secured by another little padlock behind her neck. The collar was joined to the Bikini-belt by a black leather strap that came up over her navel, divided under her naked breasts and continued up on either side to fasten to her collar at the shoulder. This arrangement cunningly raised her breasts, enhanced her cleavage and accentuated her nipples.

It was all very clever, but what would Henry say when he saw it? Oh, it was so embarrassing! She had begged Ursula again and again to take it off when she was at her home, but quite unavailingly.

'Certainly not, Emma,' Ursula had said. 'You're such a sensuous little girl that I can't trust you not to play with yourself. Anyway, I like to think of you writhing helplessly in your belt, from enforced frustration and purity.'

Yes, she thought, Ursula really seemed to understand the overwhelming psychological effect of being locked into such a belt; of always feeling it there; of always being aware of it; of always being kept not only chaste, but also pure and quite unable to touch herself.

'But my husband, John . . .' she had protested.

'You know very well,' Ursula had replied icily, 'that Doctor Anna has sent him a letter saying that you must sleep alone. You must arrange to keep yourself to yourself. And if I hear any more of your bleatings about being kept locked in a chastity belt, I'll tell Sabhu to give you a good thrashing,'

Emma had not dared to say another word.

Then there was also the humiliation of having to report once a week to Sabhu in London, even when Ursula was away, to have the belt temporarily removed whilst the grim-faced Haitian checked that her mound and beauty lips were completely smooth and hairless.

Oh yes, Emma told herself bitterly, Ursula understood only too well the abject humiliation and utter frustration that being locked into the belt caused her – and yet there was a thrill to be derived from feeling that, sexually, you were completely in someone else's power.

And now she was to experience the shattering embarrassment, but also unbelievable excitement, of meeting Henry behind the absent Ursula's back, whilst still locked into the belt.

Of course, on top of all this embarrassment and humiliation, Henry had actually turned up with another woman in tow – a woman, presumably his wife, to whom he apparently had no intention of introducing Emma. Obviously he found it all very piquant lunching with his wife in front of his mistress – and, thought Emma, a mistress who was locked into the chastity belt of her own Mistress.

Oh, how complicated life was. And how exciting! And how shocked all these other charming people here, in Henry's own club – or indeed Henry's wife – would be if they had an inkling of what was really going on under their very noses.

11

Whilst all these thoughts were racing through her mind, Emma sat quietly, not daring to turn round and look at Henry and his wife sitting on the sofa backing on to hers. She could just about hear that they were discussing a play that they had seen the night before.

Suddenly one of the club waiters came up and handed her a note. She recognised Henry's writing. He must have written it before coming to the club and then asked the hall porter to have it delivered to her now. Goodness, how Henry had planned it all!

She tore open the envelope.

As soon as you have read this note, you are to get up and, showing no sign of recognising me, you are to walk past where I am sitting and go out of the room. Then you are to go to our room, number 45, which has been left unlocked. You are then to put the 'Do not disturb' sign on the door. Then you are to lock the door – I have my own key.

Her heart racing, Emma read on.

You will find a tray with a sandwich and a glass of wine in the room . You are to have a bath and then by two o'clock sharp you are to crawl into the bottom of the bed, naked. When I arrive (my wife has another appointment for the afternoon), I shall only want to see a little lump curled up at the bottom of the bed. When I get into the bed you are to keep absolutely silent and invisible, lying between my legs, until I pull you up to worship my manhood. Even then, I do not want to hear another word, or even see you, whilst you are pleasuring me. If you are locked into a chastity belt, then so much the better, for I am not interested in your pleasure.

Emma felt a flash of anger, but she controlled herself.

12

After I have left, you are to dress yourself and leave.
Provided you have pleased me properly and humbly,
and provided you have remained out of sight and have
not said one single word, I shall leave five fifty pound
notes on the mantelpiece, as payment for your services,
and will ring your home tomorrow with further instruc-
tions. So do exactly what you are told, or you'll get
nothing!

Her eyes flashing, Emma put down the note. How dare
he treat her like this! Who did he think she was? A mere
slut – a call girl, summoned for his pleasure? She wanted
to turn round, to throw the note into his horrible
sneering face and to storm out of his damned club!

Then she began to simmer down. Two hundred and
fifty pounds! In cash! Emma had a vision of mounds of
chocolate truffles and Bentick's mixed centres, especially
the violet cream ones, and of slipping into a tea shop to
enjoy meringues and cream cakes. But then she remembered that Sabhu weighed her naked every week and
that the penalty for putting on weight was six strokes of
his terrifying long dressage whip for every extra pound.

It was a terrifying prospect. She would have to
control her craving for sweet things. Oh dear! But even
so it would be wonderful to have a secret little store of
cash that she could spend as she liked without having to
tell Ursula.

Two hundred and fifty pounds! Five fifty pound notes
that she could easily hide. And she could even use part
of it to replace the travelling money that she was
supposed to have kept for her journey up to London
again in two days' time when she was next due to report
to Sabhu.

It was all like manna from Heaven. At one stroke,
one of her most pressing problems had been solved.

Yes, she must have that money! But she'd only get it
if she remained humiliatingly hidden and silent under

13

the bedclothes. Well, perhaps after all, that in itself would be rather exciting – and the fact that she had not seen Henry for several months would make it all the more piquant and tantalising. Perhaps it would be rather amusing to play the role of an anonymous call girl, keen to earn her due payment.

Moreover, if she did as he said, then he was going to ring later with further instructions – and it would be too frustrating not to know what he had in mind! Thank heavens he wasn't going to write, for Mrs Maunder intercepted all her letters and sent them on to Ursula to read first. She could imagine the row that would ensue if Ursula found out that Henry was writing to her.

Instead she would be waiting all day in her room for him to ring her on her private number. This had no extension, so Mrs Maunder would not be able to listen in. It would all be so exciting, both now and tomorrow – and one in the eye for Ursula!

Yes, she decided, she would do as he said.

She stood up and smoothed down her silken dress. She blushed as, under its loose pleated skirt, she felt the soft leather of the tight-fitting Bikini belt and, under her scarf, the leather collar to which the belt was attached. Momentarily she put her hand on to the small of her back and then on to the back of her neck and felt the little securing padlocks – the padlocks to which only Sabhu had the key. What would the nice, well-dressed couples in the room think if they knew about them?

She saw Henry turn around for a moment, look her up and down and then turn back to his wife. Had he noticed her touching the padlocks? Was that why he had devised a scenario that enabled her to give him both physical and mental pleasure, despite the belt and its collar? What would his wife think if she ever learnt the truth?

Slowly she walked past them both, her head in the air and her heart pounding. Then without a word or a backward glance she left the room.

14

Emma's heart was in her mouth as she walked along the corridor looking for the number 45, desperately trying to keep her high heels from tapping on the floor and drawing attention to her. She tried to put on a nonchalant air, just in case a maid saw her and wondered what she was doing there. What on earth should she say if she were challenged? 'Just looking for the ladies' sounded horribly weak.

Then she saw the number on the door. She put her hand on the door handle. It was unlocked. With a gasp of relief she slipped into the room and closed the door, and paused to catch her breath. Goodness, this was certainly all very exciting! She saw the 'Do not disturb' notice and, quickly opening the door again, hung it on the outside handle.

Then she looked round the room. There was a large double bed, with a heavy bedspread. Good! It would help disguise a little creature curled up at the bottom of the bed.

But what caught her eye were the silver ladies' hair-brushes and expensive Elizabeth Arden make-up on the dressing table, and all the women's clothes hanging in the cupboard. So Henry really was staying in this room with his wife! He really was going to meet Emma here, surrounded by his wife's nightdresses and underclothes!

But supposing his wife came in unexpectedly? Supposing, indeed, she came in now, returning to look for a handkerchief? My God! Hastily, Emma bolted the door. But was that the answer? In any case she would have to remember to unbolt it by two o'clock sharp.

Henry was really putting her through it! And the swine would now be tucking into a delicious lunch, flirting with his wife and quaffing the club's excellent claret so as to be in good form for Emma!

She remembered that his note had mentioned a glass of wine and a sandwich. She looked around, hungrily. Yes, there on a tray were the remains of Henry's and his wife's little elevenses. She was really being made to feel like a hired servant, or a dog, gobbling up the remains of her Master's meal. And his wife's!

How dare he treat her in this way! But, she had to admit, the food was jolly good all the same – and, as was usual with Henry, it was all very exciting.

Emma was still highly excited when she ran a bath. She found some bath salts and, as she lay back relaxing in the scented foam, she wondered what to do to titivate herself. But why bother, she thought, if she was just to remain hidden under the bedclothes? But such was her pride that she knew she would still use his wife's make-up to make herself look lovely.

Drying herself and coming back into the bedroom, she saw a large bottle of Madam Rochas scent. His wife's! All right, if that's what he liked, she'd use that too! She began to spray it liberally all over herself. Revenge!

At last there came the noise of a key in the lock of the door.

Emma could not help giving a little tremble of excited anticipation as she lay in the dark under the bedclothes. She could feel herself becoming moist with arousal underneath her belt. Oh, how she longed to be able to touch herself! Oh how she hated Ursula's belt!

Then she heard the door being locked again and a man's footsteps coming slowly in the direction of the bed. There was a rustling noise as he paused to undress himself slowly. Oh the excitement! After all this time!

She was about to call out to him to hurry, then she remembered that if she said one word she would lose the money. Hastily, she bit her tongue. Then at last she heard footsteps slowly approaching the bed, and then veering away from it as if he was looking for a book to read. He was even humming a little tune as he did so. God Almighty! Come on! She could hardly prevent herself from screaming out aloud.

At last she heard the sheets being pulled back. There was a glimmer of light and she felt a little draught of fresh air on her bare body. Then she felt a hairy male leg being pushed down on one side of her and then the other equally hairy one on the other side.

After months of having to please women – wealthy women with soft, scented, well-cared-for skins – the contrast with this rough-skinned, hairy male was almost overpowering.

Suddenly she felt his hand reach down and grip her hair, then heard him snap the fingers of the other. This was Henry's familiar but still humiliating signal for her to commence operations.

She put out her tongue and began to lick her way slowly, very slowly, up his leg. The smell of Henry filled her nostrils. Then gradually she approached his even more hairy manhood. He raised his knees and obediently she began to lick underneath his scrotum – in the way that, she knew of old, drove Henry almost mad with delight. She heard him give a contented moan and felt his whole body jump slightly.

She continued to lick, but now used fast little movements, keeping her lips pursed. Again there came a moan of deep pleasure and again his body jumped a little. Oh, what a clever little slut she was!

She reached up with the tips of her fingers to where her tongue was wriggling to and fro, and very gently began to tickle him. Again came the moan and his whole body seemed to jerk. What an accomplished little tart she was, she thought, as well as being a slut!

She could feel his manhood surging into erection against her face, but the giving of pleasure like this was having its effect on her too. She could smell her own arousal under the bedclothes. Oh, how she longed to reach down and give herself a little relief. Oh, how cruel both Ursula and Henry were.

She felt the hand on her hair pulling her head forward

17

and upward, and again there was a commanding snap of Henry's fingers. His manhood was now under her eager mouth. Humbly, as if worshipping a god, she began to lick it up and down, whilst keeping the tips of her fingers busy on the underside of his testicles.

She could feel his manhood growing and growing, until it seemed ready to burst. She took it into her mouth and sucked, dutiful and slave-like, her head rising rhythmically up and down in the dark, under the bedclothes. It was exhausting, but she knew she had to go on. She felt his whole body tense and then suddenly she felt him explode into her mouth.

With a natural grimace of disgust, she tried to take her head away, but the hand gripping her hair held her there, held her steady. Held her so that she had to swallow every drop. It was horrible and slimy, but it was also somehow madly gratifying.

Then, bracing one of his big feet against her pert behind, Henry pushed her back down to the bottom of the bed.

Emma lay there, now quite still, under the bedclothes, whilst Henry appeared to be taking a little nap after his exertions. She could not believe it. The indifferent swine! Not one word of thanks, of kindness, or even of recognition. Was this satiated male beast really Henry? She longed to wriggle up under the bedclothes and take a look, but the two strong legs kept her down at the bottom of the bed.

Suddenly, she felt him getting out of the bed. She heard the noise of water splashing in the bathroom and then the rustle of clothes being quickly put on. She heard him brushing his hair and putting on his shoes. Then, without a word having been spoken by either of them, she heard him unbolt the door and step out into the corridor, leaving her alone in the room.

Lying under the bedclothes, she could not help but

18

begin to sob with disappointment, and with frustrated lust.

My God, she suddenly thought, his wife might come back at any moment! She rushed out of bed, washed her face, dressed and put on fresh lipstick. Hastily she looked in the mirror. Fine! But her money? Her precious money!

She looked on the mantelpiece. There, under a book, were five new fifty-pound notes. She thrust them into her bag and fled, feeling utterly outraged. Henry was just a swine, a damned selfish swine, a self-opinionated swine, a – anyway, a swine!

But, by God, he knew how to wind her up and leave her in a state of wild excitement. Just like Ursula!

3

Sabhu

Sabhu rubbed his hands contentedly and lay back on the bed in his comfortably furnished room in Ursula's London house.

Yes, he was thinking, this is the life! It was certainly infinitely better than life back in the primitive village in his native Haiti in which he had been brought up. It was even better than life as a respected animal trainer in the circus where he had been in charge of schooling and breeding the various performing animals – dogs and monkeys, as well as dangerous big cats.

It was there that Miss de Vere had seen his act and had afterwards asked to see the animals in their cages. She had then offered him a well-paid job as a trainer and keeper – not of animals but of young women, European women – her girls.

To actually be paid to do what he had always dreamed of doing – disciplining and training white women! Wonderful! Not surprisingly, it was an offer he had accepted with alacrity.

Miss de Vere's only proviso was that he must not use the girls for his own pleasure. But this did not worry him. He got his kicks from subjugating women, rather than actually ravishing them! And in any case there was always Babindu, Ursula's attractive Afro-Caribbean housekeeper. Indeed, she had only just left his room!

He was a big, strong-looking man. His sheer size and strength, coupled with his hard-looking, bloodshot eyes,

20

bristling short-cropped hair and unsmiling face, combined to give him a frightening countenance. He did not seem to be a man who would stand any nonsense – particularly from any European women in his charge.

He had just finished inspecting and depilating 'Number Four', as Emma was called, in his preparation room. To bring her into line with the other girls, he had also painted the figure '4' on her forehead for ease of identification by the clients.

Earlier on that day, she had arrived up from the country for her weekly inspection, and also to be put to work pleasuring Ursula's clients. She had, as usual, handed Sabhu her duly completed daily record book for his scrutiny and signature.

He laughed as he thought how, even when she was at her home and outwardly appeared to be a free and happily married woman, he was still exerting strict supervision over her, on behalf of his employer, Miss de Vere. Every morning and evening Emma had to ring him with an intimate account of her natural functions and body temperature, and enter them in her book, ready for his weekly inspection. Any errors or omissions and she faced a thrashing.

All this, of course, was not only to enable him to keep a check on her health and on her monthly cycle, important though these were. Equally crucial was the psychological effect that having to report to him and being kept locked into her Bikini-belt had on her. She still felt subjugated, and that she was under his control and discipline, even when she was living in her own home.

Miss de Vere had warned him to keep a close eye on Emma as she did still tend to hanker after men, and he was damned well going to make sure that she had no opportunity to remove her chastity belt and go running after them! Her only aim in life should be to please her

Mistress and her Mistress's clients, and he was going to see to it that she did just that. He regarded ensuring Emma's continuing faithfulness to Ursula as a personal challenge.

He had stripped her, and had then unlocked the little twin padlocks of her Bikini-belt at the small of her back and the back of her neck, and he had laughed as he had seen her previously compressed beauty lips open up like a flower. But then he had had to weigh the now naked young woman to check that she had not put on any weight.

Emma had been trembling as he had done so, knowing that the punishment would be six strokes for every pound she had put on. Sabhu, for his part, enjoyed beating this stuck-up young woman and had felt rather disappointed that, to her great relief, her weight had not changed!

Then, parting her beauty lips, he had carefully, and humiliatingly, checked that all was well. Consulting his own detailed notes, which he had made in a book marked 'Number Four', he had checked that her monthly cycle was in order, and then double-checked against Emma's own daily record book. These girls could be such liars! He wanted to make quite sure that her graph of her twice daily temperatures was complete and corresponded with his own record of her cycle – about which he would later report to Doctor Anna.

Then he had turned to her record of her natural functions, making sure that she was still healthy, and that her written account tallied with the daily reports she had made by telephone, which he had transcribed in his own notebook. He had asked Emma several embarrassing questions about all this, enjoying the blushing girl's obvious humiliation as she answered them, while standing naked in front of him.

This was always the part of Emma's weekly inspection that he enjoyed best, for the girl was well aware that the punishment for being caught out as having made an incorrect entry, in either her daily record book or in her daily telephone reports, was six strokes. Not until Sabhu was fully satisfied with her answers would he finally countersign her daily record book. He always enjoyed the feeling of power as he kept the nervous young Irishwoman waiting, trembling with fear, her eyes on the long dressage whip hanging from his wrist.

Then, after he had felt her breasts and the rest of her body, he had made her stand quite still, and had twice covered her mound and pouting beauty lips with his burning hair-removing lotion whilst she bit her lips with the pain. Finally he had applied his special soothing cream. Standing back to admire his work, he had smiled approvingly as he had seen that her entire pubic area was now completely soft and bald.

After replacing her belt and closing the twin padlocks again, he had checked that the number '4' painted in red on her forehead was now dry. Next he had made her brush her hair and make up her face and eyes. Satisfied that she was now looking like a pretty and heavily made-up little numbered tart, he had fastened on to her the heavy wrist and ankle manacles that so excited the clients.

Then he had clipped a lead on to her collar and had led her, crawling on all fours, up to the attic, where he had put her back into her usual cage. She was now ready to be shown off to the rather special client that Ursula had lined up for her.

Sabhu lay back on his bed and glanced at the large closed circuit television monitor. He had set the controls so that the camera would scan automatically up and down the line of half a dozen numbered cages situated along one side of the large bleak attic with its bare brick walls. A button on the remote control unit lying by his bedside enabled him to zoom instantly to any cage that caught his attention.

23

The bright lights illuminating each cage, together with the optical fibre link to the camera upstairs, ensured that the pictures on the screen were clear and sharp. They showed how the strongly barred roofs of the cages were too low for a girl to be able to stand up; instead she had to crawl around in her cage on all fours like an animal.

The screen also showed how each of the equally strongly barred floors was covered by a thick rubber mat, and how the cages were raised several feet above the floor of the attic to give a better view of it, and its contents, to anyone standing outside.

The rubber mats sloped down gently to a little shiny metal grille near the front of each cage, underneath which was a white enamel collecting tray from which a small clear plastic tube ran away to a drain in the corner of the attic. This enabled a girl's liquid wastes to be regularly collected for testing. But the sloped rubber mat and drain were also designed for the twice daily showers that Sabhu gave each girl, through the bars of her cage, with a high pressure hose – just as he had washed the animals in the zoo. Sabhu was very strict about cleanliness.

The cages were only about four feet wide and four feet deep, so the girl inside had to lie curled up on her mat. The sides of the cages, like the back, were made of rough brick. This was not only to prevent the girls from escaping, but also to stop them from being able to touch or even see each other and in particular to prevent them from playing with each others' nipples, or worse!

Shut up in their cages, Sabhu considered, the girls should be thinking only of how they might give more pleasure to their next client, and thus avoid punishment from his long dressage whip. He certainly did not want them smiling at each other or trying to form forbidden relationships. Indeed, he liked to see them just silently gripping the bars of their cages, or playing innocently with the dolls which had been issued to each of them to bring out their maternal instincts.

Having nothing else to do except wash, dress and change these beautiful little baby dolls, they soon became, like little girls, very attached to them. Indeed, it all made for a charming sight and one which often delighted a client looking down at the cages from the viewing gallery. Certainly the clients liked the sight of half-naked and grown-up young women being treated like little children – or, caged as they were, like helpless animals.

The front of each cage was barred like the roof and floor, but had a small hinged door in its centre. This ensured that a girl had to enter and leave her cage on her hands and knees and could not therefore rush out of it. Instead she had to crawl out of it with her head down, ready for the lead which hung from the front bars to be fastened to her collar. Sabhu always liked his women to be kept on a lead when taken out of their cages, and also kept them crawling on all fours – again, just like his circus animals.

As Sabhu well knew, this treatment played an important part in impressing on these women their subservient status – a status which, despite all the humiliations they had to suffer, or indeed perhaps because of them, they masochistically soon learned to enjoy.

Each barred door was kept prominently locked by a large padlock. Hanging from the bars of each cage, next to the lead, was the form on which Sabhu recorded, as he had just done for Emma, details of the young women's natural functions while they were resident in the attic. It also showed on a graph the progress of their monthly cycles, illustrated by their daily morning and evening temperatures.

These were taken when, in response to the simple order 'Buttocks!', each woman would turn in her cage and then, like a team of well-drilled performing animals,

25

they would all put their heads to the floor and press their raised bottoms against the bars of their cages. Then, at the command 'Expose!', they would all reach back with their hands and, as they had been humiliatingly taught to do by Sabhu, part the serrated edges of the small semi-circular plastic discs that were sewn into the back of their Bikini-belts to guard access to their little rear orifices, and now blushingly expose them. Then, when he was finally satisfied that all was ready, Sabhu would go down the line of cages inserting his well-greased thermometers.

Sabhu grunted with satisfaction as he saw on the screen that the large padlock for each cage was properly in place. He smiled to himself at the thought that, even if a girl did somehow manage to unlock her cage, she would not be able to escape without also getting past the door to the attic which had an electronic lock for which she did not know the combination. Moreover, the door had been specially strengthened with iron bars to prevent a girl from trying to wrench it open.

Sabhu laughed aloud. No, there was no escape for the women in his care!

He smiled as from the monitor's loudspeaker came the chinking of chains mixed with soft little moans, as the girls crawled about their low cages, occasionally silently gripping the bars and peering out – just like the monkeys used to do in their cages in the circus.

The girls were not allowed to talk to each other in their cages, nor indeed anywhere else, though he did not object to little animal-like grunts, barks, or purring sounds.

Sometimes he would press the button that automatically played soft background music in the attic to relax the girls in their cages, just as he had often played similar music to calm the caged wild animals at the circus. But he was careful to keep the level of sound down, for he did not want to stop the sensitive micro-

26

phone that hung down in front of the cages from picking up any attempt by the girls to speak to each other.

But for much of the time, as now, only the clinking of the girls' heavy chains broke the silence in the attic.

The girls never knew whether or not Sabhu was listening from another room. However, they did know that, like the pictures recorded by the watching closed circuit television camera, the sounds picked up by the microphone were being continuously taped. They also knew that the punishment for being caught talking was the usual six strokes of his long dressage whip and that the microphone was so sensitive it would detect the slightest forbidden whisper.

Whereas the circus animals in Sabhu's charge had been free within their cages, the women wore iron manacles, each pair linked by two feet of heavy chain, locked on to their wrists and ankles. It was these chains that were chinking with the girls' every movement. They were only taken off when, as a special treat, the girls were taken outside the house for a little fresh air and exercise – but always, of course, under Sabhu's careful supervision.

The continual rattling of the chains and their sheer weight, the sight of the large padlocks on the little barred doors to the cages, and the design of the cages themselves, all combined to play an important psycho-logical role in constantly reminding the girls of their abject status – as did the microphone, the ever-watching television camera, the humiliating Bikini-belts, and being deprived of contact with any man, except for the dreaded Sabhu.

Indeed, the sight of the half-naked and silent girls, manacled in their padlocked cages, was highly erotic – especially when seen from the little viewing gallery to which Miss de Vere liked to bring her clients. It was a sight that served to excite the clients greatly and this, in

27

turn, helped to ensure the profitability of Miss de Vere's new enterprise – and the size of the tips that the delighted clients gave to Sabhu.

The stark bleakness of the cages in which the girls were kept, and indeed that of the whole attic, with its bare brick walls and wooden floor, contrasted sharply, as was intended, with the comfortable and elegant opulence of the rest of Miss de Vere's house.

It was a scene that reminded Sabhu of the similarly bare cages behind the grandiose ring of the circus in which he had been an animal trainer. They too had been barred at the front and on top with solid sides and rear walls. They too had been raised up and enclosed in cases on their mobile trailers. They too had had a drain in the floor of the cage for liquid wastes. They too had been well lit to show off their occupants to interested visitors.

At the circus, he had trained caged animals to perform to the crack of his whip. But how much more rewarding it was now to train Miss de Vere's caged young ladies to do the same thing! Just as he had then liked to see the animals cringing in front of him, so he now enjoyed the sight of these intelligent white women similarly cringing.

Moreover he enjoyed treating them like little girls who were only to be seen and not heard, and who dared to open their mouths only in reply to a question from him or a client. Even then, scared of being whipped for 'impudence', they always called him 'Mr Sabhu' or 'sir', and a client 'madam'.

Yes, he certainly kept them all well disciplined!

Each girl was wearing a pretty little velvet cape, short enough to expose her intimacies and buttocks, and prominently embroidered with Ursula's 'U de V' monogram as well as with the girl's own number. The young women were, as usual, naked under their capes – except for their heavy manacles and Bikini-belts.

Sabhu smiled as he thought about the way in which

28

the belts were cleverly designed to ensure both a girl's chastity and purity and yet also to allow a lady client to obtain great pleasure from a girl wriggling under her. The pleasure came from the studded rubber pad at the front of the belt which covered a plastic grille, which in turn covered the wearer's beauty lips. This pad was cleverly attached to the sides of the plastic grille with velcro so that a girl could raise her pad to spend a penny through the grille without being able to touch her intimacies.

The pleasure she gave to her client could be further increased, thanks to the little vibrator built into the pad which a client could switch on with a little key. Moreover, the client's pleasure, Sabhu knew, would be made even greater by the knowledge that the obediently wriggling girl would not be feeling anything beneath the plastic grille. These Bikini-belts were indeed very cleverly designed!

Of course, if a client wanted to feel the girl's own little shorn beauty lips wriggling beneath her, then, for a small extra charge, the belt could always be removed. However, this was not something that Sabhu encouraged for there was always the risk that the client might let the excited girl climax – and keeping the girls almost continuously frustrated was an essential part of Sabhu's way of keeping them desperately eager to please their clients.

He liked to make the relief of climaxing a special secret treat for a girl, a treat that had to be earned, a reward for really good and obedient behaviour. For this reason, he kept in his own record book for each girl a note of the date on which she had last been allowed to climax, and details of exactly how she had done so.

Sabhu regarded himself as the guardian of each girl's purity. There was more to this than merely ensuring that they never had an opportunity of being with a man, and training them to dedicate themselves to serving women.

29

These white sluts were such lascivious little creatures that, given half a chance, they would be constantly unfaithful to their Mistress, committing what he regarded as adultery by playing with themselves or with each other.

4

A Touch of Sabhu's Discipline

Sabhu looked at his watch – it would soon be time to
give the girls their midday meal of just a little yoghurt
and sliced fruit. He wanted to keep their bellies nice and
empty, so that they could concentrate in the afternoon
on pleasing some important clients.

Early that morning, having been taken, crawling out
of their cages, they had been ordered to squat, their
hands clasped behind their necks, over a line of pretty
little brass bowls, each of which was placed on a
correspondingly numbered red spot on the floor of the
attic. Then, taking care that they were correctly positioned above the little bowls, but not actually touching
them, they had had to show Sabhu that they were
concentrating on holding back the serrated edges of the
little plastic semi-circular discs in the back of their
Bikini-belts, just as they had to do whenever he took
their temperatures whilst they were in their cages.

This time, though, standing behind them and holding
their leads, he had kept them waiting rather longer than
normal, making them crawl forward or backward until
they were in a perfect line, whilst in silence each girl
desperately tried to ready herself for what was to follow.

Finally, obedient to a sudden crack of his whip, they
had all simultaneously performed into their little brass
bowls, each of which had been half-filled with rose-
water. It had been the usual frightening and humiliating
performance for the straining women, with Sabhu

31

watching them all carefully from behind, holding their leads taut in one hand and his raised whip in the other. It had also been a simple way for him to assert his complete authority over the women in his charge.

Not until he had humiliatingly cleaned each of them with his sponge, for he was fastidious about such things, had he allowed them to release the plastic plates that guarded their rear orifices. Then, one by one, he had locked them up again in their cages.

And now it was time to allow them to spend a penny. This was something which they could, in theory, do whilst still in their cages, but they were too well trained and too frightened of his whip, to dare to do so without his permission. Moreover, making them all again perform together to his command was, once again, an ideal way of stamping his authority on them. But, he thought, as he lay back on his bed, he really could not be bothered this time to go up to the attic.

He picked up the microphone by his bed. 'Sluts!' he cried.

Hearing his usual preliminary warning order, the girls all put down their dolls and straightened up in their cages. Yes, they were a well-disciplined lot! They would all be wondering, he knew, what they were now going to be made to do. Except for Number Four, all of Miss de Vere's girls were foreigners who spoke little or no English. They had therefore to be trained to recognise and obey a limited number of simple words of command – with a little help from his long dressage whip!

'Capes!' There was a rattle of chains as each girl unfastened the neck strap of her cape.

'Off!' he ordered and each girl obediently slipped her cape off her bare shoulders and hung it up carefully on a hook on the right-hand side of her cage. He liked things to be uniform and coordinated at all times.

'Position!' The girls were all now kneeling up at the front of their cages, their manacled hands gripping the bars. Their Bikini-belts were well displayed and their bare breasts pressed through the gaps between the bars. Their eyes were submissively lowered. They made, he felt, a perfect picture of disciplined white womanhood.

Sabhu chuckled as he saw how the naked breasts of two of the girls, Numbers Two and Five, held and supported by the divided strap that linked their Bikini-belts to the sides of their collars, were showing the distinctive blue veins and prominent nipples of a woman in milk.

The two girls had been specially sponsored. Miss de Vere liked to offer her richer clients the opportunity to sponsor a girl to be put into milk, with the client paying more as Sabhu coaxed the girl's breasts into producing a steadily increasing flow.

The two girls had been brought into milk, to their own amazement, thanks to a course of Doctor Anna's special pills – another miracle of modern medicine, with which she was said to have had experimented whilst serving as a medical officer in an institution for young female political prisoners in the former communist Eastern Europe.

There was, he knew, no lack of rich clients willing to pay to sponsor a girl of their choice in this way, and the more milk the girl produced, the greater was his tip from her delighted sponsor. Although, of course, such a girl's milk was primarily reserved for her sponsor, in her absence, other lady clients were only too delighted to pay extra for the services of a lactating girl. Indeed, Miss de Vere herself frequently enjoyed their services.

He laughed to himself as he remembered how simple it had been. After the two girls had been selected and the clients had paid the initial sponsorship fee, he had discreetly slipped Doctor Anna's pills, ground to powder, into one girl's yoghurt. He hadn't even bothered to take such trouble over the other girl; he had simply told her that they were vitamin pills. Soon the unsuspecting girls had been mystified to find their breasts excitingly filling out and firming. Forbidden to talk in their cages, they had been unable to discuss it with each other and had been astounded when their now swollen breasts had started to produce milk.

Sabhu smiled again, remembering how, earlier that morning, he had, as usual, bound the two girls in their cages so that they were kneeling up, with their breasts thrust through the bars and their hands fastened above their heads so that they could not interfere with what was to happen next.

Then he had wheeled his portable milking machine up to their cages and had fastened its rubber suckers on to each pair of nervously quivering nipples. How the girls had learnt to love its slow sucking and pulsating action! Indeed, they now loved being in milk and being taken downstairs on a lead by Sabhu, their manacles clanking, to offer their milk to their sponsor – or, better still, to their beloved Mistress.

He had found the machine excellent, initially for quickly bringing on the milk of the girls after they had been sponsored, and later, used every morning, for ensuring a good flow – and for measuring it.

It was also amusing to see how proud the girls themselves were of their state, and how they competed against each other to produce the most milk – and the sweetest – with each one anxiously awaiting her Mistress's verdict after she had tried out each individual offering with her morning coffee and muesli.

Neither could Sabhu help laughing as he saw the extraordinarily elongated nipples of one of the girls in milk, Number Five, and those of another girl, Number One. Unknown to them, both had been sponsored to have their nipples lengthened – with the delighted client paying more for each half centimetre that Sabhu achieved.

This was also a technique that Doctor Anna was

alleged to have perfected in her prison camp days –
fitting over the nipple a little rubber tube attached to a
rubber bag which on being squeezed produced a vacuum which drew out the nipple to a quite extraordinary
extent. Initially, to get the right effect, Sabhu had kept
the rubber tubes on for half an hour twice daily, with
the girl blindfolded so that she could not see what was
being done to her, and with her hands again chained
above her head to prevent her from interfering with the
process. But twice a week was now sufficient to keep
them the right length.

It was a technique that delighted other clients almost
as much as it pleased the sponsor herself. They would
willingly pay more both to watch it being done and to
enjoy a girl who had been sponsored in this way. And
as for the girls concerned, they were partly ashamed at
what had been done to them, but also a little proud of
having nipples so much longer and more prominent
than those of the other girls!

Sabhu stopped the camera when it zoomed on to
Number Three. Then he regarded her with satisfaction.
There was no sign of any regrowth on her exotically
glistening bald head.

She had been sponsored to have her head shaved and
then to have it kept shiny and bald. It had been quite a
scene as, in front of the delighted sponsor and the other
girls, he had carefully shaved off the sobbing girl's long
hair and had then applied a stronger version of the
burning depilatory paste that he used on the girl's
mound and beauty lips – an application that he repeated
weekly.

Headshaving, too, was a treatment that made a girl
very popular, not only with the sponsor and with Miss
de Vere herself, but also with the other clients as well.
Not only was it a highly erotic sight, but many clients
felt that a shiny bald cranium gave more intense pleasure when gripped between their thighs than one covered

with long hair. Indeed, the sponsor was happily paying for each month for which the girl was kept perfectly and beautifully bald.

The sponsor had been even more delighted when Sabhu had subsequently tattooed a large figure '3' on to the girl's now hairless cranium, to match the number painted on her forehead. She and the other clients might not be able to see a girl's number painted on her forehead as, manacles clanking, she crawled between their legs and humbly started to pleasure them. But now, whether they were sitting up in an armchair or lying back in bed, they would, when they chose Number Three, have the excitement of looking down and seeing her number prominently tattooed on the top of her dutifully nodding and carefully polished head, as she applied her tongue to their excited, swollen beauty buds.

Sabhu then chuckled cruelly as he saw the pretty red crest of a bird that a sponsor had paid handsomely to have tattooed on to the front of the thighs of the girl in cage 5.

The sponsor had also wanted to have her initials tattooed there, but Miss de Vere had refused – unless the client had been willing to buy the girl outright. As it was, the tattoo made an attractive way of further identifying the girl for a client ringing up to make a booking. It was much easier to ask for the girl tattooed with a bird than to remember that her name was 'Number Five', and only the sponsor knew that the bird was her own private mark.

Sabhu interrupted his thoughts and stopped the camera as it panned to the cage marked '4' – the one containing Emma. Originally she had been subjected to the full rigours of being caged and trained, but now that her husband had returned, she only came up from her home once a week to be checked over and depilated – and, of course, to be put to work.

Indeed, the opportunity was taken as often as was

practical to put Number Four back into her cage and offer her to a client, to 'earn her keep', as Miss de Vere put it. She would also, thereby, earn Sabhu a substantial tip from the delighted client, or else face a thrashing. She was outwardly a well-disciplined young woman and was certainly scared of his whip, but Miss de Vere had warned him about her continuing to lust after men. All in all, he was never quite sure whether he could trust her – any more than he had been able to trust the many wild caged animals he had broken in and trained in his circus days.

Miss de Vere demanded total submission from her girls, but Number Four did not always seem to accept being in the power of her dominating mistress. Half the time, Sabhu felt, the girl resented both Miss de Vere and himself, and was longing to escape from their strict control. But, he laughed to himself, he would make certain that she never did!

He shook his head, disappointedly, as he looked at her pert little breasts. They seemed to be crying out for the gentle but substantial expansion that he would achieve if they were brought into milk. Moreover it would help her to settle down and accept her subjugation. Ah well, perhaps one day!

'Prepare to –' he ordered, and paused. He was pleased to see how each girl was straining to hear and understand his next instruction. '– Perform!' he commanded in a brisk tone of voice.

Recognising the word and looking embarrassed, each girl parted her knees on either side of the little metal grille over the drain hole in the rubber mat at the front of her cage. Then there was a ripping noise as each girl used her manacled hands to loosen the velcro fastenings that kept her studded rubber pad down between her legs and over her Bikini-belt.

'Up!' he ordered and each girl lifted up the rubber pad to reveal a white plastic grille over her beauty lips.

37

'Muscles!' he ordered. Each girl, still holding up her rubber pad, now obediently closed her eyes and concentrated on relaxing her muscles so that she would be ready to perform the instant he ordered it. Each one knew that woe betide her if her terrifying overseer noticed the slightest delay in her flow – or, for that matter, a premature little dribble.

Such was their fear of Sabhu's whip that the fact that he was not actually present, but simply commanding them by remote control, did not affect their instant obedience to his orders.

'Stand by!' There was a pause. Sabhu smiled as he saw that several of the girls were biting their lips as they strained to hold themselves back. What a wonderful way of enforcing discipline this was! He picked up his whip and raised it.

Suddenly, the girls heard on the loudspeaker the distinctive crack of their dreaded keeper's whip. It was the signal that they had been trained to wait for, for Sabhu liked to see them move and perform to the crack of his whip.

Instantly, the television camera and the microphone relayed the sight and sound of six little fountains trickling through the white plastic grilles down on to the rubber mats, then through the little metal gratings set into each of them. Down again they flowed into the collecting trays, and on via the transparent tubes to the drain in the corner of the room.

Sabhu quickly trained the television camera on each girl in turn. Checking that her flow was satisfactory, he put a little tick in the individual notebook he kept for each of his charges. Doctor Anna liked him to keep a full record of all the girls' performances – of every type.

Nonchalantly he pressed the music switch on his control box and instantly, the noise of soft gentle background music came over the loudspeaker, picked up by the microphone in the attic. After their stressful little performance, it would do the girls good to be relaxed by a little music. It was, he knew, this frequent contrast between relaxing and performing that kept them on their toes – just as it had kept the animals in the circus on theirs.

5

Emma in the Cage

A few minutes later, the heavy chain of Emma's wrist
manacles chinked as she again knelt up and gripped the
solid bars of her cage. Except for her Bikini-belt and
manacles she was naked, but the controlled temperature
in the centrally heated attic prevented her from feeling
cold. How shame-making it had been – all the girls
being remotely controlled by Sabhu to perform simultaneously in their cages, like trained animals, and
monitored by the ever-watching television camera. It
was even more humiliating being made to do it by a
man, a mere servant ... but deep down she also knew
that it was very exciting.

Oh, how she hated being put back into her cage, under
Sabhu's strict supervision, as part of her weekly visit,
after he had finished inspecting and depilating her. Oh,
how she hated the heavy wrist and ankle manacles being
put back on her – and yet, once again, how exciting!

She glanced at the little mirror fastened to one of the
walls that formed the side of her cage, and saw the large
figure '4' neatly painted on her forehead. Oh, how
humiliating! And how thrilling!

The mirror was made of metal rather than glass, as
though she and the other girls could not be trusted to
use something so potentially dangerous if broken – just
as they were not allowed knives and forks but had to eat
in their cages with their hands or with a harmless
wooden spoon.

Oh, how dreadful it all was. But then she remembered how all this, the manacles, the numbers, the wooden spoons and, indeed, being put into a cage at all, had all been ordered by Ursula, her Mistress. It all made her feel like a slave – and a slave under the orders of a cruel black male overseer. Did she, perhaps, secretly really love it all? Did the other girls secretly love it all, too? Well, she must do, or else she would not have come back to Ursula's house that morning to submit herself to Sabhu's discipline. Or was it just that, with that horrible Bikini-belt locked on to her, she simply had no other option? Oh, how complicated life was!

But then how equally dreadful, and yet equally exciting, was the humiliation, when she was at home, of having to telephone her twice-daily intimate reports – especially to a man, especially to an uneducated Haitian, like Sabhu. How she hated having to fill in her daily record book to hand to Sabhu on her arrival, so that he could check both her health and her monthly cycle.

How she hated having to stand, shamefacedly, up on a bench in front of him, not daring to say a word except in answer to one of his embarrassingly searching questions, and then peppering her reply with 'Mr Sabhu, sir', terrified that he might otherwise take offence at her tone and angrily thrash her for 'impudence'. She just had to stand there in front of her overseer, scared stiff and yet somehow also thrilled, with her head up and looking straight in front of her, her hands clasped behind her neck, her legs apart and her knees bent, so that he could more easily inspect her body.

Then, while he kept her standing there and aware of the whip in his hand, he would study her daily record book, comparing it with his own records of her twice-daily telephone reports. Occasionally, he would fire off a stream of questions in his rough half-French, half-Caribbean accent. It was a terrifying procedure, and she

41

knew that she would get the whip if he was not fully satisfied with her entries and responses.

It all seemed miles away from the sophisticated world of Henry and his wife, and the people in his club. Henry himself might well understand why, masochistically, she allowed Ursula to exert such an extraordinary degree of control over her life. But, for his wife and the other people she had seen in his club, what had just taken place would be just simply unbelievable in London, and in this day and age.

It was not merely, she reflected, that she loved to be strictly controlled and dominated, but now there was also the uncertain anticipation as to what was going to happen on each of her weekly visits. She would, she knew, have 'to earn her keep', as Ursula so bluntly put it.

Certainly, she thought, the cost of paying Mrs Maunder, the housekeeper that Ursula had put into her home, and of her journey up to London and back, must all add up. That was why, she presumed, Ursula liked to offer her as a rather special item to her more discerning and richer clients.

To whom, she wondered, would she be on offer today? Another of Ursula's overseas visitors? They would always pay more if they first saw her caged and manacled. Pay! Pay Ursula and, she thought bitterly, give a good tip to that swine Sabhu – but not a penny would come to her. Of course, she would also be made to compete against the other caged girls. She would have to try hard to attract the attention of any clients that Ursula brought up to the viewing gallery, or else risk a thrashing from Sabhu.

But being chosen by a client was not the end of the story. She would then have to concentrate on really pleasing the client and on obeying her every command, or risk another thrashing from an angry Sabhu who had not received his customary large tip.

What Emma really longed for was to be chosen by Ursula for her own pleasure, but then so did all the other girls, as they were equally besotted with their fantastic and cruel Mistress. Oh, how jealous she would feel when Sabhu took one of them down to Ursula for a little after-lunch pleasuring! Kneeling in her cage and gripping the bars in silent rage, she would imagine what would be going on in Ursula's bedroom as, still locked into her chastity belt, the girl would be ordered to apply her tongue to her Mistress' beauty bud.

Then later, she would equally hate it when the chosen girl, tossing her head proudly, would be led crawling back into the attic by Sabhu and put back into her cage. Oh, she would feel, I could have given my Mistress so much more pleasure than that girl – or any of these other ones!

The other girls! Oh, how she longed to be able to see them and to exchange little whispered confidences. It was so unfair never being able to talk to each other in the cages, being made to feel so isolated. She could only hear the rattle of their manacles as they moved about their own cages. She thought of them all as her friends, even though they were also her competitors – and even though they seemed to be constantly changing as Ursula brought in new blood for Sabhu to train and for her clients to enjoy.

What happened to the ones who disappeared? She had never managed to find out. Had they been sold to clients whom they had particularly pleased? She had once asked Sabhu and he had angrily given her six strokes of his whip for impertinence, and then told her that it was none of her business.

Earlier on, whilst being put back into her cage by Sabhu, she had caught a glimpse of another new pretty face staring at her through the bars of the end cage, the one marked '6' – like the number painted on the girl's forehead. Emma gathered that her real name had been

43

Sofia – what a pretty name! But, poor thing, now she was just Number Six, as Emma herself was now just Number Four.

She wondered how the girl had been trapped by Ursula. Had she, too, been ensnared by Ursula's obvious wealth and sexual blandishments? Had she, too, been lured by Ursula's almost incredible ability to make pretty young women become besotted with her? Besotted, just as Emma herself had been – and still was! And as all the other girls still were!

Poor thing! Had she, too, thought she was starting a lovely life as Ursula's pet companion, only to find herself being turned over to the tender mercies of Sabhu? Well, she too would now have to settle down to a life of being kept frustrated in a chastity belt, and of being kept manacled in a cage when she was not being taken out to please one of Ursula's rich clients. As she was such a pretty girl, it would not be long, Emma guessed, before she was in demand for sponsorship of one kind or another.

Meanwhile, there would be the humiliation of being taken down every morning by Sabhu with the other girls to the small gymnasium in the basement for a period of strenuous exercise under his whip. There would also be the even more humiliating intimate training periods in which Sabhu would teach her exactly how to please women and to obey instantly the standard words of command printed in English on the lists used by the clients.

Had Sofia yet got used to never seeing or hearing another man, other than Sabhu? Had she yet got used to being put on a lead, like a little dog, whenever Sabhu took her out of her cage? Had she yet got used to living in constant fear of his long dressage whip? Had she yet learnt that he would use it on any girl showing the slightest sign of recalcitrance, or even of dumb insolence – never mind any sign of embarrassed hesitation when made to perform her natural functions in front of him and simultaneously with the other girls.

She would also soon learn that he would use his whip if he ever felt that a girl was not doing her utmost to attract a client when paraded for her inspection, or if the girl did not do her utmost to please a client who had chosen her.

Poor thing, indeed! Emma had once noticed how, looking scared stiff, Sofia had shrunk back in her cage, her manacles clanking, when Sabhu had come up to it. Did she have any idea of what she was in for? Or did she perhaps, like herself, also secretly find it all wildly exciting?

Emma longed to speak to the girl, but the walls separating the cages prevented them from even smiling at each other. Then, of course, there was the strict no talking rule in the attic, enforced by means of the sensitive microphone that hung down in front of the line of cages. It was connected to a tape recorder as well as to the loudspeaker in Sabhu's own room. One little whisper and Sabhu would come and take the girls concerned out of their cages and thrash them.

Sabhu only allowed the girls to play with their dolls, or, as a special treat, to look at a children's nursery picture book. Hence, deprived of conversation and of access to the radio, television and newspapers, and only occasionally taken out for a carefully supervised little walk in the fresh air, the caged girls had no idea of what was going on in the real world outside. Instead, as Emma knew only too well, the women, kept relaxed by the soft background music, and never seeing or hearing a man other than Sabhu, lived in a totally artificial world of their own. It was a world dominated on the one hand by their love for their wonderful mistress, and on the other by their fear of Sabhu's whip.

That clever swine, Sabhu, Emma realised, just wanted each girl to be alone with her thoughts. He knew that they would be thoughts of how she could best attract and please a client or, if she was lucky, her beloved Mistress, and so avoid another thrashing from her terrifying overseer by earning him another good tip!

Emma also longed to hear how the girls who, to use Ursula's cruel euphemism, had been 'sponsored' in various ways by rich clients, were getting on. It must have been an awful shock for two of them to find themselves mysteriously in milk and not allowed to ask how it could have happened. And how awful for the girl who had been been sponsored to have her head shaved – and for the girls whose nipples had been elongated, and for the girl who had had a sponsor's crest tattooed on to her thighs.

It must all, she realised, have been very exciting for the sponsors and for the other clients. And indeed, how exciting, in the unreal world of Ursula's cages, for the girls themselves.

It would all be part of the power game that Ursula and her clients so enjoyed playing with young women. Indeed, the power to select a girl for sponsorship, and then to watch her subsequent progress, must indeed be thrilling.

Sponsorship in its various forms was also a threat that was always hanging over her, too, but was it really such a frightening threat? Might it not, on the contrary, be an exciting way of coming closer to her Mistress? Certainly, it must be an astonishing feeling to be in milk or to have one's nipples elongated, and she could always wear a wig back at home if they decided to offer her for sponsorship to be made bald! But how could she explain away a prominent tattoo?

Back at home, of course, the mere idea of any such sponsorship sounded quite appalling. But here, kept in the artificial environment of the cages and of pleasing Ursula's lady clients, it seemed quite different. Here, it seemed quite natural, and even thrilling, for a slave-girl to be used in these ways by her Mistress!

46

Indeed, every time she came to London, she found herself being overwhelmed with jealousy as she watched Sabhu leading a sponsored girl out of her cage and then proudly taking her downstairs to be paraded in front of her Mistress and her sponsor. Oh, how she hated the sight of a chosen girl being led, crawling on all fours, past the other girls still in their cages, her nose disdainfully in the air, her manacles clanking, and her now heavy breasts or elongated nipples swaying. It was a sight that, as was intended, made Emma and the other girls jealously long to be sponsored, too!

It was probably, she reflected, the fact that she was a married woman with a house and a husband – albeit one who was rarely at home – that had saved her from being sponsored so far. But for how long? One never knew what clever plans were being mulled over in Ursula's fertile brain – or being discussed with the clever Doctor Anna. Certainly money would be no object, for the sponsorship payments might be very large – payments, of course, to Ursula, not to poor Emma!

The thrilling fear that she might, unbeknown to herself, have already been chosen for sponsorship by a rich client was with her always. She knew, even if those other girls had not, that Sabhu, or even Mrs Maunder, might at any time start mixing Doctor Anna's ground-up pills in with her food. She knew that on any day she might find her breasts strangely growing and producing milk. She knew that at any moment Sabhu's clippers might be applied to her head or his vacuum device to her nipples.

She knew that a proud sponsor, her friends and other clients, and indeed Ursula herself, would find any of these changes wildly exciting – and that, just like the other girls, she would, too.

Once again, she thought of the people in Henry's club, and of her own friends in the country. How horrified and astonished they would be by all this. In the real world outside it would indeed all seem ridiculous and even distasteful, but not here in the dream world of Ursula and her cages. Here it all seemed different, almost natural and inevitable.

Indeed, here she found herself constantly dreaming of discovering herself to be in milk and of being made to give the milk from her swollen breasts to Ursula, or to – No! Yes! To Henry!

Henry! What on earth he would say to all this?

Being such a cynical cad when it came to women, he would probably laugh and say it served her right for letting herself get involved with Ursula and her secret world.

Henry! Oh, Henry! Her train of thought had changed completely, now.

Oh, how she was longing to meet Henry again. But how on earth could she get out of her belt and join him next week?

She could still remember his every word when he had telephoned her the day before: 'Go to Gatwick in a week's time, next Thursday at three o'clock in the afternoon and go to the desk of the French airline Inter Air. They will have a ticket waiting for you. And don't forget to bring some cool clothes and your passport. If that bitch Ursula has confiscated it, then get a temporary travel document from your local Post Office. No arguments. Just be there!'

No mention of where they were going – just 'go to Gatwick'. No mention of how she was going to escape Ursula's strict surveillance – just 'be there'!

Thursday was, coincidentally, the day when she would be next be up in London to report to Sabhu. But how could she escape from him? And how would she get out of her belt? Oh, it was all so impossibly difficult, and yet so exciting.

Oh, Henry! You've just no idea of what awful situations you get me into! Or did she really just get herself into them by her ambivalent attitude towards Ursula? Oh, why couldn't she simply face up to making a clean break, for once and for all, with Ursula, with her cages, her awful Sabhu and her unremitting control over every aspect of her life? Yes indeed, why not? But deep down she knew that she never could.

The truth was that Ursula was like a drug. Emma simply could not give her up, and when she tried to do so she soon found herself crawling back to her, like a naughty child. She hated Ursula, just like she hated that swine Sabhu, but there was a difference. She was also besotted with Ursula!

It was, she realised, all a strange and unreal dream world. Ordinary people walking or driving past Ursula's apparently innocuous house would never imagine what went on in it. Even nice normal people visiting Ursula's house to see her pictures, or to discuss the progress of one of her pet charities, would never guess that up in the attic was a line of silent, caged and manacled young women nervously, and yet also excitedly, waiting to be chosen to please clients of a different sort.

Dream world or not, the fact was that being under Ursula's control had been just about the most exciting thing in her life.

But now she longed to go away with Henry – and damn the consequences.

6

Ursula

Ursula was smiling as she ushered the tall Maharani into the warm little attic viewing gallery.

The aristocratic Indian lady had a gracious air and was wearing a beautifully embroidered sari of scarlet silk. It contrasted vividly with Ursula's own discreet black business suit.

Ursula herself, a tall, angular figure, with short dark hair cut in a masculine style, a hard looking face and steely eyes, might have been a successful business-woman, or a rich and dominant lesbian who stood no nonsense from her girls, or even a rather exotic foreign artist. She was, of course, all three.

The viewing gallery was under the high side of the sloping roof of the attic and looked down on the line of cages and the little display area in front of them. Unlike the bleak cage area with its brick walls and bare wooden floor, the gallery was comfortably furnished with armchairs surrounding a small coffee table on which was a tray with a cut glass decanter of dry sherry and several tall sherry glasses.

Ursula politely offered the Maharani a comfortable chair and poured her a glass of sherry, but she was clearly so overwhelmed by the erotic sight before her that she hardly noticed. Ursula smiled. This was the normal reaction of a new client, and one that augured well. The Maharani, she knew, was extremely rich.

Indeed, Ursula saw that the Maharani could hardly

take her eyes off the raised row of small cages, each of which contained a pretty white girl, naked except for her Bikini-belt and her heavy wrist and ankle manacles. Each girl was silently looking up at the viewing gallery as she knelt up, gripping the bars of her cage with her chained hands.

Western women, chained and caged! And one had even had her head shaved! Her erotically bald cranium was glistening under the bright light that illuminated her cage.

Her eyes widened further as Sabhu stepped into the arena. He was wearing his circus animal-tamer's costume of black leather boots, tight white breeches that set off his jet-black skin, a tight sky-blue jacket festooned with gold lace, and a peaked military cap. He was also holding a long dressage whip with a little red loop at the tip. His black skin and brightly coloured uniform contrasted sharply with the near nakedness of the white women and their black leather Bikini-belts.

Sabhu bowed towards the Maharani and then turned to the cages. 'Show respect!' he shouted, cracking his whip.

The women silently flung themselves down on to the floors of their cages, their manacled hands positioned on either side of their heads, with the heavy chain across the backs of their necks, their foreheads touching the rubber flooring, their long hair – with the obvious exception of Number Three – flung forward over their heads and their little bottoms, encased in the soft leather of their Bikini-belts, raised high in the air.

A strong feeling of pride of ownership surged through Ursula as she looked down on to the line of humbly prostrated young women. They were all hers! She owned them, body and soul! She used them for her purposes and prevented them from having any contact with men other than the frightening Sabhu.

Moreover, thanks to the Bikini-belts, she also

51

controlled their sexual urges, keeping them pure and innocent until she or a client decided otherwise. Quite apart from the tremendous feeling of power that came from controlling their sensuality, she just could not tolerate the idea of one of these sluts being free to play with herself. In any case, it was much more exciting for Ursula herself, or for one of her clients, to have a girl lick her whilst she was physically prevented from giving herself relief by the tight enclosure of her beauty lips.

Ursula laughed at the thought that, whereas there was no counting the number of times she herself enjoyed an orgasm, Sabhu kept an exact record of the dates of the rare occasions on which her desperately eager girls had been allowed to climax.

She laughed again as she saw the erotically shiny bald head of Number Three. Yes, these girls were hers to do with as she liked. Oh, how exciting it was, having such power – wildly exciting! There was just nothing like it!

And as for the girls themselves?

Who cares, Ursula thought, what the little sluts felt! She certainly felt no remorse for the way they were treated. Indeed the greater the discipline these girls were subjected to, the more they all adored her!

Ursula laughed again as she thought how easy it was to find highly-sexed young women who quickly became so besotted with her that they willingly entered her service. Usually, they were Eastern European girls, scarcely speaking any English, lost in Western Europe and completely dependent on her. But she also enjoyed English girls – or well educated Irish girls, like Emma, she thought with a smile, who had married into good English families.

She was certainly adept at spotting a young woman who, like Emma, secretly longed to be controlled and dominated, and to have all her decisions made for her. So many women, as Ursula well knew, were masochists at heart. Her girls, she laughed to herself, might not always enjoy being kept caged here and disciplined by Sabhu, deprived of any contact with any other man, and known by just a number, but they were certainly being controlled and dominated beyond their wildest dreams!

Moreover, before entering her service and being turned over to the tender mercies of Sabhu, each of her girls, including Emma, already seduced by her and carried away by her commanding ways, had willingly signed a humiliating contract. It was this contract that reduced the girl to the level of a numbered, nameless slave, with her Mistress being able to do whatever she wanted with her.

The girls were not legally Ursula's slaves, of course – in this day and age, slavery had been abolished. But, to all intents and purposes, they were just as much her adoring slaves as had been the concubines of a Turkish Sultan.

Although the girls would not have understood the significance of the wording, the contract also mysteriously specified that in return for the Mistress taking the girl into her unpaid service, the girl agreed that her Mistress 'could accommodate and feed her in any way that her Mistress might decide, could ensure her purity, could arrange for her to give her services to a third party, or allow her to be sponsored by a third party for any purpose that her Mistress might in her wisdom decide upon, and could at her sole discretion dispose of the contract to a third party.'

The Mistress also had the right to 'take any steps necessary to ensure that any such services or sponsorship were duly completed to the satisfaction of both herself and the third party.'

Thus, like real slaves, the girls were effectively hers to use for both her pleasure and her profit. They were hers to thrash, or have thrashed, at the slightest sign of disobedience or sulkiness. Hers to have slimmed down or fattened up. Hers, above all, to have trained and put to work to earn her large sums of money by pleasuring her women clients, or by being sponsored for the titillation of one wealthy client or, perhaps, even by being sold to her.

Yes indeed, the feeling of power that came from having complete control of these attractive young women was very exciting!

Like the effective overseer he is, Sabhu certainly keeps my girls well disciplined, Ursula thought, as she continued to look down at the line of women still silently grovelling in their cages. What a relief it was being able to leave their day-to-day supervision to him. Perhaps his native Haiti's strong historical links with the slave trade had somehow given him an instinctive idea of the duties of an overseer, and of how slaves should be treated. Certainly, she could rely on him to cope with their monthly cycles and to keep them fit, well trained and submissive, and also beautiful, wellgroomed and eager to please both herself and her clients.

Like herself, her clients wanted both beauty and instant obedience in a girl. With Sabhu's help, this, and the occasional opportunity for different types of sponsorship, was precisely what Ursula so profitably offered.

What was the secret of Sabhu's success? The answer, she knew, was the way he disciplined her caged girls, and trained them to earn their money by performing tricks, just she had seen him discipline and train the caged animals at the circus – and all through fear of his whip! His real name was Aristide Beaumarchais, but at the circus he had been given the name of Sabhu, and Ursula had asked that he keep it on when he had come to work for her. It sounded so suitable!

How lucky it was too, Ursula reflected, that Sabhu and Doctor Anna got on so well, and had such confidence in each other's different abilities. Certainly Doctor Anna's previous experience in a women's prison had thrown up some fascinating possibilities for her and Sabhu to work on together.

When communist rule had collapsed, Doctor Anna had thought it best to flee to to England. Here, as an another confirmed lesbian, she had met Ursula who had helped her to establish a thriving private practice, specialising in looking after the kept girls of rich older women, and indeed men, of different nationalities. Ursula and her girls formed an important part of this practice and, moreover, one that often enabled Doctor Anna to make use of her accrued experience.

Of course, Sabhu was an overseer and not a trained male nurse, but he had quickly learned the basics of everyday nutrition and gynaecology from Doctor Anna, just as he had learned the simplest rudiments of veterinary medicine at the circus. He could therefore be safely left to keep the girls healthy and, much to their embarrassment, to cope with their minor female complaints and any problems arising from their sponsorship or extra sponsorship.

Doctor Anna could also be certain that, when she periodically inspected Ursula's girls, Sabhu would produce comprehensive daily records of each girl's health and intimate functions.

Ursula again glanced down at the line of cages to check that Emma was in cage Number Four, as was usual on a Thursday. She had already decided that Emma would be the ideal girl for the Maharani. She nodded in approval as she saw that Sabhu had fastened the heavy wrist and ankle manacles back on to her, and had painted the figure '4' on her forehead. These all played an important and erotic role in exciting clients, as well as in making a girl accept her subjugation.

It was annoying, of course, that Emma's husband was now only going abroad for short periods, which meant Ursula could no longer keep Emma caged in the attic on anything like a permanent basis. With her blonde beauty, Emma had always been very popular with the clients, especially those who were visitors from overseas.

But the embarrassing twice-daily telephone reports to Sabhu, the humiliation of having to fill in her daily record book for his subsequent inspection, and the presence of her Bikini-belt all helped ensure that, although she was now living at home, she still felt as controlled and disciplined as when she had been kept here, with the other girls, manacled in her cage.

Ursula smiled at the thought of how, with a little judicious encouragement from Sabhu's whip, Emma had turned out to be a good little money earner. And now that she only came here once a week, it was normally important to make sure that she was offered to more than one client – or, even better, booked by several of them in advance!

Today, however, in view of the potential importance of the Maharani as a new client, or even perhaps as a potential sponsor, Ursula had given orders that Emma was to be kept free for her alone.

Sabhu turned back towards the viewing gallery and bowed again. The Maharani gave a little burst of delighted applause.

Then Sabhu turned back to the cages. 'Up!' he ordered.

There was a noise of rattling chains as the six women now knelt up straight, their manacled hands gripped behind their necks, their elbows back, their chins raised, their knees and their manacled ankles parted, their eyes fixed straight ahead, and their full breasts quivering.

The Maharani took a sip from her glass of sherry and then gave a little gasp of excitement as she saw that, judging from the large size of their breasts and the blue veins visible on them, two of the girls appeared to be in milk. One of them, and another girl, had nipples which had been excitingly elongated, and what seemed to be some kind of crest had been tattooed on to the thighs of another!

Ursula mused that she had always liked to have a

little coterie of adoring, pretty and well-disciplined young women around her and in her power, and had made enough money to indulge her fantasies. She was a very successful artist, mainly known for her pictures of half-naked nubile young women, for which she used her girls as models. She had also enjoyed offering her girls to her friends. From that it had only been a small step to charging her clients for their use – and what a success that had proved!

Of course, the great financial success of the venture was at least partly due to her not having to pay the girls themselves anything. Ursula kept for herself the large fees she charged for the use of her girls and, of course, the much larger ones she charged for sponsorship.

Moreover, with the girls being kept half-naked in bare cages and fed on just yoghurt and fruit, her expenditure on them was minimal.

This new enterprise had more than made up for the drop in sales of her pictures during the recession. It had also been very enjoyable. But now she was under pressure from art dealers around the world to hold exhibitions again. Not surprisingly, she was hesitant about giving it all up and concentrating purely on her pictures once again. Then again, another of the joys of having Sabhu in charge of her girls was that it gave her time to paint.

Ursula looked down again at the erotic sight of the manacled Emma kneeling up in her cage. The fact that she was a married woman had made her seduction and subsequent caging, and, of course, maintaining strict control of her when she was at home, all the more exciting and challenging. Indeed, Ursula always felt a wonderful feeling of power surging through her at the idea of actually enjoying the wife of an unwitting man – and of putting her into a chastity belt to prevent her from sleeping with her husband! The fact that the husband, in his innocence, actually asked Ursula to look

57

after his wife whilst he was away abroad made it all the more piquant!

She frowned at the notion that Emma was probably still attracted to the male sex – men were strictly out of bounds for Ursula's girls. But she was confident that Emma was now too scared of Sabhu's whip to try to get up to any of her old tricks!

Ursula turned to look at the girls whose swollen breasts were in milk, her eyes lingering on Number Five's specially elongated nipples. Yes, it was a joy having an experienced overseer who knew how to handle her girls even when they were going through the initial mystery and excitement of different types of sponsorship.

Here, too, she could rely on Sabhu playing a key role when an often unsuspecting girl was being prepared by Doctor Anna to be offered to a rich client for sponsorship of one type or another.

It was a role that would continue afterwards when, to the delight of the sponsor, and indeed of Ursula, and to the astonishment of the girl herself, her milk would, almost immediately, be brought on artificially, or else she would find that her nipples had been strangely elongated.

The sponsor would find it unbelievably exciting to have the naked girl pleasure her. Pushing the girl down on her knees between her legs she would grip her by her head whilst she licked and sucked, as she had been humiliatingly trained to do by Sabhu. Not only would the physical pleasure be intense, but so, too, would be the mental pleasure as little glimpses of the girl's swollen breasts, or elongated nipples, or of the number tattooed on to her shaven scalp, or the crest tattooed on to her thighs, would remind the sponsor of what she had paid to have done to the girl.

The feeling of power experienced by such a sponsor would, Ursula knew only too well, be almost overwhelming. And if the girl did not fully understand what was happening to her, then it would be all the more exciting. The sponsor would feel like a god. A god with the power of life itself!

Meanwhile, of course, Ursula herself would also be enjoying the sponsored girls. She might, for instance, in a sponsor's absence, sit a lactating girl on her knee and enjoy her delicious, rich milk straight from her breasts. Moreover, although a sponsor and her friends would be given priority over the use of 'their' particular girl, other clients, too, would happily pay considerably extra for her services – and would bring *their* friends along!

Meanwhile, the Bikini-belts would ensure that the girls were kept in a state of purity, until their sponsors decided otherwise.

Yes indeed, Ursula laughed to herself, sponsorship of different kinds certainly played an important role in her operation. It was both wildly exciting and deeply satisfying to women like herself – the very apogee of a mistress's power over a helpless younger woman, and something that her clients would pay handsomely to enjoy.

Ursula smiled again as she remembered that she was planning to travel out, next week, to see a villa she had taken for a month on a privately owned small island in the Aegean. She would be able to complete several paintings there, and several of her clients and sponsors were planning to come and stay, with the intention of enjoying her girls. Once everything was ready, Sabhu would bring the girls out. Indeed, they were already thrilled at the thought of getting away from their manacles and from the cages in the attic – and at the prospect of their hated Bikini-belts being removed.

How wonderful, they were thinking, it was going to be to have a lovely comfortable bedroom overlooking the sea and the freedom to excite themselves whenever they desired.

Ursula had not had the heart to tell them that it

would not be lovely bedrooms that awaited them there, but rather a line of dog kennels in the garden of the villa, each with its own attached collar and chain. And neither did she mention that, once they had safely arrived, Sabhu would quickly be putting their Bikini-belts back on!

As Emma's husband was still around, it would be too problematic to take her out to the island with the other girls. No, she would have to stay behind, living at home, but still locked into her Bikini-belt to make sure that she behaved herself, and was kept frustrated and longing for the return of her Mistress!

Although there would be no clients visiting the house the following Thursday while Ursula was away, she saw no reason why Emma should not report to Sabhu as usual for a final depilation and inspection before he came out to the island.

7

Emma is Chosen to Please a Client

Ursula snapped out out her reverie and turned to the Maharani. 'Would you like any of the girls to be paraded for you?' she asked, her fluent English pronounced with a distinct Slavonic accent. 'We have a good selection of girls here, of different ages and types of beauty.'

The Maharani's eyes glistened.

'The girls all come from different countries, but I think you said you were particularly interested in finding an upper-class British woman?'

'Yes!' replied the Maharani speaking with emphasis in her sing-song Indian accent. 'I'd love to come back and try out the others another time, but what I really want now is to humiliate a girl from the race and class that so dominated us in India for two centuries. I was brought up to admire them and they seemed almost god-like figures. How exciting it would be now to humble one of them by making her pleasure me!'

'Then, in that case,' said Ursula with an innocent smile, as if she had not been planning this all along, 'Number Four is just the girl for you! Although she's not an aristocrat and is Irish by birth, her husband – the man she chose to marry – is very much from the elite class that went out to rule India.'

'Her husband!' queried the astonished Maharani. 'You mean she's a married woman and yet she comes here to be offered to other women?'

'Yes,' laughed Ursula, 'she certainly does, though her husband thinks she just comes here to study art!'

'Better and better!' murmured the Maharani

Ursula turned and called down to Sabhu, 'Parade Number Four!'

Sabhu bowed and went up to the cages, unlocked the padlock on Emma's cage, and opened the little barred door. 'Number Four!' he ordered, 'Out!'

There was a clinking of chains as Emma crawled out of her cage.

Sabhu reached down and snapped Emma's long leather lead on to the ring at the back of her thick leather collar. Then, holding the lead in one hand, he stood back and, with his other hand, cracked his whip. 'To your spot – go!'

Pulling on her lead like an eager little dog, Emma now scuttled on all fours to her red spot in the display area just below the viewing gallery. The spot, like her forehead, was marked with the figure '4'. Once there she assumed what Sabhu called the Position of Respect, with her hair flung forward, her forehead to the floor and her little bottom raised, whilst he stood behind her, keeping the lead to her collar taut.

Ursula looked at the Maharani. Once again the Indian woman's eyes were glistening as if she could not believe what she was seeing – the humbling of a manacled upper-class woman by a foreign overseer who was holding her on a lead. The Maharani was used to treating her own lower caste Indian servant girls as if they were mere chattels, but this was something more – much more.

'Stand-by for inspection,' ordered Sabhu in his harsh voice. There was a pause. The Maharani saw Emma tense her body. Then suddenly Sabhu cracked his whip. Like a well-trained animal obedient to the whip, Emma jumped up, raised her head, and fixed her eyes on the wall below the gallery. Then she parted her manacled ankles slightly, bent her knees, clasped her manacled hands behind her back and, pursing her lips, stuck out her little pink tongue. This was another of the positions Sabhu had taught her to assume on his command.

'She's certainly very well disciplined,' said the Maharani admiringly, turning to Ursula.

'Yes, we aim to please,' replied Ursula with a laugh.

The Maharani saw how the soft black leather Bikini-belt around the girl's hips, with its diamond shaped cutouts, contrasted with her white skin. She wondered about the black rubber pad prominently displayed over the girl's beauty lips and admired the thick leather collar – studded like a dog's – round her neck. It was joined to the Bikini-belt by a black leather strap which came up over her naked belly, divided under her quivering bare breasts, and continued up on either side to fasten to her collar just above the shoulder.

How cleverly, Ursula thought, this simple arrangement raised the girl's breasts, enhanced her cleavage and accentuated her nipples. 'A fine picture of a well-trained, subjugated society woman, silently and obediently waiting to please her Indian Mistress!' she whispered enticingly.

'Oh yes,' murmured the Maharani, breathing heavily, 'that's the one I want!'

'See how she's trained to wriggle the rubber studs on her Bikini-belt to give pleasure to a woman lying on top of her and holding her down,' explained Ursula giving Sabhu a nod.

'Wriggle!' he ordered, raising his whip menacingly. Immediately, Emma began to wriggle her hips to and fro, and up and down, in a lascivious and wanton manner.

'Imagine her wriggling under you as you pressed your intimacies down on the studs,' breathed Ursula.

'Goodness!' exclaimed the Maharani, biting her lips with excitement.

'But, for no additional charge, there's more!' said

Ursula, giving another nod to Sabhu. Sabhu inserted a little key into the back of the Bikini-belt and immediately there was a low humming noise.

'Now, imagine not only that the girl is wriggling under you, but also that the little rubber studs are vibrating against your own beauty bud. Many of my clients find the combination wildly exciting! Would you like this additional service?'

'Oh yes,' the Maharani replied, 'oh yes'. Then she paused for a moment. 'But won't the girl also be getting pleasure? I thought the whole point of this belt was that she feels nothing.'

'Exactly!' laughed Ursula.

'Oh? What do you mean?' asked the Maharani, puzzled.

'Well, the belts have been cleverly designed so that, when a client switches on the integral vibrator, it's only the little rubber knobs that actually vibrate. The girl herself would still feel nothing as she was made to writhe under you.'

'Brilliant!' laughed the Maharani. 'How clever!'

'And there are two other additional and optional services I can offer to heighten your pleasure this afternoon. Using them on a pretty young woman like this one would make you enjoy your feeling of power all the more – though I shall have to charge extra for them!'

'Oh?' said the Maharani intrigued.

'Well, Option One is . . .' She began to whisper into the Maharani's ear. The Maharani's eyes opened wide and she licked her lips.

'Oh yes,' she said, 'I'll certainly pay extra for Option One. What about the other?'

'That's something rather different,' Ursula said with a conspiratorial smile, 'and something I myself greatly enjoy using on Number Four!' She opened a little cupboard, and pointed to something black with leather straps. 'That is Option Two!' she announced.

'Well!' cried the Maharani, 'I see what you mean. Oh yes!'

8

The Maharani

Holding Emma's lead and his whip in one hand, Sabhu
knocked at the door of the guest room. Behind him,
with the clip of the lead now fastened to the ring on her
collar, stood Emma herself, still naked except for her
manacles and the Bikini-belt.

'Come in!' said the voice of the Maharani.

Sabhu opened the door. 'Prance!' he ordered, as he
entered the room. Emma was led in behind him, obediently raising her knees high in the air, to the full extent
of the heavy chain attached to her ankle manacles. Her
manacled wrists were again clasped behind her neck,
and her breasts were bouncing wildly. She breathed
heavily with the effort, but, at the same time, it was clear
that prancing was something she had been made to
practise over and over again

The Maharani, sitting in a chair in the corner and now
clad in only a simple cotton sari, watched with mounting
excitement as Sabhu, now standing in the middle of the
room, let out more of the lead and, cracking his whip
behind her bottom, made Emma prance round and round.

'Halt!' he finally called out. Her bosom rising and
falling as she got her breath back, Emma stood quite
still, her eyes lowered demurely, her ankles pressed
together and her hands now at her sides, so that the
manacle chain between them was touching her knees.

What was going to happen now? she wondered.
Normally at this stage, Sabhu bowed, handed the lead

to the client and left the room. But there was no sign of him leaving and he was still holding her lead himself.

With his whip, Sabhu pointed to the back of a special chair near the Maharani. Then he smiled and, speaking slowly and deliberately as if to a child, he ordered, 'Bend over! Yes, over the back of that chair!'

'Oh no!' Emma could not help gasping. 'Oh please, not that!'

It was some time since Ursula had offered the spectacle of Emma being beaten by Sabhu to titillate a client. She did not like her girls being marked and it was something that she offered to only the richest and most extravagant of her clients – for the thin leather of the Bikini-belt gave little protection to the girl's buttocks.

'Silence!' shouted Sabhu, secretly pleased with Emma's terrified protest as it could only serve to heighten the spectacle for the Maharani. 'Move!'

Scared almost out of her wits, Emma rushed towards the chair and bent over its low back. Then she reached down with her manacled hands to grip its arms. She was, she realised, ideally positioned to be thrashed.

'Head up! Look straight ahead! Tongue out! More! Up on your toes! Present your buttocks for the whip!'

With each order, Emma felt more and more humiliated and ashamed. But, as was always the case when she was going to be beaten, Emma could also feel herself becoming aroused under her Bikini-belt. The thought of being whipped in front of this tall and attractive-looking woman heightened her excitement even more and, as Sabhu flexed his whip, all her thoughts of Henry, his commanding masculine ways, and her plans to try to go off with him, suddenly seemed very remote.

Her buttocks, only partly covered by her belt, were thrust back, her head was raised, her tongue thrust out, and her breasts hung down prettily towards the empty seat. It was a position that she had often had to adopt in the early stages of her training by Sabhu.

Still holding her lead with one hand, Sabhu tapped her belly with his whip, making her raise her bottom slightly and part her legs a little wider. Then he turned and bowed to the Maharani. 'Permission to carry out Option One, Madam?' he asked, ingratiatingly.

Oh God! Emma was thinking, how many strokes has the Maharani paid for? She did not dare to look around and did not, therefore, see Sabhu smiling and holding up six fingers to the Maharani.

The Maharani, in turn, could scarcely believe what she was seeing: a married woman, and part of the arrogant upper class, was about to be thrashed by an uneducated and comparatively low-born man. She could feel herself becoming wet with arousal.

Sabhu raised his whip, took careful aim and brought it down across the soft-skinned backs of Emma's thighs – just below the line of the Bikini-belt.

Emma gave a scream of pain as a long red weal began to appear. She longed to rub her bottom, to ease the pain, but she did not dare to break her position. As she absorbed the pain, she blushed as she felt herself becoming even more aroused. But all she could think was how many more strokes was she going to get?

Two more strokes slowly followed and then there was a pause. Still not daring to look around, she felt Sabhu fitting a key into the little padlock at the small of her back, and then into the one at the back of her thick collar. He was going to take off her belt!

Normally, the feeling of relief as the tight belt and collar were removed and her firmly compressed beauty lips relaxed was wonderful, but now, bent over as she was for a thrashing, she could not help trembling as she felt the air on her newly bared bottom and between her legs.

With his whip, Sabhu made Emma spread her thighs slightly further apart, and then, with a respectful gesture, he smilingly invited the Maharani to come and feel what was in between them. He reached down and separated the now well-exposed beauty lips.

Emma blushed scarlet with shame, as she felt the elegant Maharani's hand on her soaking wet intimacies. Oh, why did being beaten always have this shameful effect on her – even when it hurt like mad! She heard the Maharani give a contemptuous laugh and then go back to her chair. At heart these upper-class society women were just low-caste sluts!

Sabhu adjusted Emma's position again and then, holding her lead taut with one hand, took careful aim, this time bringing the whip down across her soft bottom. Three times the room was filled with Emma's screams, and then Sabhu replaced her Bikini-belt, closed the padlocks, bowed to the Maharani and left Emma alone to her mercies.

'Lick, you beautiful lady, lick!' cried the Maharani as she knelt on the large bed over Emma's face.

Emma, lying on her back with her manacled wrists fastened to the head of the bed, gave a little jump of pain from the weals on her bottom. Then doing her best to keep herself from crying out, she reached up with her tongue and began, very gently, to lick up and down the Maharani's own well-aroused beauty lips. She could hear the Maharani crying out with pleasure, and mumbling in a strange tongue – presumably her native Urdu, which had been the language of her country's Moslem rulers.

'Go on, you stuck-up girl!' the Maharani now called out, reaching down and pulling Emma's face up to her own eager body. 'And think what your husband would say if he could see you now – you slut!'

But it was not only of John that Emma was thinking with shame, but of Henry as well.

'Wriggle, you arrogant little bitch! Wriggle!' came the Maharani's hoarse voice as she clasped Emma to her again. Oh, the feeling of power from the sight of the helpless young woman lying manacled beneath her! Two hundred years of humiliating colonial rule were being avenged!

She inserted the key that Sabhu had given her into the Bikini-belt, and the little black knobs started to vibrate deliciously as she pressed her beauty lips down on to them. Oh, the sheer bliss – and, moreover, a bliss that was further heightened by the thought that the blonde woman obediently writhing under her could feel nothing except the stripes across her bottom! Oh, the ecstasy! Oh, the feeling of power! Oh, the exhilaration!

It was indeed not long before the Maharani climaxed, with a shrill scream of delight, and then collapsed on to the soft figure below her.

There was a long pause and then the Maharani reached for the house phone. 'Come and prepare her for Option Two!' she instructed Sabhu and then went into the bathroom.

Through the open door, the Maharani could hear Sabhu silently taking off Emma's belt again and then oiling her in between her legs, getting her ready for what was to happen next. Having once again made Emma lie down on her back on the bed, he fastened the chain linking her wrists back on to the ring at its head. That would prevent her from interfering with Option Two! Then the Maharani heard him leave the room.

She looked down at her own slim, taut body, and at Option Two, the well-oiled double dildo that she had strapped on to her thighs. She could feel one of the two manhoods inside her, whilst the other one jutted forward from between her legs, in a realistically masculine way. Any movement of her hips caused the manhood inside her to excite her wildly, and also made the black rubber appendage protruding in front of her sway provocatively, so that the little knobs at its base rubbed even more thrillingly against her own beauty bud. Oh,

69

the double pleasure! Oh, what a clever dildo this was! She could hardly wait to drive it up the proud beauty lying bound and helpless next door!

But that was not all, for she could also feel the weight and size of the rubber testicles that hung down below the manhood. They were heavy from the fluid that they held – ready for the squeeze of either hand that would jet the liquid of the user's choice into the girl as she herself reached her climax – or climaxes!

'Moreover,' Ursula had explained, 'the insulated rubber testicles have been been carefully designed so that each of them can be loaded with something different. I usually like to have warm milk loaded in the right testicle for the final eruption. You will find, however, that the left-hand testicle has been specially loaded with a harmless stinging lotion that will really make the girl jump every time you give the testicle the slightest squeeze with your left hand. You'll also find that her sudden writhing and screaming will make things even more arousing for you.'

'How thrilling!' the Maharani had cried.

'Yes, but you must be ready to hold the girl down as you ride her whilst she bucks and writhes underneath you. The burning feeling will make her want to throw you right off, and so you will have to bear down very hard.'

'Oh, I'll do that alright!' laughed the Maharani.

'Then,' went on Ursula, 'when the girl's quietened down again, all you have to do to stimulate her back into action is give another little squeeze with your left hand. So you can spin it out for a long time if you want to, until you are ready for a final climax when you get a different but equally exciting reaction from the girl by giving a good long squeeze of your right hand to get the warm milk jetting into her.'

'Oh, what an exciting idea!' gasped the Maharani, clapping her hands with delight.

70

'Well, that's Option Two – a rather expensive option, but most women find it worth the price.'

'Oh, the extra cost doesn't bother me – I can see that the sheer excitement will make it all very worthwhile!'

Emma lay on the bed, her body writhing, and her mind, once again, in turmoil. On the one hand, she felt unbelievable excitement at finally being free of her awful belt and at feeling a manhood, albeit a rubber one, up inside her. On the other, however, the pain from the weals on her bottom as the Maharani pressed her down against the mattress was just as acute.

She had also recognised the dildo as one which Ursula had frequently used on her. Ursula would often cruelly tease her by refusing to tell her whether or not it was loaded with the awful stinging lotion.

What was it loaded with now? Oh my God, had Ursula hired her out to the Maharani to be made to really writhe? Emma found her excitement was mounting fast, overcoming the pain from her well-striped bottom.

Then, suddenly, she gave a scream and jerked wildly as the Maharani, with a cruel smile, drove the first little jet of the stinging lotion up inside her. Desperately, Emma tried to bring her manacled hands down from above her head to push the Maharani off her, but the manacles were too firmly fastened to the bed. All she could do was try to buck the woman off her – and thereby give her even greater pleasure.

'Take it,' cried the Maharani hoarsely, as she held the frantically writhing Emma down, 'take it, you upper-class slut, take it!'

A few minutes later the same scene was repeated, as the Maharani again put her left hand down to squeeze the rubber testicle.

Listening at the door, Sabhu rubbed his hands together with delight. Emma would, he felt sure, have earned him an extra big tip this time!

71

9

Emma Makes her Plans

It was a very sore and contrite Emma whom Sabhu
drove back to the station just in time for her train home.

He did not say a word – not even when he put her
into an uncrowded carriage. Indeed, there was nothing
to be said. Emma had been examined and depilated by
him and then, as usual, put into her cage for the day.
She had then been put to work, and made to pleasure
the Maharani. It had been a pleasuring that had included both Options One and Two, so she had earned
quite a fee for her Mistress and a generous tip for
himself – but nothing, of course, for herself.

Emma sat down in the train, but immediately jumped
up with a little cry. Her bottom was still smarting after
her beating – or her spanking, as Sabhu humiliatingly
described it, as if she were just a naughty little girl who
had been smacked on her bottom. Some spanking!

She would, she realised, now have to travel standing
up – and sleep on her tummy that night. What a swine
Sabhu was! Or was the real swine Ursula who had
apparently offered to have her beaten by Sabhu to get
more money from the Maharani? How could her Mistress have been so cruel?

As the train pulled out, Emma could not help but
think what Henry would say if he found out what had
happened to her that day. What a muddle it all was!
Here she was loving, and yet at the same time hating,
being one of Ursula's unpaid tarts, subject to Sabhu's

terrifying discipline – thrilled to be one of Ursula's slaves and yet detesting her. What a muddle indeed!

Would the marks of her beating wear off before her next rendezvous with Henry in a week's time? More to the point, would she really be able to get away to meet him?

Oh, how she longed to go off with Henry once again – and to get away from the clutches of Ursula, exciting though they often were. She remembered what Ursula had said when Sabhu had taken her to report to her after the Maharani had left. 'You've been a good little girl, Emma, and the Maharani was very pleased.'

Emma had blushed with pleasure at being praised by her Mistress. Oh, how she longed to please her! But she had been dismayed when Ursula had gone on, 'I shall have to think seriously about having you thrashed by Sabhu before you service all your clients in future. It seems to make you far more eager to please.'

Eager to please! Just scared out of her wits, Emma thought bitterly, would be a more accurate description.

Then Ursula had told her about the villa, adding, however, that she, Emma, was going to be left behind.

'Nevertheless, little Emma,' Ursula told her, 'although I shall be away, which means there'll be no clients to service, you're to report to Sabhu next Thursday for him to check you over, for the last time for a couple of weeks, before he brings the other girls out to join me at the villa. But don't you dare start slackening off with your reports – just remember I shall be expecting to have a good report from him about you.'

At first, Emma had been dismayed at the idea of being left behind by her exciting Mistress. But then she remembered that Henry had told her to meet him that very Thursday. What an opportunity! But how could she get away from Sabhu? And how could she get out of her belt? Feverishly, she began to wonder . . . and wonder.

Yes, a clever little plan was beginning to form in her brain. It would need careful and secret preparation, and not a little luck, but she had never been short of that.

10

Emma Escapes

'Up!' ordered Sabhu. Quickly, Emma stood up high on the bench in the training room.

Sabhu unlocked the small padlocks of her Bikini-belt at the small of her back and behind her neck. Then he slipped off the belt itself and the stiff studded leather collar. As usual, however, he had already put her heavy wrist and ankle manacles back on to her. Except for them, she was now stark naked.

'Present!'

Blushing with shame, Emma immediately parted her legs and bent her knees so that her bare beauty lips were now level with with Sabhu's eyes. At the same time, she raised her wrist manacles, clasped her hands behind her neck and, looking over Sabhu's head below her, fixed her eyes on the wall. She must not, she knew, say a word, and neither must she look down. But she could feel him using a shaving brush to work his special depilatory cream into a lather over her mound and down over her beauty lips.

She bit her lips as she felt it beginning to burn. Then she felt him wiping it off and rubbing his hand down between her legs, feeling for any signs of stubble, before repeating the whole process again for good measure.

Oh, how she hated this being done by Sabhu – it was so embarrassing. It was one thing having it done by a nice friendly girl in a beauty parlour, but having it done by a man, and especially by this rough uneducated

Haitian, was awful. It made her feel like an animal – an animal in the intimate charge of a terrifying trainer. Of course, she reflected, that was precisely why Ursula insisted on it being done by Sabhu.

Then, apparently satisfied, he parted her beauty lips and began, as usual, to feel up inside her.

She remembered her plan – the plan on which so much depended. She plucked up her courage.

'Permission to speak, Mr Sabhu, sir?' she said, still holding her position of Present – presenting her beauty lips for inspection.

'What do you want, girl?' came the gruff reply.

'Please, Mr Sabhu, sir,' said Emma, feeling very brave. She knew that the slightest failure to treat this horrible man with the utmost respect would result in twelve strokes for 'impertinence'. She put on her best little-girl wheedling tone. 'I've got to go to the vaccination centre at Westminster at noon.'

'What!' cried Sabhu angrily, immediately suspecting a ruse to avoid having the Bikini-belt put back on. Then, assuming it was something to do with Emma's monthly cycle, he took out his record book for Number Four and studied it carefully.

'Nothing wrong with you,' he announced, in his strong half-French, half-Caribbean accent.

'No, no sir,' cried Emma, praying that she would sound convincing. 'It's not that at all. It's just that John, my husband . . .'

'What about him?' queried Sabhu contemptuously. 'He no reason for you not wearing chastity belt.'

Sabhu knew that to make sure that Emma was not unfaithful to her Mistress, her chastity belt was kept locked on her, even when her husband was at home. Sabhu had often laughed at the thought of Doctor Anna sending Emma's booby of a husband a letter saying that his wife was not fit to undertake her conjugal duties and that she must sleep in a separate room.

76

'Oh no, sir, it's not that.'

'Well then?' Sabhu asked, belligerently. He did not like Emma's husband. Even if he was a booby, he was the reason why she now only came to the house to meet a client once a week. It was because of him that the tips Sabhu was getting for Emma's services were now greatly reduced, despite all the hard work he had put into training and subjugating her.

'It's just that he has asked me to be ready to join him for a week or so at an international oceanographic conference he thinks he will be going to in – in . . .'

Emma was becoming flustered as she lied.

'In . . . San José, in . . . Costa Rica.' She finally remembered her story.

'Costa Rica?'

'Yes, sir,' Emma was now getting more sure of herself. 'And you see, you have to have a yellow fever vaccination to go there. And you can only get one at the vaccination centre when they open a batch of the vaccine. So you have to have a special appointment. My husband's office has arranged for me have one at noon today.'

'Why you not tell me this before?' asked Sabhu suspiciously. 'Why you wait until Madam not here?'

'Oh, oh . . . because I only heard about it from my husband's office this morning, just as I was leaving. And,' she added hopefully, 'they said I was very lucky to get this appointment. Someone else cancelled. If I miss this chance, it will be too late.'

Emma saw that Sabhu had taken seriously what she had said. Good! Now was the time to make her story really sound true by taking advantage of the absence of the sinister Doctor Anna, whom Ursula had taken with her to the Aegean, in case any of her girls fell ill during their time abroad.

'Doctor Anna knew about it,' Emma lied. 'It was she who said I must have it if I were ever to go out there. She said I was too valuable to risk not having it done.'

77

It was these words that persuaded Sabhu.

'Alright!' he said. 'But I'll drive you there, wait for you and take you on to the station for your train home.'

Emma gave a gasp of relief. He had fallen for it! 'But, sir, I must have my Bikini-belt off – and my manacles.'

'Manacles off? Alright!' Sabhu grunted. He would, in any case, have had to have taken them off when they arrived at the station. Emma could hardly wear them at home or on the train. But remove her Bikini-belt? Certainly not!

'Why, you silly girl,' he asked suspiciously, 'you need to have belt taken off for simple injection into arm?'

'Because, Mr Sabhu, sir,' said Emma, putting on an air of great respect for this awful man, her enemy, 'you see, the injection has to be into my bottom – and what would they all say at the vaccination centre? Anyway, even if they did agree to give it to me in the arm, how could I hide the stiff leather collar and its connecting straps?

There was a long pause as the still suspicious Sabhu thought everything through.

'And anyway,' continued Emma, brightly, 'if you're frightened I'm going to run away you can put the belt back on now. Then you need only take it off, temporarily, and the manacles, too, when the car arrives at the centre. Then you can hold them ready for me to put on again, as soon as I come back out. I shall only be in there for ten minutes or so.'

Sabhu grunted.

Emma bent down, picked up her bag and opened it.

'And look! I've hardly got any money – just my return ticket to the country. How can I possibly run away? Anyway, you've got my passport!

'Alright,' said Sabhu, picking up the belt.

Emma looked back at the car in which Sabhu was sitting and pressed the vaccination centre's doorbell. I was part of a much larger building. So far so good, but supposing they asked if she had an appointment? Luckily, it was a remotely operated door.

'Come in and go up to reception on the second floor,' came a flustered woman's voice. She was obviously too busy to ask any more questions. Good!

Emma rushed in and then, seeing a door marked EMERGENCY EXIT, rushed out again at the back of the building. Wonderful!

If later questioned by Ursula, she would simply say that she had got lost in the huge building, and that she must have left it via the wrong door. She had looked all around for Sabhu, but he and the car seemed to have disappeared. He had abandoned her! Then, finding herself all alone and knowing that Ursula, like her husband, was abroad, she had made her way to the house of an old girlfriend who had taken pity on her.

That sounded like quite a convincing story, she thought, and it might even get that swine Sabhu into trouble! In her heart she wondered if Ursula would smell a rat, but that was all in the future. Anyway, perhaps she would break with Ursula and never see her again! All that mattered now was that she had escaped! She was free – and on her way to meet Henry!

Out in the street again, at the back of the building, Emma looked around. An empty taxi was coming down the street. Her luck was in!

'The Grosvenor Hotel, Victoria,' she told the driver, and got in.

Then, to her horror, she saw that the driver was taking the taxi around to the front of the building. She had a glimpse of Sabhu, still sitting in his car – and still, presumably, holding her Bikini-belt and the manacles.

She lowered her head and started to adjust a shoe so that he would not see her. Emma's heart was pounding as the taxi drove right past him.

She did not dare to look up for a whole minute. Then

she looked behind her, through the rear window. There was no sign of Sabhu following the taxi. What a relief!

She started to feel down through a little hole in the pocket of her coat and extracted from the lining a crumpled-up ten-pound note – change from one of the fifty-pound notes which Henry had given her. Knowing that Sabhu would check her handbag, she had secretly hidden it there.

When the taxi arrived, she thrust the note at the driver, and quickly looked up and down the street. There was no sign of Sabhu or of the car. Without waiting for her change, she rushed into the hotel.

Oh thank God! There was the kind porter to whom she had given five pounds earlier that morning in return for looking after her suitcase.

Smiling, he now handed it back to her and she rushed out again, this time into the station itself, struggling to tear open a hem in which she had hidden a crumpled up twenty pound note.

She rushed to the Gatwick Airport ticket office, and bought a ticket. A train was about to leave. She looked up and down the platform. There was no sign of Sabhu. She threw herself into a seat on the opposite side of the train to the platform, and flung open her case. There, on top of her clothes, was the temporary passport she had managed to buy without Mrs Maunder knowing.

She sat back in her seat as the train pulled out of Victoria. Oh, the feeling of relief! And the sheer excitement! And the bliss of no longer being locked into that ghastly Bikini-belt! Being quite naked underneath her dress, she could feel that how her beauty lips were no longer tightly compressed. They were free to open like the petals of a flower, as Sabhu liked to say when he unlocked a girl's belt.

For the first time in months she could actually touch herself. She could play with herself! The very idea made her moist with excitement. She could hardly believe i

80

was true, and had to drop her hands discreetly into her lap to reassure herself that it was! As she did so, a little thrill ran through her body.

She was free! A free young woman! A highly sensuous young woman on her way to meet her lover! This was what life was all about!

She looked about the compartment at the holidaymakers also going to Gatwick. What would they say if they had any idea of what she had been through? What dull lives they probably lived – and what a amazing and thrilling one she led.

11

Off with Henry!

The svelte French booking clerk handed Emma her ticket.

'And I've got this envelope for you,' she said with a smirk.

'Emma' was written on the envelope in Henry's handwriting. Hastily, Emma opened and read it.

> *You are to play the role of Miss Smythe, a temporary secretary whom I have hired from an agency to help me on my trip. You will address me as Mr Fortescue on all occasions, and keep your distance. You are to be attentive and helpful to me at all times. I will contact you at the appropriate moment. Meanwhile you have your ticket and should board the plane when the flight is called.*

Oh Henry! At least life was never dull when she was with him!

She was about to join the queue to check in when she saw him ahead of her. But with him was his wife!

Emma's heart sank. Was she really just coming out as a secretary? Would Henry also have his wife with him? Had she gone through hell to escape from Ursula and Sabhu merely to play the role of gooseberry?

Then her heart sang again as she saw Henry kiss his wife goodbye and, without even so much as a glance back towards Emma, stride off to the departure lounge.

His wife, Emma realised, must merely have driven him down to the airport to see him off. Oh the relief!

Still wildly excited, Emma kept seeing Henry in the departure lounge, in the duty-free shops, in the bar and as they queued up to to board the plane, but, remembering her instructions, she did not dare to approach him.

Once on board, she found Henry sitting in the seat next to hers in the business class section. Her heart was in her mouth. She longed to fling herself into his arms. 'Ah,' he said politely, 'you must be Miss Smythe?'

'Yes, Mr Fortescue,' Emma replied, nervously.

'Well, I'm sure we will get on very well during this trip. Have you brought your typewriter?'

'No, sir ... No,' replied Emma, feeling idiotic.

'What!'

'Well ... I – I mean the agency ... never mentioned that,' stammered Emma, 'I didn't think –'

'But you can take shorthand?' he said, irritably.

'No – no!' Emma was almost ready to burst into tears. She had been so geared up to escaping and this wasn't at all what she had been expecting, not at all what she had been so looking forward to.

'Ah well, never mind,' laughed Henry, gently taking her hand, 'I expect you've got some other skills I can make use of! At least they've sent me a pretty girl!'

Emma thrilled to his touch and to his smile. Oh, what a horrible tease he was!

'But you don't seem to be wearing very many clothes,' Henry went on. 'Did you have to leave in rather a hurry?'

Emma blushed. Had Henry noticed that in fact she was stark naked under her dress?

'Yes – yes, sir.' How could she ever explain the humiliation of Sabhu taking off her belt in the car when they arrived at the vaccination centre and then just buttoning up her dress again before sending her inside?

'Yes, it was all rather rushed, sir,' she laughed. 'But I'm here now!'

'Well, my dear, you'll have to tell me all about it, later on,' Henry said gently, stroking her hand.

Again Emma thrilled to his touch. But how could she ever tell him what she had been through? Tell him of her humiliating inspection and interrogation by Sabhu? Never! She wanted to keep all that a secret – a secret part of her life. But could she really keep it all from Henry?

On their arrival at Bordeaux airport, Henry picked up a waiting hire-car, and they drove down along the straight road through the huge pine woods of the flat Landes. It was all new to Emma and she was delighted – and even more delighted to be with Henry, although he was still keeping up the pretext of having hired her as a temporary secretary.

Indeed, Henry said little during the drive and she was grateful, for she wanted to unwind and put all thoughts of Ursula, of the cages in the attic, and of Sabhu behind her.

He did, however, say that the following morning he would be picked up by a chauffeur and would spend the day at a business meeting.

As he was talking, Emma suddenly saw the spectacular sight of the Pyrenees appearing through the mist and haze, high up and surprisingly near. Oh, how thrilling this was!

Emma was equally enchanted with the little fishing port of St Jean de Luz, and even more so with the château where Henry had booked a suite of rooms in an old tower. They looked down on to a pretty French formal garden of small square-shaped flower beds, each edged with a clipped miniature box hedge and separated from adjacent beds by narrow gravel paths.

'Oh, this is wonderful!' she cried happily, her eyes sparkling. She turned towards Henry and, unable to restrain herself any longer, flung herself into his arms. Oh, how she had waited for this moment! Oh, the thrill of feeling a man's strong arms around her again – so different from a woman's.

'Oh, Henry! Darling! Alone at last,' she murmured.

She felt his hands unbuttoning her dress. She remembered how Sabhu had coldly and deftly also done so, to unlock and remove that horrible Bikini belt. But Henry was much more gentle, just like a lover should be.

Soon she was standing naked and excited in his arms. Then Henry turned and, having opened his suitcase, handed her a pair of long black gloves and a black suspender belt and fishnet stockings. With a delighted cry, she rushed into the bathroom and put them on. They made her feel even more excited and even more naked. She went back into the drawing room, where Henry was now sitting in a large armchair.

She sauntered provocatively towards him. She could feel her beauty lips becoming moist between the straps of her suspender belt. Henry, she knew, would approve of their smooth hairless appearance, but could she ever tell him that it was Sabhu who had kept her so carefully depilated?

'Now,' he said, 'come and sit on my knee like the good little girl that you are.'

A good little girl? Oh, yes! With a deliriously happy cry, Emma threw herself on to his knee. She'd never grown out of being dandled and fussed over on someone's lap, and Henry had brought exciting new grown-up elements to the innocent games she had played as a child. Older and wiser than Emma, Henry was physically much bigger, too. Literally someone for her to look up to.

'Yes,' she lisped, putting her arms around his neck and kissing him passionately. She could feel her naked nipples becoming erect. She felt his swelling manhood pressing against her.

Henry lowered his hands. She found herself opening her legs wantonly. He touched her hot moist beauty bud, his finger caressing and teasing it, and then slipping in and out of her.

85

'Now tell me all about it,' he ordered.

No! No, she told herself. It was all to remain a secret – and especially from Henry. But, as she became more and more aroused by Henry's fingers on her now throbbing beauty bud, she began to pour it all out. Prompted by his questions, she found herself telling him about the cages and the other girls, about Sabhu, about the clients, about the awful Bikini-belts, about Mrs Maunder, and about how she had escaped.

'Oh, I know,' she whispered, 'it sounds quite mad, here with you. How can girls like me really submit to being treated like that? Well, I can only say that at the time, it all seems quite different, almost natural. The fact is that it's very exciting for a girl like me to be completely in someone else's power.'

'Well, you're in mine now!' laughed Henry, sliding her down on to the floor so that she was on her knees between his legs.

She knew what she had to do, and with her gloved hands she unbuttoned his trousers and eased out his surging manhood. Humbly and reverently, she began to kiss it and, with a wet tongue, to lick its head.

Then Henry pointed to a beautifully wrapped package lying on the sofa.

As excited as a little girl on Christmas Day, Emma ran over and began to undo the parcel. Wonderful! A really sexy red basque! And a gorgeous black nightdress!

'Oh, darling,' she cried, and dropped down again on to her knees and took his manhood into her mouth in a gesture of humble gratitude.

Henry gripped her hair and held her head in place. Emma was thrilled. Then he pushed her away. 'Your next task, after I've shaved, will be to attend to your Master in his bath. Now run off and get it ready!'

Master! First sir, thought Emma joyfully, and now Master. Was she his secretary or his little slave? Both sounded equally exciting.

Moments later, she was happily scrubbing his back.

'Now go and make yourself beautiful,' he ordered. 'Put your hair up. We're going out to dinner at the port. Be ready in fifteen minutes!'

Emma was thrilled, as they dined in the Place Louis Quatorze, by the port, outside a little restaurant. The food was mouthwatering. But after months of only being allowed little more than fruit and yoghurt by Sabhu, she could hardly touch it.

She just looked adoringly at Henry, her Master, as he told her about the little town and of how the King of France, then still a young man, had come here to marry the Infanta of Spain. But she hardly took any of it in, for she could only think of that beautiful nightdress and Henry's proud and unsatiated manhood.

Meanwhile, the square had filled up. A band was playing in the bandstand. Young people were dancing the fast-moving Paso Doble with its stirring and jerky rhythm.

Suddenly, all the lights went out. There were excited cries of anticipation from the crowd. Then there was a sudden burst of fireworks as a leather bull with real horns, carried by a running man whose upper body was concealed inside it, rushed through the screaming and laughing crowd.

'It's called a *Toro de Fuego*, a Bull of Fire,' explained Henry.

Like a little girl, Emma took Henry's hand and excitedly led him out into the crowd, dodging the bull and laughing. Oh, what fun it all was!

Ursula, Sabhu, and the cages, were all very far away . . .

Suddenly, the bull stopped and stood there on its wooden legs. More fireworks were lit and finally a ring of fire soared up into the sky and burst in a dazzle of falling stars.

'I'm taking you to Pamplona in a couple of days' time

to see a real bullfight,' announced Henry. 'It's the *Feria* there – the annual bullfighting fiesta. The bulls run through the streets in the morning to the bullring and the bullfights take place in the afternoon.'

A bullfight! Emma had never seen one, but she had heard about them from friends – and about Pamplona.

Emma was looking gorgeous, she knew, as, wearing the transparent black nightdress, she knocked on Henry's bedroom door.

'Come in!' called a strangely muffled voice.

The room was in almost total darkness.

She made out a male figure standing in the middle of the large room. It turned slowly towards her. She could feel herself becoming aroused, like a bitch on heat ready to be covered.

Then she screamed. She saw it was not Henry but a black man! And he was holding a whip! Sabhu had followed her here! He had come to take her back! Back to her cage! She hadn't escaped after all! Overwhelmed with the shock, she collapsed on to her knees and burst out crying with a mixture of terror and disappointment.

'Come here and kiss me,' laughed Henry, pulling off the very realistic black plastic mask.

Her heart pounding with relief, Emma crawled over to his feet. She felt herself being lifted up and carried to the huge four poster bed.

Oh, the wonderful feeling of a real manhood inside her! It had been so long!

Her hands were firmly gripped above her head, as she wriggled beneath Henry's heavy weight. Oh, the sheer excitement! She seemed to have been climaxing again and again, as Henry brought her to one peak after another. Then he suddenly gripped her even tighter, and she felt him erupt inside her, making her ecstatic with his pleasure.

Oh, give me a man any time, she thought. Give me Henry! But did she really mean it?

12

The Croupier

Emma lay suspended between sleep and wakefulness. Bright sunlight showed around the edges of the heavy blue linen curtains. What a night! What a man!

She felt across the bed with her foot – no Henry! But there were noises coming from the bathroom, and moments later Henry came into the bedroom fully dressed, picked up his watch and small change, closed his briefcase and glanced round the room.

'I'll be back around midnight. Be wearing your red basque with your nipples showing and painted to match it, and put on those fishnet stockings and high heels – oh yes, and put your hair up again. Meanwhile, you can use the car to explore a little. Go off to the casino at Biarritz if you like. Here's a little money to play with!'

Then he was gone.

What on earth am I to do by myself until midnight? thought Emma. My God, what a night, indeed! I bet his wife misses out on all that sort of caper. But I certainly didn't. And I adore it. Hurry up midnight!

That afternoon, Emma walked into the casino. The room was magnificent with red brocade walls, huge gilt-framed mirrors, and a parquet floor. The gaming tables were surrounded by seated players, both male and female, mainly above middle age and smartly dressed. She sat down as a chair was vacated and watched the ball spin round the roulette wheel, diminish speed, flicker up and down and then rattle into the number 8 slot.

Rakes, which reminded Emma of the food pusher she had used as a child, scooped up the round chips and varying amounts of them were then pushed towards the positions of the winners. There was a pause and then again came the rattle of the ball, followed by '*Rien ne va plus*' from the croupier.

Emma glanced at him and caught a quick sensual look in return. He had classic Mediterranean looks, she thought, and felt a response deep inside herself and then a little gush. 'Oh Lord, now I can't get up because my dress will be moist – and there'll be a damp patch on my chair,' she thought. Henry had had an active night inside her and always produced copious amounts when he climaxed!

Well, she told herself, now that I'm stuck here, I'd better start playing.

She pushed a hundred francs towards the croupier and received her chips from the end of the rake.

'Thank you.'

The look that she received made her hand tremble as she sorted the chips into three even stacks in front of her.

The supervisors, sitting on tall chairs behind the croupiers, were changing over. Her croupier gave a meaningful glance at the wheel as if to indicate something significant and, as the ball clattered round, passed her a casino card.

'You might find this a help, mademoiselle,' he said with a smile, in an attractive French accent.

Mademoiselle! She looked down at her bare hand. Ursula had, of course, confiscated her wedding ring and replaced it with the simple anklet that all her girls had to wear.

She took the card from the gorgeous croupier. Their fingers touched and the thrill of it turned her tummy

90

over. He spun the wheel and flicked the ball free. Seconds later it fell into number 3.

Emma had tentatively put a chip on the nearest square to her croupier – number 3. To her delight, he now pushed a pile of chips to her. Emma was thrilled and with her pen marked the number 3 on the wheel on her card.

An hour passed and the supervisors behind the croupier changed over again. Emma looked at her croupier and the glance that he shot her again resulted in the familiar thrill and the sensation of a flow inside her.

She looked at her wheel card. How curious! A pattern was forming. Number 7, then 22, then 2, each separated on the wheel by half a dozen slots, and then, when the supervisor settled in and was concentrating, the ball went random again.

My God, thought Emma, he's showing me that there is no direct supervision for the three or four numbers that come up whilst one supervisor is climbing down off his high chair, and before his relief then climbs up to take over, adjust his spectacles and settle down.

Indeed, more than that, she realised, her friendly croupier was telling her that, during these hourly change-over periods, he could flick the ball so that it came down into one of several adjoining numbers on the wheel. She looked again at the wheel card he had given her. It had been divided up into seven marked segments, each of some five numbers. So what her friend was doing in each changeover period was flicking the ball, so that with each throw it fell into a higher segment than the previous one.

Goodness, Emma realised, all she had to do was wait for the changeover period and then, for the next couple of throws, cover the five numbers in the next highest segment.

She widened her eyes at her croupier, and with a secret smile acknowledged her awareness of how he could allow her to win.

Whoopee, thought Emma, now I know what Henry means when he talks of beating the system, but I bet he didn't have the world's sexiest croupier helping him.

As the afternoon wore on, Emma found that, indeed, when the supervisors changed over every hour, it was guaranteed that, if she covered the five numbers in the right segment, one of them would be correct and she would receive 35 chips. Then she would stuff the bulk of her winnings into her bag, and idly play black or red, or just the occasional number, until it was changeover time again.

The croupier gave Emma the most sensual smile that she had ever received and then left the room for his break.

Emma collected her winnings. She was up by over a hundred pounds!

There was no sign of her croupier, but he might have been on the terrace, smoking a cigarette, as she walked back to her car. Later she learnt that this was the favourite gathering place of the casino's employees.

That evening, she made her way back to the roulette table. Good! There was a free chair – but alas still no sign of her friendly croupier! Was it because she had not been to thank him? She felt disappointed and depressed. Was this because he had let her win, or because he was so incredibly sexy – or was it both? Winning money was such an aphrodisiac.

Then, suddenly – oh joy! There he was! He looked quite something in his white dinner jacket – so smart. And what a sensual mouth, and those smouldering eyes!

Emma's senses were now alert, aroused and overwhelmed by her response to this man who, once again, was letting her win lots of money.

Time passed and it was getting late. She was doing better and better. But her mind was divided between the thought of Henry returning shortly and of this devastingly attractive croupier. She would have to keep an eye on her watch, for Henry had told her to be waiting for him at midnight, and to be at her most glamorous.

Suddenly, her croupier got up to leave, his shift over. Emma was up by another two hundred pounds. Time for her to go, too!

She left the marble and red plush of the casino entrance and walked to the sea front. A slight surf lapped the white sand. There were few cars and the air was pure. The oleander flowers were scentless, but there was a faint breath of pine. A few people were wandering along under the plane trees, illuminated by occasional street lamps.

She was only slightly startled when a hand took her arm and turned her around to look into the smiling and sexy eyes of her croupier. He touched the backs of her fingers with his lips. 'Mademoiselle, good evening once more,' he said, in his delightful French accent. 'Let us make our way to a café.'

He led her to a bustling street with tables on the pavement. 'Pernod, mademoiselle?'

Emma found the drink rather nasty, but she enjoyed the glow inside her as she and the croupier discreetly discussed his ability to spin the wheel and release the ball so that it fell into a specific segment. He emphasised that it was strictly forbidden and that he had run a great risk on her behalf.

'I have to return after my break,' he said and, thinking that they were leaving, Emma followed him. But as they walked through a passageway, he took out a key and opened the door to a small apartment. Holding her arm, he gestured to Emma to enter.

The door shut and the Yale lock clicked. Then, with Emma's back to the door, he kissed her passionately and silently, his tongue in her mouth and his hands unbuttoning her dress – yet again, she kept thinking. The dress fell to the floor and his fingers touched her nipples.

He seemed to be in a desperate hurry as, at one moment, he was caressing her back, then sliding his fingers between her buttocks, and then, bringing them around to the front again, he used them to roll her nipples. Emma gasped for breath under his hot lips, his questing tongue and the expert touch of his hands.

Then he slipped her panties down over her thighs. He lowered his head to her beauty bud and licked and sucked, whilst she leant backwards. French kisses! The expression raced through her mind as she climaxed almost at once and then again.

Sex whilst standing up seemed twice as intense as in other positions, and she was totally lost in the sensation when, suddenly, in the back of her consciousness, she heard a church clock beginning to strike. She found herself trying to count. My God! Was it eleven or twelve?

She snapped back into reality. She wanted to be beautiful for Henry and everything would be spoilt if she were not there when he returned. Understandably, he would beat her, instead of sharing with her the tender side of his personality – which he had shown her last night for the first time.

But the croupier was intent on enjoying her and it occurred to Emma that perhaps he might want some of her money. Was he a gigolo? Or was he now merely taking his just reward for letting her win? She let herself be moved to the bed – awkwardly, because her knickers were down around her knees. Then the croupier eased one of her legs out of her panties. Now, putting both of her legs over his shoulders, he thrust into her again and again – and again.

'Pretty good!' thought Emma, though her only real concern was that he should hurry things along. However, he then turned her over, raised her hips and again penetrated her – this time slowly pulling out and then ramming his manhood back into her with impressive force.

Good doggy! Emma considered crying 'Woof!' like

she sometimes did for Henry, but what she really wanted to say was, 'Do get a move on. I know you think you're giving me a wonderful time, but honestly I am so fussed about Henry that I can hardly feel a thing. I just want to go.'

Now she was facing him on her side, and in he went again, kissing her, and rolling and pulling her nipples, with her leg bent awkwardly over him. But there was no sign of him finishing. He was, she realised, a wonderful lover, but he seemed wasted on her that night.

At last she was on her back with her legs apart, and his thrusting was becoming increasingly urgent. And, as he plunged ever harder and faster into her, she found, to her shame, that she, too, was responding more and more passionately to him.

Suddenly, it was all over for them both. 'My boy-friend is returning any moment,' she said frantically. 'Thank you so much!'

She left her croupier prostrate on the bed and fled, buttoning up her dress and pulling up her panties as she went. She could still smell the croupier's musky odour on her body as she ran to her car.

Emma parked the car outside the chateau and rushed up to their suite. It was in darkness. Henry had not yet returned! All was well. She would give him back his money and tell him that she had simply explored a little and then spent the evening in their suite.

Hastily she undressed and washed, before putting on her basque and painting her nipples, just as Henry had ordered her to do. Quickly, she hid her winnings. Then in strode Henry!

Clearly, a day spent discussing business had left him feeling more virile than ever. The sight of the almost naked Emma turned him on and she felt herself being thrown on to the bed.

Two men in one evening! What a tart she was, she thought, thinking of the precious three hundred pounds hidden in her case!

13

El Mercurio

There was deathly silence in the huge arena, and Emma caught her breath as the slim figure, dressed like a peacock in his brilliantly coloured *Traje de Luces*, with its gold and silver embroidered short jacket and tight red satin breeches strutted slowly and arrogantly up to the angrily pawing black Andalusian bull.

He was, she knew El Mercurio, the up-and-coming young *torero*, and the darling of the bullfighting crowds. In his right hand he held the gleaming flat-bladed *estoque*, the killing sword, and in his left the small red cloth *muleta* on which the bull's eyes were fixed and on which his life largely depended.

He was bare-headed now. His black bicorne hat was being prominently held by a beautiful woman to whom, only moments before and with a graceful gesture and set phrases, he had formally dedicated the death of the bull. She was seated in the front row only feet away from Emma and Henry. Emma could not help glancing at her jealously, and wondering whether she and this gloriously handsome young man were lovers.

Neither could she help casting glances down to where El Mercurio's manhood was outlined in his tight crimson silk breeches. What a man!

Henry had explained to her that the theory was that the bulls, who had been reared without ever seeing a man on his feet but only on horseback, would take about twenty minutes to realise that the distracting red *muletas* and capes were not part of the bullfighters' bodies. After that, they were too dangerous to fight, for they would charge not at the cape, but straight at the man.

But these bulls here in Pamplona had been raced through the streets to the bull-ring that morning whilst numerous young men had risked their lives by running in front of them. Emma had seen them doing it earlier that very day, and had heard how, only the day before, one young man had tripped – and had been killed.

How, she wondered, could they be sure that this bull had not already realised the truth and would not, as soon as he got his breath back, charge straight at El Mercurio?

Emma then gasped, and it was a gasp which was echoed by the thousands of other spectators, as the slender figure dropped to his knees and flung his arms wide open, exposing his body, in its silken and multi-coloured dress, to a sudden charge by the infuriated bull.

Even Emma, who had never seen a bullfight before, realised that this man's life depended on his having correctly assessed that he now mentally dominated the bull.

Her concern was clearly shared by the *torero*'s own team of *banderilleros*, his assistants, who were anxiously standing back on either side of the bull, ready to dash in and try and to save their master by distracting the creature with their capes.

Then slowly, El Mercurio stood up again. A hush descended on the bull-ring as, unbelievably, he turned his back on the bull, and slowly, very slowly, as if challenging it to charge, walked away.

The whole arena burst into applause and cheers. Bands struck up and soon everyone was standing up and waving their red Basque handkerchiefs, the emblems of the Pamplona fiesta.

Emma was standing and cheering wildly with the rest. Such an act might have had little to do with the finer points of bullfighting, but it showed a degree of sheer bravery that she had never seen before. What courage! What a man indeed!

And if he could so dominate an infuriated bull, she was thinking, what more could he do with a woman like her!

Minutes later, having, to the delight of the spectators, killed the bull cleanly and instantly, El Mercurio was doing a lap of honour around the arena with his *banderilleros*.

As he passed by them, whole sections of the crowd would rise to their feet and applaud. Numerous *botas*, the soft leather Spanish wine flasks, were thrown into the arena to be picked by the *banderilleros* and offered to the smiling and triumphant young *torero*, who would take a swig from one or another, and then throw it back to its rightful owner.

Emma felt completely overcome – emotionally exhausted. Earlier on, outside the bull-ring, Henry had bought her a rose to put in her hair. As the handsome El Mercurio came up level with their seats, she impulsively plucked it from her hair and threw down it at him.

Laughing, one of the *banderilleros* picked it up and handed it to his young master. As he did so, he pointed out Emma, with her distinctive honey-coloured hair.

El Mercurio, still sweating from the fight, clasped the flower in his hand and, looking Emma straight in the eyes, kissed it and thrust it into his short jacket. It was a gesture that brought more applause from the crowd around the blushing Emma.

Outside the arena, there was a huge and happy crowd, drinking and cheering their favourite bullfighters as they made their way, with their teams, out of the bull-ring.

Henry and Emma found their car hopelessly blocked in by other vehicles, and by a low barrier between it and the street down which the crowd was slowly moving. Henry told Emma to wait in the car until the situation eased. He, meanwhile, explained that he had to return to their hotel to make some urgent business telephone calls to England.

She was sitting in the passenger seat wondering what to do, when a crowd of drunken young students came by, saw her problem and, to her astonishment, promptly lifted both her and the car high in the air, over the barrier and into the main street.

Emma got out to thank them, and it was just at that moment that El Mercurio, accompanied by his team and by numerous half-drunk supporters, all cheering and shouting, passed by.

She was recognised as the honey-bonde woman who had thrown their hero a rose and, before she could say a word, she had been lifted up on to the shoulders of the laughing young men and taken off in the procession to El Mercurio's nearby hotel. What Henry would say to this she shuddered to think, but she was quite happy to let herself get – literally – carried away.

Arriving at the hotel, she could not make herself understood, and neither could she understand quite what was being said as, protesting helplessly, she was carried up to the suite of El Mercurio and his team.

There seemed to be constant drunken cries of '*la rubia guapa*', which seemed to mean 'the beautiful blonde', and of '*la rosa*' which seemed to refer to the rose which she had so impulsively thrown to the *torero*. And now, in their inebriated state, they clearly thought they were doing the right thing by reuniting them!

The door to the room in which El Mercurio's men were changing out of their brilliant bullfighting kit was flung open, and Emma was thrown on to the bed. Before she could do anything, her wrists were tied to the head of it, and her now well-spread legs by the ankles to its foot. Several pillows were thrust up under her hips. She started to ask what they thought they were playing at, but their laughter drowned out her voice.

Her dress was pulled up and soon she was naked. There were cries of delighted astonishment when her hairless mound and beauty lips were exposed.

The team members, still wearing their tight red satin breeches, thrust the laughing young students out of the door and turned to Emma. She was, she realised, going to be their reward after the dangers and excitement of the bullfight.

'El Mercurio, help!' cried Emma, but the half dozen *banderilleros*, *picadors* and *chulos* just laughed. Clearly, their master was still downstairs. Clearly too, they felt it was their duty to prepare her for him!

Three of the men now removed their breeches and climbed on to the bed. Others bent down over her. She felt hands all over her body, prodding her, feeling her, examining her – and, most humiliating of all, stimulating her.

First one, and then another thrust into her, arousing themselves to a climax. Each of them was young and virile and Emma realised she couldn't take much more of this without a pause for breath. Again she screamed for the dashing El Mercurio to come and save her.

Suddenly, the door opened, and there he stood, still dressed in all the finery of the bull-ring, his black bicorne hat back on his head. He waved his assistants aside. He looked down at the naked and bound Emma.

'You were the girl who threw me this!' he said in heavily accented English, and produced the rose from inside his short embroidered jacket. Clearly he, too, had been drinking, celebrating his success in the bull-ring.

Emma remembered noticing his manhood under his tight silken breeches in the bull-ring. She glanced down at it now and could see that the sight of her naked and helpless body had aroused him considerably. And the sight of his arousal aroused her, much to the amusement of the watching men standing around the bed.

One of the *banderilleros*, apparently El Mercurio's right-hand man, put out his fingers and felt her now soaking wet beauty lips. He raised his hand to his nose and nodded to his master. The girl was now ready, he seemed to be saying.

'So you, an English Miss, want me?' the handsome young man laughed. 'Well, I shall certainly have you!'

Before she could say a word, he had flung himself down on to her, and had silenced her with passionate kisses. She felt his tongue in her mouth. A shiver of excitement ran through her body and she found herself arching her hips to him. The handsomest bullfighter in all of Spain, she told herself. What a conquest for her – even if the circumstances were rather unusual.

Suddenly, the young bullfighter got up off her. She could not help moaning in disappointment. He said something to his men and Emma found herself being untied from the bed and then turned over, so that she was now kneeling on it. Once again her wrists and ankles were tied, but numerous other hands held her up in position with her bottom raised and the side of her head resting on a soft, plump pillow.

Out of the corner of her eye, she saw El Mercurio strip off his tight breeches, leaving himself dressed in only his short, stiffly-embroidered coat. His now exposed manhood was erect and huge.

Horrified, she felt several fingers rubbing lubricant on to, and then into, her rear orifice. Oh no!

Then, whilst she was still being held by the men, El Mercurio climbed back on to the bed and knelt behind her. She yelped as she felt his manhood driving into her, but seconds later she could not help moaning with pleasure as, clasping her from behind, he rubbed her nipples with his hands. She was, she felt, an English sacrificial lamb to Spanish masculinity.

* * *

101

Half an hour later, Emma tottered out of El Mercurio's hotel and found her car in the now empty street. Nervously, she drove back to the hotel. Henry, she knew, would be waiting for her by now. Waiting to take his pleasure.

My God, she thought, it had been two men, Henry and the croupier, only two days ago. Today it had already been three – no, more than that!

What an ending for her wonderful little holiday with Henry!

14

A Strange School

It was now two weeks after Emma's little escape with
Henry, and she was enjoying life at home again. It was
early summer and the garden was looking lovely,
though there seemed to be so much to do to keep it
looking that way.

John was frequently back and forth as he travelled
around Europe attending symposiums and giving lec-
tures. Mrs Maunder whom Ursula had installed to run
the house in Emma's absence had disappeared, and so
it seemed had Ursula herself. She, Emma realised, was
still away in the Aegean with Sabhu and the other girls.

She had written a postcard to Emma saying that the
villa was lovely and that she was looking forward to
seeing Emma again soon. Not a word about Emma
giving Sabhu the slip! How strange, Emma thought.

Henry was often on the telephone, and the memory
of their little holiday together was never far from
Emma's mind. How lucky she had been to have escaped
from Sabhu and to have gone off with Henry whilst
Ursula was away.

But did she want Ursula back in her life? Did she
want to be one of her girls again – one of her slavegirls
more likely! Did she really want to return to the humiliating life of the cages, the Bikini-belt, the manacles, of
Sabhu's awful supervision, of having to please the
clients, and the constant threat of being chosen for
sponsorship?

It all seemed very far away as she looked around her lovely garden – as did the sheer shame and indignity of having to make those twice-daily reports to Sabhu, of writing up her daily record book for him, and of having him closely supervise her monthly cycle for Ursula.

Had it all been a dream? Did that sort of thing really go on in secret in this day and age? Had she just imagined it, or subconsciously exaggerated it? Anyway, she would keep her distance from Ursula in future!

Her relationship with Henry seemed much more firmly rooted in the real world. Indeed, she was wondering whether to ring him and suggest taking advantage of John's next absence to go off for a weekend together, when suddenly the telephone rang in her bedroom.

It was her private number. Was it Henry? Her heart was pounding as she ran upstairs to answer it before he rang off. But it was a woman's voice. Emma's heart jumped as she recognised the rather cold metallic tone and distinctive Slavonic accent. Ursula!

'So how's my little Emma? Have you missed your Mistress? And have you been a good girl?'

Emma's heart began to thump. She caught her breath. Her Mistress! Her exciting Mistress! Suddenly, she forgot all about Henry and all about her thoughts of not seeing Ursula again. Her Mistress had rung her and was being nice and affectionate!

'Yes, Madam,' Emma lied happily.

'Good. Well, I thought it would do you good to get away for a little time. I'll come and pick you up tomorrow morning at eleven.'

'But –' whimpered Emma. It was a very exciting prospect to be together with Ursula again. Was it to be another honeymoon? Goodness! But she needed a little time to arrange things, to put Henry off, to . . .

'No buts, Emma! Eleven o'clock!'

The phone went dead. How long was she going to be away for? What clothes should she bring? She must find out! Should she send a message to John to say that she was going to be away, or had Ursula, who enjoyed discussing Emma with John behind her back, already done so?

And she had promised to ring Henry in a couple of days' time. Well, she laughed to herself, going off for a long weekend with Ursula should not prevent that! There were so many questions she wanted to ask, but she realised she did not even know from where Ursula had rung. She might still be abroad and only arriving back at Heathrow in the morning. With Ursula's energy and natural secrecy anything was possible.

She rang Babindu, Ursula's housekeeper, but she would not say any more than that the Mistress was away.

Ursula always assumed that a girl could drop everything and come running whenever she snapped her fingers. She was so selfish, so uninterested in her girls' own little problems. But, all the same, how exciting it all was!

The rest of the day was one mad rush as Emma arranged for the gardener to come in every day to air the house, cancelled a supper party she had arranged for some neighbours, and stopped the milk and the newspapers.

All night she tossed and turned, driven almost mad with the excitement and anticipation of seeing Ursula again the next morning, and of wondering what she would wear, and how she should do her hair and make up her face.

Ursula, unlike Henry, did not like to see Emma made up like a sophisticated woman, with her hair up. She liked to see her looking like a much younger girl, with her long silky blonde hair brushed down her back, and dressed in jeans or a gymslip by day and in a party frock in the evening. Alright, that's how she'd be!

Indeed, the next morning, wearing her jeans and a T-shirt, she really felt just like an excited teenager when she saw Ursula drive her car up to the house. She was surprised to see that Ursula was wearing a dark business suit. She rushed out to greet her, but Ursula was strangely cool.

'What shall I bring?' Emma asked.

'Nothing!' was the cold reply, and Ursula silently pointed to a small suitcase on the back seat.

It was a suitcase that Emma recognised only too well. It was the one that Ursula had frequently used to pack the clothes that she had decided Emma should wear and the 'toys' that she was going to use on her. It was a sight that had so often preceded an exciting time together.

Ursula said virtually nothing as they drove for some two hours to a part of the country that was unknown to Emma. Emma did not understand Ursula's strange mood. She assumed that Ursula must have suddenly received worrying news about her plans for more exhibitions of her pictures.

Suddenly, while they were driving through a rather remote part of the countryside, she swung the car towards some closed iron gates set in a high stone wall. Then she stopped the vehicle and blew the horn three times. Emma saw a small television camera discreetly trained on the approach to the gates.

There was a pause and then, suddenly, apparently by remote control, the gates swung open and Ursula steered the car down the drive to what looked like an old Victorian vicarage. Emma was wondering why on earth they had come here, but with Ursula in such an odd mood she did not like to open her mouth.

Ursula parked the car. 'Come!' she said, in a hostile tone, and strode up the steps to the front door.

'Do come in,' said a tall, dapper man, looking to be in his forties. His voice sounded cultured.

Emma was surprised to see that he was dressed in a

khaki military uniform jacket with gleaming buttons and large patch pockets, a military cap, khaki breeches and highly polished brown riding boots. An equally highly polished leather Sam Browne military belt, with a leather strap over his right shoulder, and a long leather swagger stick tucked under his arm, completed the picture.

'You must be Miss de Vere,' he said. 'We have spoken several times on the telephone making the necessary arrangements.'

Ursula nodded and he pointed to Emma.

'And this, I presume, is the intended ... pupil?' He seemed to be eyeing Emma's slim figure up and down with interest, which made the girl blush.

Again Ursula nodded, and he led the way across a large hall to an office in which a tall, unsmiling woman, also appearing to be in her forties, was sitting at a desk. Her brown hair was cut in a short, mannish style, and she wore a dark dress buttoned high up to her neck. She reminded Emma of one of her school headmistresses. Behind her was a door covered in green baize. Emma wondered what was kept behind it.

'Shut the door, please, Randolph,' said the woman to the military-looking man. Her voice sounded educated but, thought Emma, what an unusual name he had – Randolph!

'Of course, my dear,' he said. Were they husband and wife? But what a strange pair! And, Emma wondered, what did they do in this house?

To Emma's surprise, the man locked the door which led into the hall with a key. Then, turning back to Ursula, he politely drew up a chair for her in front of the desk, before sitting down alongside the woman. He made no attempt to produce a chair for Emma, and she was left standing awkwardly to one side, the only one casually dressed in jeans and a T-shirt, and feeling very out of place.

'I think, Miss de Vere, my husband, the Major, has outlined to you our services here at the Private Offenders Rehabilitation School?'

But what on earth did that mean? thought Emma. The phrase Private Offenders worried her. But evidently Ursula understood.

'Yes, Headmistress,' she said.

So, thought Emma, she is a Headmistress. But of what kind of school?

'And you have kindly sent us your cheque for the initial period. Our aim here, in this rehabilitation centre for private offenders, is to achieve complete rededication, after unfaithfulness, through confession and a period of stress and punishment. We also, of course, aim to ensure that the guilty party is both brainwashed into accepting the desired situation, and is far too frightened to dare to risk reoffending!'

Unfaithfulness! Oh my God, Emma thought, remembering her little holiday with Henry, and the sex she had enjoyed with the croupier, never mind with all those bullfighters! Was that why she had been brought here? To confess all? To rededicate herself to Ursula? My God! To be punished?

'Oh no! No!'cried Emma, suddenly realising the significance of being brought by Ursula to this strange school for 'private offenders'. And she had thought she was going off with Ursula for a second honeymoon!

She must have been mad to imagine, she now realised, that Ursula would condone her behaviour. Ursula's girls belonged to her and to her alone, and she required both complete obedience and loyalty. Loyalty! Ursula might hire her girls out to other women, but woe betide a girl who even looked at a man. Emma had broken all the rules and, as Sabhu was abroad, Ursula must have brought her here to be punished!

My God! I can't stay here, she decided, I must get away. I must escape! Now!

She turned and ran towards the door and tried to open it, wrestling with the handle and forgetting that it was locked.

'Young woman,' called out the Headmistress calmly, as if they had been expecting such a reaction. 'There's no way out for you. So go and stand in the corner of the room whilst we discuss you with your Mistress!'

Emma caught her breath, but she was too frightened not to obey.

'No!' called out the Major. 'Stand in the corner facing the wall – and up on your toes!'

Scared almost out of her wits, Emma did as she was told. She felt just like a naughty schoolgirl.

'Thank you, Major,' she heard Ursula say.. 'As you can see, the girl does seem to have quite a guilty conscience.'

'Don't worry,' came the voice of the Headmistress. 'We'll get the full story out of her and then invite you here to hear it in her own words. She'll stay here until we are completely certain that we've got the truth out of her, using Total Control if necessary, and that, thanks to our strict regime here, she is really contrite and will not re-offend.'

Emma heard the noise of papers being turned over on the desk.

'Yes,' Emma heard the woman say, 'I think we have enough of the story to make a good start in interrogating the girl whilst her normal keeper is away in the Aegean, supervising your other girls. Yes, let's see . . . she appeared, deliberately, to give her keeper the slip on the excuse of needing a vaccination, and you are naturally concerned about what she then got up to –'

'No! No!' Emma could not help crying out. She remembered the story she had fortunately prepared. 'It wasn't like that, I got lost and couldn't find him. He abandoned me! I –'

'Silence!' ordered the woman. Then the now quiet

Emma heard her say, 'Miss de Vere, we like to give our pupils numbers rather than names. Do you have a number for her?

'Yes!' answered Ursula abruptly. 'The ungrateful wretch is called Number Four.'

'Number Four!' repeated the Major. That will do very nicely here, too. Well, Miss de Vere, I think you can safely leave Number Four in our hands. We will be in touch with you!'

Emma heard Ursula shake hands with the Major and his wife, the Headmistress. She heard the Major unlock the door and, without another word, Ursula left the room.

Oh my God, Emma thought, still standing in the corner like a child being punished, how did I let myself be tricked into coming here?

15

The Short Sharp Shock

Suddenly, a bell rang harshly in the dormitory. It was the beginning of Emma's third day in the terrifying establishment.

The Major's authoritative voice rang through the room. 'Last one out of bed gets six!'

Emma flung herself out of her bed. All day long it was 'Last one gets six' and every time it meant someone getting six strokes on the bare bottom from the Major's swagger stick, which had a flat leather end. She had learnt only too well how much it stung.

She rushed to line up with the others in this strange establishment where the inmates all lived, slept and worked together, irrespective of age or sex.

In the front row were four other inmates – two very pretty young girls in their twenties, an attractive and sophisticated-looking older woman in her forties, and a very good-looking youth.

They had all been sent here by jealous rich men, their Masters, for suspected unfaithfulness. Emma knew their stories by now – how scared they were of their Masters, how the women had all fallen in love with another man, and the youth with a girl. They were all now having this love thrashed out of them, so that they could be returned to their Masters as good little slavegirls or slaveboys – loving, servile and utterly faithful.

Emma felt so sorry for the good-looking youth for he was surely brainwashed into accepting that there was now no question of him enjoying normal heterosexual love for a pretty girl. His destiny now was to love and please men: his cruel Master and his Master's friends. He would stay at this terrifying institution until he had clearly accepted this, and until his manhood remained unaffected by the near nakedness of the many pretty girls at the establishment.

Several times, Emma had noticed him eyeing her body appreciatively as they were made to take a nude shower together. He would be biting his lips in an attempt to control his manhood, for the slightest sign of arousal would earn him the inevitable six strokes.

Emma had also felt sorry for the older woman. How terribly embarrassing it must be for a sophisticated woman of the world to be treated like this in front of much younger girls.

In the second row, alongside Emma, were two lovely girls and a handsome young man, a toyboy. They, too, had been sent here for unfaithfulness – to have their illicit love thrashed out of them. But they had not been sent by rich men, but by equally jealous rich women – their Mistresses. The toyboy, Emma learnt, had been caught by his Mistress with a younger woman and the girls by their Mistresses with young men.

All the inmates were dressed identically in short cotton tunics and nothing else, except for a triangular black leather purity pad that was locked over their intimacies, whether they were male or female. It was a more simple type of chastity device than the Bikini-belt, but it still prevented them from playing with themselves or each other. It had, however, to be removed for spending a penny – or anything else.

Emma breathed a sigh of relief. This time it was one of the girls in the front row, and the boy in the back row, who were judged to be equal last, and who had to lift up their tunics and bend over in front of the others to be given six by the Major. Both were crying by the end.

112

Oh, how embarrassing it was being beaten by a man in front of the others – especially in front of the young men. But then, Emma had learnt that half the object here was to so humiliate them all, both girls and toyboys, that they would think twice about being unfaithful again to their Masters or Mistresses – knowing that, if caught, they would be sent back here, this time for a double sentence.

'Strip,' ordered the Major. Quickly, they all pulled off their tunics, and stood in line again. Then the Major, his boots and Sam Browne belt gleaming as usual, passed down the two lines and unlocked the inmates' belts, which dropped to the floor. They were now standing rigidly to attention, stark naked.

Emma had noticed that, like herself, the others, both boys and girls, had all been completely depilated. The manhoods of the boys were now well displayed, but everyone was too terrified of the Major's swagger stick to do anything other than stand still, waiting for the next order.

'Bathroom! Last one there gets six! – Go!' There was a mad rush as the terrified inmates struggled to get through the narrow door into the bathroom and then struggled again to queue up to spend a penny.

This time it was the other girl in Emma's group who got the six strokes. Soon she too was crying – and this was scarcely the beginning of a long day. Oh, what a really terrifying regime they ran here!

Emma now had only one aim in life – to persuade Ursula to take her away. She would have a chance that afternoon, when Ursula came down to discuss Emma's 'progress and reports' with the Major and the Headmistress. Oh, how she longed to be taken away from this awful place! But meanwhile there was plenty to get through.

Next came showers, with the stark naked women and men having to soap each other, without showing any sign of arousal. The lady Physical Training Instructress, a cruel-faced woman, now came to take over from the Major, who handed his swagger stick to her.

Still stark naked, they had to put on running shoes and rush outside into the cold morning air. Once there, they had to run around a quarter of a mile exercise track, complete with high hurdles over which they had to jump, hanging rubber tyres through which they had to crawl, and a steep switchback, up and down which they had to run.

It was indeed an exhausting circuit, and they had to complete it ten times. 'Last one back after the next circuit gets six!' called out the P.T. Instructress. Emma tried desperately hard, but the tyres were so high off the ground that they delayed her. Straining with the effort, she tried to catch up on the switchback, but was just pipped at the post by one of the young men.

She was not even allowed to get her breath back before being made to bend over in front of the others to take her six strokes. They stung like mad, and soon she was in floods of tears and begging, in vain, for mercy from the steely faced P.T. Instructress.

Then it was time to run back into the house to have another communal shower, have their belts put back on, and to put on their tunics. This time Emma escaped being last by a hair's breadth. My God, she thought, to have had another six just after the last lot . . .

Now came breakfast. After Sabhu's meagre meals, Emma was delighted to be allowed food which was a little more substantial, but, she realised, she was being made to take much more physical exercise than when she was kept locked up in the cages.

For the next two hours it was lesson time in the classroom. They had to share little desks – boys and girls all mixed up. First came lessons in Greek from the Major, which meant having to master a new alphabet and strange new laws of grammar. The slightest mistake

114

and the culprit had to bend over his or her desk for another six. It was terrifying, and Emma found herself concentrating as she had never done before.

Then the Headmistress took them for Composition. The essays they had to write were always on very relevant subjects, such as: *Why I Love my Master/Mistress More Than Anything Else in the World*, *How I Will Always be Faithful in Future*, and, more embarrassingly, *How I Will Give Pleasure* and *Why I Will Never be Unfaithful by Masturbating*.

The aim, Emma soon realised, was simply to brainwash the inmates into adoring and humbly worshipping the Master or Mistress who had sent them there. At first, Emma had treated this as bit of a joke, but each inmate had to read out their essay no matter how embarrassing or personal its content. If an essay was not considered to be sufficiently fervent, or if there was too much repetition of what had been written the day before, then the customary six strokes would be given to its author.

And, of course, there were always six strokes for the essay judged by the Headmistress to be the dullest. She demanded from her pupils, both boys and girls alike, complete openness in describing explicitly how the writer would give pleasure to his or her Master or Mistress. Full details had also to be given of exactly how the mere thought of a Master or Mistress made the slave, male or female, highly aroused, and how they promised to keep themselves pure in future and never, ever, touch themselves. It was all so humiliating, thought Emma.

Just as was intended, Emma soon found herself thinking all day about what she was going to write in her next essay to avoid getting six. The prospect of such a beating was terrifying and preyed on her mind all day. Her biggest concern was making her prose read sincerely – how could she pretend to adore Ursula, when really she was longing to meet Henry again?

115

Essay writing was, however, only just one of many trials that Emma had to face. After an early lunch, followed by another ten circuits of the track and a shower, all the inmates had to rest in their beds. Supervised by the P.T. Instructress, they were not allowed to talk or to read, but just had lie there, never knowing when it was going to be their turn to be called out to a special interrogation session with the Major and the Headmistress.

These sessions were, more accurately, a mixture of interrogation and brainwashing, and were much feared by everyone. The women or the young men summoned would return with their eyes red from weeping. Strangely, they would also be rubbing their bottoms, even though these bore none of the usual marks from the Major's swagger stick. Emma heard murmurs about something called Total Control and wondered what it was – it clearly had a terrifying effect.

In her own sessions, despite all the harsh questioning and threats of a thrashing, Emma simply stuck to her original story as she stood to attention every day in front of the Headmistress's desk, dressed in just her skimpy tunic, whilst the Major walked up and down alternating between tapping his swagger stick menacingly against the palm of his hand and against her buttocks.

She had got lost, she insisted; had failed to find Sabhu, had assumed that he had abandoned her, and had taken refuge with a girlfriend. Then she had gone out to join her husband in Costa Rica and had only got back a couple of days before her Mistress had brought her here.

She had even made up a long story about going up the volcano that Henry had told her was the main feature in Costa Rica. And yes, of course, she loved her Mistress and had missed her very much.

It all sounded fairly convincing, Emma thought, as

she finally recorded this on to a tape that was going to be played to Ursula when she arrived that evening.

'Absolute nonsense!' was Ursula's reaction when the tape was played to her in the Headmistress's study, whilst Emma stood, as before, in the corner with her face pressed to the wall. 'I don't believe a word of it. She was off with some man! She's just pulling the wool over our eyes. And she's not nearly contrite enough. I want her really feeling she's my property; my slave to do with as I like. I want her really hating all men.'

'Right!' said the Major. 'Then can we have your permission to use Total Control on her?'

Total Control, thought Emma. That was the expression she had heard the other inmates whispering in horror as they waited their turn to go in for interrogation – an interrogation that, up to now, she had found surprisingly mild.

'Do what you like,' came Ursula's angry voice, 'but get the truth out of her and break her spirit. I want to have her crawling at my feet! I'll come back in three days' time to hear just what she's really been up to.'

16

Total Control

The frightening figure of the Headmistress appeared around the door of the classroom, pointed silently at Emma, and beckoned her out.

Emma caught her breath. She had been waiting for this moment with utter trepidation. Feeling like a lamb being led to the slaughter, she followed the woman whose long, severe dress contrasted with the simple pinafore that she herself had to wear during classes and which scarcely covered her intimacies, leaving her back and buttocks bare.

As the Headmistress led the way down a stone-flagged corridor to the back of the house, the heels of her shoes clattered menacingly – in contrast to the shuffle of Emma's little slippers. She flung open a stout door.

'In!' she ordered, closing the door behind them both.

Emma looked around the room in astonishment. It was whitewashed and barely furnished. It looked more like a private chapel than anything else, with copies of Italian Renaissance pictures of the suffering of saints on the walls.

Standing in the middle of the room was the Major, dressed as always in his quasi-military uniform. But, instead of his swagger stick, he was holding a small electrical control box with several black knobs. One long lead led from the control box to a plug in the wall. Another one, thinner this time, led to one of the big patch pockets of his officer's khaki tunic.

He picked up what looked like part of a leather harness. Emma saw that it included a leather collar and that there was some lacing hanging down from it. He handed it to the Headmistress.

'Put it on her, my dear,' he said. Then, turning to the terrified Emma, he said: 'Hands behind your back! Now grip your forearms.'

Scared, Emma did as she was told. The woman fastened the leather collar around her neck. Then she went behind Emma and wrapped the other part of the harness around her wrists, tightening the lacing so that they were bound together. These were then joined to her collar by a strap which went down her back.

Emma felt the strap being tightened so that her wrists were held, still bound together, firmly against her back, and her head was held rigid by the collar. She felt quite helpless.

'Ever seen one of these before?' asked the Major, pulling a small plastic ball from his pocket. Emma saw that the ball was attached to the thinner electrical lead that ran back to the control box. It rather reminded her of the two electrically controlled vibrating balls that Henry had sometimes used to arouse her.

'No, sir,' she said.

'Well,' the Major added with a cruel laugh, 'you're going to see how it gives me total control, not only of your body but, more importantly, of your mind as well. Now turn around and bend over.'

Emma blushed with shame as she presented her naked bottom to him. She saw the woman going behind her with a small jar of lubricant in her hand. She felt a finger smearing a little of it on her rear entrance. Then she gasped as the Major pushed the little plastic ball up inside her, but only a tantalisingly short way.

'Now you see,' he said, as if talking to a child, 'I can pull the little ball most of the way out by the electrical lead.'

119

Emma gasped as she felt her muscles being stretched. It was horrible. She tried to lower her hands to reach the ball, but the strap between her wrists and her neck prevented her from doing so.

'Or I can push it back again.'

Emma felt his hand on her bottom as, with one extended finger, he pushed the ball back in again. She gave a little moan of relief as her muscles relaxed.

'But that's just by the way, little girl. Let's see what happens if I repeat the process with the current switched on!'

With one hand he turned one of the knobs on the control box and with the other he gave a little jerk to the lead behind her.

Emma gave a little scream as this time she felt not only her muscles being stretched, but also a little shock as the ball was pulled down.

'Yes!' murmured the Major. 'And if I push the little ball back in again?'

Again, Emma gave a little scream as she felt another slight shock. Her eyes filled with tears. She realised that the shocks only came when the ball was moved, either inward or outward. The Major did not turn a hair; his finger seemed somehow to be insulated against the shocks.

The Major was now standing to one side of her, with one hand on her bottom. Oh, for God's sake, she thought, please don't let him move the ball again!

She saw that the Headmistress had placed a tape recorder on a table in front of her.

'I think it's time for a little confession,' she said, switching on the machine. 'Now, first of all, who's Henry?'

'Henry?' said Emma, bristling. 'I don't know anyone called Henry.'

Instantly, she felt the little ball being moved. She gasped as she got another shock.

'Oh, but we think you do,' insisted the Major, pushing the little ball back in again and ignoring Emma's scream.

'In a moment I'm going to ask you that question again,' said the woman, harshly. 'And this time you're going to give me a proper answer, aren't you?'

The ball moved. 'Yes, yes,' Emma heard herself screaming through her tears. She could also feel sweat running down her face.

'Now, think for fifteen seconds of what you are going to say when I repeat the question – so as to avoid another little shock!'

Emma's mind was in torment. She would, she knew, now say anything to avoid another shock, mild though it was. There was a long pause. Emma was very conscious of the little ball. She tried to expel it with her muscles, but the Major's finger kept it in place.

'No, little girl,' he laughed cruelly. 'We'll just keep it there nicely at the entrance – ready to be activated again if we have any more little lies!'

The silence continued. It was driving Emma mad.

'So, let's start again,' said the woman suddenly. 'Who's Henry?'

'He's an old friend,' cried Emma.

Instantly the ball moved and Emma got another shock.

'You know very well, little girl, that you hate all men. You just live to please your Mistress. So he can't be a friend, can he?'

The ball was moved back again. Again Emma screamed. My God, this was total control alright!

'No, I hate him!' Emma heard herself cry.

'Good! That a good start,' said the woman. Through her tears, Emma saw the Major switch off the control box. She felt him remove the little ball.

'Now,' said the Headmistress, 'we're going to take you back to your lessons and then in an hour's time it will be your turn again with Total Control – and this time we shall want to hear exactly how Henry contacted you, how you planned to escape with him, and everything you got up to with him.'

'And,' added the Major, 'just remember, the slightest hesitation, and the little ball will be moved! So you've got a whole hour, whilst you're copying out those Greek words, to think about your next interrogation. You're going to tell us the whole truth!'

Moments later, a still sweating and tear-stained Emma, clasping her bottom, staggered back to her desk.

'Get on with your copying,' she was told, 'and don't make any mistakes!'

But how, Emma was thinking, am I going to be able to concentrate on copying out these strange Greek characters whilst all I can think of is that in one hour's time it will be my turn to go back to the interrogation room?

By the end of the day, after three more sessions of Total Control, Emma had finally taped a full and very contrite confession of how she had met Henry in his club, and of what had happened under the bedclothes. Then she had revealed how she had schemed to get her Bikini-belt taken off so that she could run off with him, and finally she had given all the details of the holiday she had spent with him.

They made her record it over and over again until it was word-perfect. With each session of the brainwashing interrogation, her confession become increasingly full of hatred towards Henry and towards all men.

'And tomorrow,' the Major said, 'we shall want to achieve a word-perfect recording of your attitude towards your Mistress. I shall want to hear how you sincerely long to serve your Mistress, utterly abjectly, and in any way she chooses.'

'And,' cut in the Headmistress, 'I shall want to hear you confess that you are a complete slut and that she is quite right to keep you in a purity belt and unable to play with yourself.'

'Oh!' gasped Emma.

'And,' went on the Major, in a menacing tone of voice, 'you're going to say how you love being under Sabhu's harsh control, how your Mistress is quite right to prevent you from sleeping with your husband, and how you really love earning your Mistress money with your body. I shall want it all spelt out in detail.'

'And, as a little extra surprise for your Mistress,' added the Headmistress with a smirk, 'by the end of the day we shall want a word-perfect recording of you saying that you deserve to be punished for your unfaithfulness. Then you're going to add that you are just her little dog, a little bitch she can do with as she likes. You're going to admit that you are very jealous of her other girls – of those whom she has had sponsored to be put into milk and, of course, of those who have been sponsored in certain other ways too. That's something you'd really love to have done to you too, isn't it? You'd love to be sponsored to be brought into milk or to be totally bald with a number tattooed on to your scalp, or to have your nipples considerably elongated, or to have your Mistresses's crest tattooed on to your body. Sponsorship is what you're secretly longing for, isn't it? Well?'

Emma hesitated for a moment before replying. It was enough to make the Major push the little ball back into her. 'Yes, yes,' she found herself screaming out aloud, 'I really do want to earn my Mistress a large sum of money by being sponsored –' Emma paused for breath, but immediately she felt the ball being moved again. 'Yes, yes,' she screamed, 'I long to be sponsored. It would be so exciting!'

'And?' came the Major's relentless voice, accompanied by another movement of the ball.

'And,' cried Emma desperately, 'and I deserve to be punished.'

123

'How, little girl? How?' asked the Major in an apparently innocent tone, as he turned the knob on the control box, making Emma scream yet again.

'By being brought into milk for my Mistress,' she shouted. But there was no letting up.

'And?'

This time the words came out in a rush. 'And for her clients, too. I should be so proud to be shown off to them, once my Mistress has had me sponsored, and has put me back under Sabhu's control.'

'And?' There was the same inexorable voice and the same tingling shock.

'And I beg my Mistress to have it done to me, too.'

'Good!' came the voice of the Major as he removed the ball. 'I think that will do for the time being. We'll see you again in an hour's time, and this time I will want to hear a really fluent and fervent plea to your Mistress about it all, without any prompting from me – just from the little ball! And I shall want to hear you sounding far more contrite and genuinely penitent about deceiving your Mistress. Then tomorrow we'll see about making a full recorded confession.'

The awful thing was, Emma reflected later, that she really had meant it all – at the time, anyway. She was being thoroughly brainwashed, she realised. But she was dreading having to make a full recording about it the following day.

All night she tossed and turned, thinking about it.

The three days were up. Emma knelt on all fours in the corner of the room. She was naked except for a large feather that protruded from between the cheeks of her buttocks.

The tip of the feather swayed with her slightest movement, making the cork, into which its other end had been inserted, move inside her anus – reminding her vividly of the terrifying movement of the ball of Total Control.

Sitting in the armchair in front of the desk in the reception room, with her long legs crossed, was Ursula. The Major put the tape recorder on the desk.

'Listen to this!' said the Headmistress to Ursula. 'We got the whole truth out of her alright, but I'm afraid you're not going to like it.'

She switched it on, and soon Ursula was looking furious as she heard Emma confessing how Henry had contacted her under Ursula's nose, how she had slipped up to London to meet him, how despite the Bikini-belt she had still satisfied Henry, and how she had subsequently managed to trick Sabhu before finally escaping with Henry.

My God, Ursula thought, the scheming little bitch! Well, for a start, she'd certainly have that private telephone in Emma's bedroom disconnected. And, as being locked in a chastity belt was clearly not enough to keep the little slut faithful to her Mistress, she'd just have to make sure that Emma didn't leave her own house in future without permission.

Emma lowered her eyes as she listened to her own voice going on to describe all that had happened on that wonderful holiday with Henry. Ursula, meanwhile, looked as though she was about to have a heart attack as she heard about the croupier and the bullfighters.

Ursula's eyes softened a little as, next, she heard Emma denouncing Henry and all men, and they glinted with satisfaction as the girl then claimed that her only purpose in life was to serve her Mistress abjectly and humbly, and that her heart's desire was to be offered for sponsorship.

'Well,' laughed Ursula mysteriously, 'I might well have a rather unusual sponsor for the girl.'

Emma gasped in horror. What did she mean? But then, as if to test the girl, Ursula snapped her fingers. With a well-rehearsed little bark, Emma, still on all fours, bounded over to Ursula and began to lick her

125

shoes. Still listening to the tape, which was now repeating Emma's pleadings about being sponsored, Ursula raised her shoe so that Emma could lick its sole clean.

Yes, Ursula was privately thinking, in the absence of her other girls, who were still in the Aegean, Emma would make a very suitable contribution to the special event that her half-German, half-Japanese friend, Ingrid Marburg, had been commissioned to organise in two weeks' time – with a very large payment in advance.

She and Ingrid had already made all the necessary arrangements, which meant that she could now return to the Aegean for another ten days. The clients who had arranged to stay at her villa and enjoy the services of her girls had now arrived, and she wanted to make sure that their every need was being satisfied. Then, leaving the girls safely locked up under the eye of Babindu in their kennels in the villa's grounds, she would return to England for a few days, along with Sabhu and Doctor Anna, just before this special event was due to take place.

She would keep Emma on tenterhooks about it, but without, of course, giving her any idea of what she was being let in for. Let her think that she was going out to join the other girls in the villa in the Aegean, or even that she was off on a second honeymoon with her Mistress!

This special event would pay very handsomely indeed but Ursula had been loath to expose her other girls to Ingrid's sadistic male clients. However, she felt quite differently about Emma – especially after hearing the confessions that Total Control had extracted from her.

Indeed, this newly subjugated Emma, with her class background and her striking good looks, would, no doubt, make a popular star performer at the special event – and, as such, be a top money earner! But despite all of Emma's apparently passionate assurances could Ursula really relax back in the Aegean, with her other girls and the visiting clients, and wait until Ingri gave her the signal that the special event was about to start?

Could she be sure that this apparently penitent and well-disciplined Emma would not, despite being back under the discreet supervision of Mrs Maunder, be getting up to any more tricks? She looked down again at the little creature humbly licking the soles of her shoes. Her Mistress' obedient little dog! Dog? Yes, that gave her an idea. And it was one that Ingrid might like to adapt for the special event, too!

'Right!' she said briskly, taking her cheque book out of her bag, 'I must congratulate you on a very satisfactory result. However, in view of what I have just heard, there are certain steps I must take immediately to ensure that this wicked little girl doesn't slip back into her old ways – no matter how much she may be protesting her adoration for me at the moment.'

'You mean . . .?' began the Headmistress.

'I mean that I want this unfaithful little bitch really put through the hoop here. I want her scared out of her wits at the mere possibility of being sent back here. You've got another three days. Then I shall come back and pick her up. I don't think there is anything more to get out of her, so you can let her off Total Control and just concentrate on really putting her through it physically!'

Emma felt like a prisoner being sentenced as she heard these words. Oh, what a fool she had been to have gone off with Henry! Oh, what a fool she had been to have imagined that Ursula would not exact some kind of terrible revenge!

'Oh no, Mistress, please,' she sobbed. 'No more. Please. Please take me away now. I'll be a good girl, I promise. I'll . . .'

She fell silent as the Major gripped her arm, pulled her up on to her feet and led her away.

The Major and Headmistress looked at each other and smiled.

17

Emma's Smart New Collar

Those last three days at the special school had been sheer hell.

The phrase 'Last one gets six' now seemed to be graven on Emma's heart. Invariably, it seemed, it had always been she who had had to bend over and present her bare bottom to the Major's swagger stick. Never in all her life had she had to run, to crawl, to sweat so much – around the grounds, or the cross-country course, or in the house. And always there had been that fear: 'Last one . . .'

And as well as exhausting her physically, the staff had also demanded that she continue to concentrate her mental energies on worshipping her Mistress . Her head ached as she thought of all the essays she had had to write, and of the little speeches she had had to make in front of her equally scared companions of both sexes – oh, the brainwashing never seemed to stop!

Then, at last, those three days had been over. Dressed according to Ursula's instruction, she was once again taken into the reception room where her Mistress was waiting. Emma stood there shyly, like a schoolgirl whose parents had come to take her out for the day.

This time Ursula seemed all sweetness and light, but then she produced a strange-looking dog collar and asked the Major to lock it around Emma's neck. Unlike the collar attached to the Bikini-belt, which was fastened by means of a normal padlock and key, this colla fastened at the back of the neck with a small combination lock.

The collar was nearly three inches wide and was made of stiff red leather, strengthened by shiny metal studs. To make it even stronger and to stop anyone from simply cutting it off with a knife, it was fitted with curved metal rods at the top and bottom. It had a ring on the front, and there was a curious little box on the back, near to the combination lock.

Emma saw that there was a small keyhole in the box, as if for switching something on or off, or for unlocking the top of the box so as to put something in it. Precisely what, she did not know.

Before putting the collar around her neck, the Major showed her that on one side was a small flat plate. Emma blushed, with a mixture of horror and excitement, as she read the inscription: EMMA. PROPERTY OF MISS U. DE VERE. REWARD FOR RETURN. Below was Ursula's telephone number.

Emma was even more horrified, and yet also secretly thrilled, to read on a small plate on the other side of the collar the engraving: NO. 76645. LOST DOG DEFENCE LEAGUE. PLEASE TELEPHONE IF FOUND. Again there was a telephone number.

There was a sinister click as the Major closed the combination lock behind her neck, securing the collar firmly around her throat. Only someone who knew the combination could take the collar off, Emma realised ruefully. Clearly it was now intended to remain on her permanently.

Ursula smiled as the collar was locked around Emma's neck. Now Emma was indeed hers again. The collar marked the girl as her property; hers to do with as she pleased.

Emma gasped, however, as she felt how wide the collar was and how it forced her to keep her chin up high. Clearly she was going to be constantly aware of it, even when it was hidden under a scarf.

129

Ursula was very quiet as she drove Emma back to her home, as if she was planning something exciting. Emma wondered what it could be and whether she would be involved. Oh, I do hope so, she thought.

Emma had not liked to question Ursula about the collar she was now having to wear and, when she had finally plucked up the courage to ask if she would have to wear it permanently, Ursula had reacted angrily.

'How dare you start questioning me,' she had replied. 'You just exist to do what you're told, when you're told, instantly and unquestioningly. Nothing else is any of your business. I don't like inquisitiveness in a girl, and if Sabhu were here in England I'd have him thrash you for impertinence!'

After that tirade, Emma had not dared to say another word. At least, she supposed, it was better than a Bikini-belt, and she wondered whether, with Sabhu out in the Aegean and Ursula apparently about to fly back there, it was intended as a more permanent and practical substitute. Certainly, those embarrassing inscriptions had a profound psychological effect. Oh, how humiliating they were!

Luckily, Ursula had given her a scarf to tie around her neck to hide the collar. Now she would always have to wear such a scarf, she realised. She put her hand up to touch her neck and felt the scarf, and below it the awful collar.

Suddenly, as if she had made up her mind about something, Ursula started to talk about an exciting forthcoming house party that she was arranging with Ingrid, a half-German half-Japanese friend of hers. Cunningly, she started making Emma very jealous, by saying what fun she would be having there with some other girls. With an innocent air, she mentioned that she was wondering whether or not to ask Emma, too. Not of course, that Ursula wasn't perfectly aware of how much Emma hated being left out of a party.

130

Emma's heart began to race. Her Mistress was considering inviting her to come and join her – not telling her to come, but inviting her! And Ursula's parties were always so exciting. The mention of other girls had made her feel jealous – she certainly wasn't going to abandon the field to her rivals for her Mistress's affections!

Perhaps, she thought, she would be taken out to the Aegean to join Ursula's other girls in her villa. Perhaps Ursula was inviting some special guests there. Yes, that must be the plan, she decided. How exciting! She had been so disappointed and jealous of the other girls when Ursula had originally left her behind, because of her husband coming back home again. But now everything would be alright after all.

'Oh, Madam,' she said, with genuine fervour. 'Yes, I'd love to come. Yes, please.'

'Oh, I'm not sure,' replied Ursula, with her tongue firmly in her cheek, 'whether this party will really be your form, Emma.'

In reality, of course, Emma, like her new girl Sofia, would be playing a key role, but she did not want to let on about that! Then she had woundingly added, 'For one thing, I don't think you are beautiful enough! But I suppose I might take you there as the ugly duckling.'

Ugly duckling! She was beautiful! Not quite as striking, of course, as her Mistress, but certainly not an ugly duckling!

But, thrilled at being included at all, Emma had suppressed her fury. At least her fantastic Mistress had agreed that she could come. But she had no idea what it was all about – or at whose house it would be held. All she knew was that Ursula had told her that she would be away for over a week. A week with her Mistress! How wonderful!

Arriving at her house, Emma noticed a line running across the drive, as if it had recently been dug up for a pipe or cable to be laid. Ursula, she presumed, must have told the jobbing gardener for whose services she paid to carry out some kind of modification. She wondered what it might be, but she did not dare to ask. Ursula was always so fiercely secretive!

Parking the car in front of the house, Ursula curtly told Emma to remain in it, and then went off to have a quick word with the gardener. Emma heard them talking.

'Yes, Madam, I've laid that special wire in a trench around the garden, just as you said. I hear it's very effective at stopping dogs from straying, but what sort of dog are you thinking of sending up here?'

'Oh, probably quite a large and valuable one,' Ursula replied with a laugh.

What on earth were they talking about? Emma had wondered.

Then Ursula had gone into the house, saying that she wanted to have a word in private with Mrs Maunder. Mrs Maunder! So she was back! Emma's heart sank. She could have done without her.

Soon Ursula came back to the car and told Emma to get out. Then she inserted a little key into the small box attached to her collar.

'And in future, Emma,' she said, 'I don't think you'll feel like straying out of the garden!'

Emma was mystified.

'But why not?' she asked. 'What do you mean?'

But Ursula ignored her question. 'I shall be back in an hour. Go and have a look at the garden. Then get ready to serve me lunch and afterwards we'll have a little fun. I'm in the mood!'

Leaving Emma standing there, her mouth open with astonishment and excitement, Ursula disappeared in her car.

Curious to know what her Mistress had meant, Emma went for a walk in the garden. Nothing very much seemed to have changed but, as she approached the end of the drive, where she'd first noticed the trench that had been dug for the wire, she felt a series of little shocks in her neck. Hastily, she backed away and the shocks ceased.

Then, when she went across to the other side of the garden, near to where it merged with the surrounding fields, she saw more signs of a recently dug trench, and suddenly the shocks started again. Again she backed away and the shocks ceased.

Horrified, she followed the line of the trench. It went right around the garden, and every time she went near it the shocks started.

There was, she realised, no way out; she was a prisoner in her own garden. She was the 'large and valuable dog' about which she had heard Ursula talking to the gardener. She was going to be confined to her own garden, just like a dog. She was certainly going to be prevented from straying, with Henry or with anyone else.

Oh, how humiliating! And yet how exciting! Ursula never ceased to amaze her!

And how difficult things were going to be when John was home. He and Emma didn't, of course, sleep together, as Ursula had arranged for Doctor Anna to write to him saying that she was not fit enough to undertake her conjugal duties. She would always have to wear a scarf to hide the collar from his eyes, but what excuse could she make when he suggested they went out? Thank heavens he was away again for the time being.

But there was more to follow, as she discovered when she went up to her room. Her private telephone, her secret link with the outside world, the number on which Henry had contacted her, had been removed. Now, she realised, all calls, both in and out, would have to be made via Mrs Maunder's phone.

Not only was she now a prisoner in her own home, but she could not even, without permission, have any communication with the outside world.

She remembered Ursula saying, after hearing her confession at the Major's terrifying establishment, that there were certain steps she would have to take to ensure that 'this wicked girl' did not slip back into her former ways. Goodness, it was exciting being under such strict control!

With a sudden start, she saw that laid out on her bed was a skimpy French parlour maid's outfit. She remembered Ursula saying that she would be back in an hour, and that she would expect Emma to be ready to serve her lunch. But she had not realised that Ursula had also meant her to dress for the part; that must have been what she had been speaking to Mrs Maunder about – how embarrassing!

And Ursula would be back here at any moment! And after lunch they would make love!

Emma was over the moon with excitement as she slipped into the knickerless and provocative black silk outfit, with its white pinafore and matching starched cap. She began to feel moist with anticipation. It had been so long since she and Ursula had . . . For good luck, she also painted her nipples to match her lipstick, and then simply could not resist doing the same to her now eager beauty lips. She had already rouged her cheek bones and now, giggling to herself, she also rubbed a little of the rouge into her soft and still almost hairless mound.

Suddenly, she heard wheels on the gravel. Ursula must have returned. There was a sudden imperious ringing of the front door bell. Hastily, Emma put her hand up to her hair and ran downstairs.

Passing a mirror she felt even even more aroused as she saw how, below her prominent shiny collar, the transparent blouse of the maid's uniform accentuated her otherwise bare breasts and scarlet nipples. She blushed as she saw how the little pinafore scarcely hid her naked rouged mound and her scarlet beauty lips. Yes, she decided, she looked a really lovely little creature – and one that Ursula would simply not be able to resist!

The bell rang again. Emma rushed down and opened it, closing her eyes humbly as she did so and making a little curtsey.

Then she gasped, for there, standing on the mat in front of her lowered eyes, was not just one pair of smart women's shoes, but two!

'Ingrid, my dear,' came the voice of Ursula, 'this little creature is Emma, the girl I was telling you about. Now let's go in!'

18

The Maid Called Emma

Emma stood back against the wall, a napkin folded over
her left arm. She was jealously watching Ursula and her
friend, Ingrid, as they tucked into the delicious lunch of
filet of beef which Mrs Maunder had produced, and
which Emma had just had to serve to them.

She looked hungrily at their plates, and wondered
whether she would be able to steal any leftover scraps.
She felt half-starved, and *filet* – well!

Emma had been highly embarrassed at being seen by
Mrs Maunder in the revealing French maid's outfit, but
the housekeeper had made no comment. She had also
been embarrassed by the presence of Ursula's petite and
rather rather oriental-looking friend. Ingrid ... the
name rang a bell. She must, Emma realised, be the
friend of Ursula's with whom her Mistress was arranging the mysterious special event. She certainly looked
like she might be half-Japanese.

Ingrid, too, had made no comment about Emma's
erotic appearance, as though the sight of a half-naked
chatelaine waiting at the table with painted nipples and
body lips was quite normal in an English country
house. She was, however, very impressed, just as Ursula
had intended her to be, by Ursula's evident power and
authority over an attractive and well-connected young
married Englishwoman – or Irishwoman, as Ursula had
laughingly corrected her. If, Ingrid thought, Ursula

would bring this young woman to the special event, then they would be home and dry!

The two women were chattering away in German, which Emma could not understand. Then she remembered that the woman Ursula had mentioned in the car, in connection with the house party, was half-German and half-Japanese. This had to be her!

From time to time, Ursula would point at Emma, making her wonder what they were saying. But perhaps it was as well that she did not understand.

'You see, the club members are so demanding,' Ingrid was saying.

'I'm not surprised, in view of what they're paying,' Ursula laughed. 'I think I've been in the wrong business! My women clients pay very well, but not like these men.'

'Well, you'll be doing very well out of them if you produce this girl and Sofia to back up my two. They're certainly going to love Emma, as a slightly older girl, being made to perform. But are you really sure about putting her through it? After all, she is married and lives in this country.'

'Yes, and she is still my property and under my control,' replied Ursula with sudden vehemence. 'She'll damned well do exactly what I want!'

'But what will happen when her husband comes back?' insisted Ingrid.

'Well, although she does not know it yet, her husband has confided in me that he's going to be abroad again for several months. He hasn't told her yet as he did not want her to be upset! But he's asked me to keep an eye on her and break the news to her gently – and, meanwhile, to keep her busy.'

Ingrid burst out laughing. 'Keep her busy! Oh yes, I'm sure you can see to that. She'll soon have something else on her mind! But seriously, if you're going to keep her here, won't there be the risk of her trying to run away?'

'Oh no, she can't escape. Let me show you!' laughed Ursula. 'Have a look at her collar.'

Ingrid got up to take a closer look. 'Well?' she asked. 'It's just like the dog collars that many Mistresses like to see their girls wearing.'

'But this one's special,' laughed Ursula again. 'Watch!'

'Now Emma,' she said in English, pointing to a clump of trees just outside the garden, 'would you like to run across the lawn and over the garden fence to those trees?'

'No, Madam, no! I can't!' cried Emma in genuine alarm. 'My collar – it won't let me!'

Ursula smiled at her friend. 'You see?' she said.

Emma saw Ingrid nod her head pensively. 'That's brilliant!' she said in German, her eyes sparkling. 'You mean she can't leave the place? She can't escape? Well, perhaps I should use the same system for the special event. It'll make security that much better.'

'Yes indeed,' agreed Ursula, also now speaking in German again. 'It's a technique I've already used in similar circumstances – for my girls in the garden of the villa in the Aegean. I was worried that they might try to escape, but these collars certainly put any question of that right out of their heads. Psychologically, too, they make a girl feel, even more, that she utterly belongs to her Mistress.'

'And yet it seems so simple,' said Ingrid.

'Yes, it is, once the cable has been laid around the house, and you've still got plenty of time to get that done.' Ursula paused and then said in English, 'Well, my dear, I think we've finished talking business, so why don't we enjoy ourselves with Emma?

Ingrid beckoned Emma over and then, with a well-manicured hand, began to stroke the girl's cheek. 'Keep still,' she said, in a strange German accent, and started to run her hands down over Emma's breasts and on to her belly.

'Yes,' she said turning back to Ursula. 'I think that would be a splendid idea. How should we use her?'

'Oh,' Ursula laughed, 'she thinks she's very good at giving pleasure whilst she is hidden under the bed-clothes, don't you Emma?'

Emma blushed as she realised that Ursula was alluding to the way she had been forced by Total Control to confess how she had first pleased Henry in his club. 'Yes, Madam,' she said with a little sob.

'So off you go upstairs. Draw the curtains and then, still wearing your maid's costume, get into the big bed and hide yourself down at the foot of it, until you're told to start working your way up! Now go!'

With a little cry, Emma rushed out of the room and up into the spare room with the big bed – the room in which Ursula had so often slept when staying there.

Curled up under the bedclothes at the foot of the large bed, Emma did not know whether to feel deeply humiliated at having Ursula treat her in this way in front of a stranger, or to be wildly excited at the thought that, within a few minutes, she would be pleasing her Mistress.

It was so long since she had been called to Ursula's bed on anything like a regular basis. When she had been kept in the line of cages in Ursula's house, she had had to compete with the other girls for Ursula's attentions. Then, when her husband had come back to England and she had been sent home, Ursula had only come down to enjoy her on the occasional weekend.

Suddenly she heard the door opening, and the voices of the two women, still speaking in German, as they made their way across the room to undress in the bathroom. She felt a sudden burst of arousal surging through her. She heard feminine laughter coming from the bathroom. Evidently, Ursula found the fragile beauty of her half-Japanese friend very stimulating. Emma began to feel jealous.

'You'll find her well trained in the art of pleasing a woman,' she suddenly heard Ursula say from alongside the bed. 'Look, here's the list of commands which she's been taught to obey. They're in English, but alongside each of them is a description in German. I've brought it especially for you! So we can both use her as a stimulus for our own love-making!'

Emma gave a little gasp. She was going to be used by Ursula and Ingrid just as she was used by Ursula's clients! She did not know whether to feel disappointed or excited.

The two women now sat on the edge of the bed, naked under their satin negligees, and kissed. Emma could hear both of them uttering little moans of pleasure and, jealously, she began to imagine what they were doing. Then, suddenly, she heard them laugh and felt the top of the bedclothes being pulled back on either side, but instead of a pair of hairy legs like Henry's reaching down towards the bottom of the bed, she felt two pairs of soft, feminine legs brushing and rubbing up against her body.

'What have we here?' she heard Ursula laugh. 'Ingrid, why don't you reach down and put it properly in position, and then use the list of commands?'

Once again, instead of Henry's strong masculine hand, it was Ingrid's well-manicured female hand, with its long, carefully painted nails, that reached down and gripped her hair. She felt her head being slowly drawn up and then placed carefully in position.

'Worship!' she heard Ingrid say, and immediately she obeyed, kissing the woman's beauty lips reverently and respectfully, as if she were indeed worshipping them. She was aware that Ursula and Ingrid were meanwhile kissing each other passionately and playing with each other's nipples. She could taste Ingrid becoming more and more aroused.

'Lick like a dog!' came the next order, and obediently Emma began to waggle her tongue up and down the

140

length of Ingrid's beauty lips. She could hear her crying out in ecstasy.

'Part lips!' came the next order. Emma reached up and parted the beauty lips and inserted her tongue. The woman gave a little cry, and then she clasped her thighs around Emma's head.

'Lick it up!' came the order as the woman lay back and relaxed.

'My turn now,' she heard Ursula say, and she felt her head being pulled over to Ursula's beauty lips whilst the two women started to kiss and play with each other again.

Ursula put her through the same routine, with the same result.

Poor Emma was now beginning to feel exhausted, as she lay still hidden under the sheets, whilst the two women lay back and caught their breath. Oh, how she longed to throw back the bedclothes and join in their fun! But she did not dare to do so.

'I'll show you another exciting way of using her,' Emma heard Ursula whisper, after a brief respite.

She felt Ursula roll over and lie on top of her friend.

'Part your legs, darling,' she heard Ursula murmur. Each woman's beauty lips were now rubbing against the other's, as they clasped each other, kissing passionately. There was a pause as they excited each other more and more.

'Come behind!' she heard Ursula say, harshly. It was an order that the hated Sabhu had repeatedly trained her to obey. Still keeping the bedclothes over her, Emma knelt up and moved in between Ingrid's outstretched legs, whilst straddling Ursula's closed ones. Then she lowered her mouth and applied her tongue to where the two highly aroused pairs of beauty lips met.

She was rewarded by both women giving a series of little jerks of sheer ecstasy, as their juices mixed together under the stimulus of Emma's hot little tongue. She felt them once again becoming more and more aroused, then finally there was a cry from Ursula that was almost immediately matched by one from Ingrid.

 Emma felt both excited and tormented by their response. She was wildly aroused herself, but would she, too, be allowed a little relief? At least she was not locked into a frustrating Bikini-belt, as she would normally have been with Ursula's clients.

Had she really pleased them? Sabhu's training had ensured that this question was uppermost in her mind. The threat of his whip always seemed to hang over her, even in his absence. The slightest sign from a client that she was not fully satisfied with a girl's efforts had invariably meant a degrading thrashing in front of the other girls. And now, she knew that Ursula herself would thrash her if she or her friend were in any way not fully pleased. Desperately, she re-applied her now flagging tongue.

Suddenly, she heard Ingrid whispering something in German to Ursula, and then Ursula's answering laugh. Leaving her concealed underneath the bedclothes, the two women got up. She could hear them doing something and laughing. Now what was going to happen? Both women got back into bed, one on either side of her.

'Up you come, little girl,' ordered Ursula.

With a little cry of delight, Emma wriggled her way up between the two women. Oh, the lovely feeling of fresh air! Eagerly, she turned on to her side in the half-darkness towards Ursula. She could feel Ingrid's naked body behind her. She put her hands lovingly around Ursula's neck, just as she had so often done in the past.

'Grip me!' ordered Ursula. It was another order that Sabhu had trained her to obey. Still lying on her side in the soft bed, she gripped Ursula's waist between her thighs. She was, she realised, now wide open. She gave a little startled jump as she felt two well-greased rubber

142

dildos, strapped on to the women's hips, pressing against her between her legs. As she felt Ingrid's pressing against her rear orifice, she tried to move her hand to push it away, but Ursula gripped her wrists firmly.

'Relax your little bottom for my friend, like a good girl,' ordered Ursula. Then, further aroused by the sight of Emma's collar, she began to kiss her passionately on the lips.

Seconds later Emma gave a little cry, though it was muffled by Ursula's lips, as Ingrid's dildo finally penetrated her behind. She felt Ingrid's hands excitingly gripping her nipples from behind as she held Emma to her, forcing the dildo deeper into her. Wantonly, Emma found herself beginning to press her body back against Ingrid and accept the entire length of her dildo.

Moments later, she again tried to cry out as she felt Ursula's dildo beginning to part her beauty lips and then penetrate her. Ursula was now holding her still by the waist as she, too, drove her dildo deep into her.

Doubly held and doubly penetrated, Emma could hardly move. Oh, the discomfort and pain! But, oh, too, the sheer shame-making excitement! And the feeling of utter helplessness!

Ursula and Ingrid were now thrusting hard into her, both of them highly stimulated and aroused, mentally and physically, as the strategically-placed rubber knobs at the base of their dildos tantalised and tickled their beauty buds.

Emma, her hands again around Ursula's neck, found herself beginning to respond to their thrusts. Soon the women were rewarded by hearing the girl's own little cries of ecstasy mingling with their own . . .

19

A Terrifying Journey to a Special Event

Emma was pacing up and down her bedroom, occasionally looking out at the beautiful garden with its carefully tended lawn. It was remarkable how much it had all improved since Ursula had started to pay for a regular jobbing gardener, even if his duties had apparently included burying the cable which triggered off her collar.

For two whole weeks she had been confinèd to the house and garden, thanks to the collar. She wondered whether driving out of the grounds in a car would be a way of beating the underground cable that surrounded the house, but her husband was away abroad and Ursula had taken the keys to her car off with her.

If she wanted to go anywhere, she had to ask Mrs Maunder to call a taxi, and invariably the housekeeper replied, 'Oh, I don't think Miss de Vere would want to pay for that.' Nor, with her private telephone removed, had she been able to make any outside calls.

So she really had been a prisoner in her own house this past fortnight. A prisoner with nothing else to do except think of the thrilling forthcoming special event, as Ursula had mysteriously described it.

She had had to start keeping her daily record book again, just as Sabhu had used to make her do. It was humiliating, but at least she wasn't, to her delight, locked into the awful Bikini-belt that she had last seen in Sabhu's hands in the car outside the vaccination centre. She had been rather surprised that Ursula had made no mention of it.

Perhaps the frightening Doctor Anna had advised Ursula that, while she and Sabhu were in the Aegean and therefore unable to supervise Emma or deal with any emergency that might arise, it would be unwise to lock her into it. Or perhaps the collar was regarded as a simpler alternative. Certainly she would not want anyone, not even Henry, to read those degrading inscriptions.

Perhaps she was now considered 'safe' after her terrifying brainwashing at the Major's special school. Of course, she knew that it was not for her to question Ursula's actions or decisions, but, whatever the reason, it was a lovely liberated feeling. At first, she had thought she would be free to play with herself to her heart's content, just as she had done before Ursula had taken her to the school. Strangely, however, she now felt herself mentally inhibited from doing so. Had she really been brainwashed into wanting to keep herself pure for her Mistress – pure for whatever was going to happen at the special event?

She had not heard another word from Ursula, but surely it must now be about time that Emma joined her? It had all sounded so exciting. But when was it going to start? And how, and where?

Suddenly her thoughts were interrupted by the telephone ringing in Mrs Maunder's room. Oh, how she hated not being able to answer it herself – it was so humiliating!

Moments later, Mrs Maunder appeared. 'Miss de Vere is on the telephone for you, my child!'

Oh, how she hated being called that! But never mind, Ursula was on the line! Her Mistress wanted to speak to her!

She rushed downstairs to Mrs Maunder's room. 'You will be picked up today at noon,' came Ursula's cold voice, 'and don't forget to bring your daily record book!'

Then, before Emma could say a word, Ursula had hung up. From where had she rung? Was she still abroad? Was she now on her way here? Goodness!

She saw Mrs Maunder wave an admonishing finger. 'Now, my child, just compose yourself and get ready to be collected.'

But what should she wear? What she should she take? What sort of climate was she going to? Would Ursula be angry if she took anything at all? She normally liked Emma to come naked under her dress and to bring nothing, so that she could then be dressed from scratch, like a doll. Perhaps just a loose frock would do, and a scarf to hide her collar.

Emma's tummy churned with excitement as she heard the drawing room clock downstairs chime twelve. Moments later, there was the noise of a car on the drive. She looked out of the window. It was Ursula's car! Oh, how thrilling!

But she felt a cold shiver of apprehension when she saw that the car was being driven by Sabhu, dressed in black and wearing a chauffeur's hat.

Sabhu! She had imagined that he was still out in the Aegean looking after Ursula's other girls. She had even begun to hope that he was now out of her life for ever.

Would he ever forgive her for the way she had tricked him before escaping with Henry? She knew he would have taken it all very personally. A mere chit of a girl had succeeded in deceiving him! He would would certainly want to get his revenge sooner or later.

She was even more horrified when she saw he was alone. Had Ursula deliberately sent him, knowing the effect his mere presence would have on her? She gave a little start when she saw that he was carrying a leather lead – just like the dog leads he used when he took a girl out of her cage in Ursula's attic and downstairs to show off to a prospective client. Emma looked at it fearfully. Like his dressage whip, it had been a symbol of his authority over her.

Her heart was now beating fast. She longed to run away, but how could she? Gradually, she regained control of herself. She reminded herself that she had been invited by Ursula to join her for this exciting-sounding special event! What harm could Sabhu do her? No, she thought, she would just try to be very brave and ignore him.

'My child –' the voice of Mrs Maunder interrupted her thoughts, '– that nice Mr Sabhu has come to collect you.' Dumbly, Emma followed her downstairs and out into the drive.

'I'll go and get a cup of tea ready for you, Mr Sabhu,' Mrs Maunder said, cheerfully. 'I expect you've got a long drive ahead of you.'

Emma heard Mrs Maunder walk back into the house. She saw that Sabhu was contemptuously looking her up and down. She gave a little shiver of fear. She was about to cry out, 'You can't do anything to me. I'm Madam's guest!' when suddenly he gave her an order.

'Handbag!' She handed it to him without question. He opened it and took out the little record book. He glanced at it and, apparently satisfied, put it carefully into his inside pocket. Then he threw her handbag into the car.

'Hands behind your back!' Nervously, she obeyed, and instantly felt him grab her wrists. She tried to twist away, but he was too strong for her. He snapped a pair of handcuffs on to her wrists. She was in his power again!

She felt herself trembling as he came slowly round in front of her again. She tried to back away as he raised

147

a hand to feel her breasts through her dress, and then her waist and her belly. Was he checking whether she had put on any weight, or just indulging himself?

Then, sneering, he pulled off her scarf, revealing her collar. With a contemptuous laugh, he snapped the lead on to the ring at the front of it. Then, holding the lead with one hand, he used the other to open a rear door of the car.

'Get in,' he ordered. Struggling awkwardly because of her handcuffs, but too scared to say a word, Emma sat down in the car. She saw him fasten the other end of the lead on to a hook above the window. Then he pulled a soft leather mask out of his pocket. Emma gave a gasp as she recognised it. It was just like the one that Ursula had sometimes enjoyed putting on to her when she took her to bed.

'No, not that, please!' she cried, but Sabhu did not reply. Instead, grinning cruelly, he let it dangle in front of her face. Clearly he was enjoying his revenge! She longed to push him away, but with her hands cuffed behind her she was quite helpless.

Deftly, Sabhu slipped the mask over her head. Eyeholes had been cut into it, but hinged over each one was a blinker which Sabhu quickly snapped down and clicked into place. She could now see nothing.

She was about to cry again, when she felt a zip fastener over her mouth being closed, pulling her chin up and effectively muzzling her. She could still breathe through two little holes below her nostrils. She felt Sabhu tightening the lacing of the mask at the back of her head, and realised that she would not be able to shake it off. She was now in total darkness except for a glimmer of light from the two little breathing holes.

'Madam not want you to see where I take you,' she heard Sabhu laugh, cruelly. 'And I not want to be disturbed whilst driving.'

She heard him unhook the end of her lead from above

the window, and then she was pushed down on to the floor of the spacious car. She heard the lead being clicked on to a ring low down. She tried to sit up but was held down by the lead. She felt a rug being thrown over her. Anyone looking in through the window would simply see a rug on the floor of the car, with perhaps a dog playing underneath it.

The door was slammed shut. She heard Sabhu lock the driver's door from the outside, and the locks in the other doors clicked shut too.

Then she heard Sabhu stride off, presumably to enjoy his cup of tea with Mrs Maunder, leaving Emma blindfolded and muzzled, with her hands fastened behind her back and her collar firmly secured by the lead to an attachment on the floor of Ursula's locked car.

Never, she thought, had she felt so helpless. Was this all an exciting game of Ursula's to get her into the right frame of mind for their eventual reunion at the special event? Or was this just Sabhu making sure that he got his revenge in early?

After what seemed like ages, she heard Sabhu's footsteps on the gravel of the drive. She heard the driver's door being unlocked, and then the car shook slightly as Sabhu settled himself into his seat and fastened his safety belt.

She heard another click and realised that he had locked the child safety catches on the doors and windows. She would not now be able to open either, even if she did somehow manage to get her hands to the right place. She heard him start the engine and felt the car move off down the drive.

Her heart was in her mouth again, as she realised that the car must be being driven down towards the line marking the trench at the end of the drive. She gritted her teeth, expecting a nasty series of shocks from her collar.

But nothing happened! Soon she heard the noise of

the wheels changing as the car swung from the gravel drive on to the smooth tarmac of the road. Clearly, as she had half-suspected, the collar did not work inside a car!

For what seemed like hours Emma lay on the floor of the car, helpless and hidden under the rug. Where was she being taken? And why like this? She had to admit that it was all rather exciting.

Again and again, she wondered whether Ursula had ordered her to be treated like this simply as a build-up to the mysterious special event. Surely her presence could not be so important that Ursula was taking no chances in getting her there? Or, more likely, was it just Sabhu's unauthorised revenge for being made to look such a fool when she had escaped with Henry?

She heard the car stop at what she guessed must be a petrol station. For a moment, as Sabhu got out and before he locked the doors, she heard voices – the voices of ordinary people. What would they think, as they queued up to pay behind Sabhu, if someone told them that in the back of his car was a gagged and chained woman, a woman who was highly excited at the thought of being taken off to meet her Mistress? They would never believe it!

She was tempted to cry out, but she knew that, behind the mask zipped across her mouth, she could only make little moaning noises. Moreover, with all the windows shut no one would be able to hear her. In any case she could, she felt, put up with any amount of degradation from Sabhu. The fact was that she was thrilled at the thought that soon she would be meeting her Mistress again – and, so far as she knew, as her guest!

She heard Sabhu get back into the car and, without a word to her, start off again. Time passed slowly . . .

Suddenly, Emma felt the car swing off the road and on to another gravel drive. It seemed very long – much longer than hers! Then, at last, the car stopped. She heard Sabhu talking to someone – a man. He, too, seemed to have a strange oriental accent.

She heard the door being opened and her lead being unfastened. She felt the rug being lifted off her, and heard the other man laugh. Then hands reached down and lifted her out of the car. They held her up by her arms, but propelled her forward. She could see nothing.

She felt herself being dragged up some steps and then down a stone staircase. She heard a creak as a door was opened, and then felt herself being thrust through it and down on to a stone floor.

Her hands were unfastened and pushed into strange padded gloves which seemed to immobilise her fingers. Her shoes were taken off. She blushed under the mask as her dress was slipped off. She was now barefoot and stark naked – except for her gloves and collar.

Under her feet, she felt straw on the floor. The lead was unfastened from her collar and she heard the click of a padlock as a heavy chain was fastened to it instead.

She heard Sabhu and the other man leaving the room, and then the sound of a heavy door being slammed shut and locked.

She was alone, but where? And why? Desperately, she tried to untie the lacing of her mask and get it off. But she found she could not grip anything with her now helpless hands which were encased in what indeed seemed to be some kind of heavily padded boxing glove. But it couldn't actually be a boxing glove, she realised, as her thumb was bunched up with her fingers, rather than being separately enclosed.

She would not, she realised, even be able to play with herself now, even if she wanted to!

She wanted to cry out, but the mask prevented her from doing so. Frantically and ineffectually, she began to rub her head against the floor like a dog trying to rid itself of a muzzle. Then, tilting her head right back, she tried to peer down through the little airholes in the front of the mask.

She seemed to be in total darkness. Then, slowly, she began to make out a little line of faint light – as though from under a door. She tried to crawl over towards it, but the heavy chain attached to her collar pulled her up short. It did not even allow her to stand up.

She was, she realised, crawling on little flagstones. She felt back along to the end of the chain. It was securely fastened to a ring set low down in the wall.

She felt a tiny pile of straw. Was this intended for her wastes? How awful!

Suddenly, she heard the two men's voices outside her door. They were laughing cruelly. Then came the noise of other doors being opened and then slammed shut. She thought she heard a little moan, a female moan, as though from behind a mask like hers.

Were there other girls chained up in similar dark cellars? Was this all part of the special event? Who was the oriental-sounding man? Was Sabhu exceeding his orders by treating her in this way like an animal, or had she been tricked by Ursula? My God! But why? For what purpose?

20

Emma Meets her Companions

Just how long Emma lay there she did not know. She slept for some of the time.

Then suddenly she heard the door being unlocked and footsteps, again as of two men, approaching her. She made little moaning noises behind her gag and then felt her hooded head being raised and then firmly pulled back so that, had she been able to see, she would have been looking straight up at the ceiling. She could not move her head at all. Then she felt the zip-fastener over her mouth being opened very slightly – not enough to allow her to speak, but just enough to allow the lip of a little medicine glass to be put to her mouth and its contents quickly poured into her throat.

It tasted oily and horrible, and she tried to spit it out, but the zip-fastener had already been closed again. Her head was still being held right back and now she felt a hand stroking her throat, like a someone making a dog swallow a dose. Satisfied that she had indeed swallowed the oily liquid, the unseen hands released her head, and she heard footsteps going away from her. Then came the sounds of the door being slammed shut and locked again.

She heard other doors being unlocked, and little feminine moaning noises like those she herself had made, shortly followed by the sounds of the doors being slammed shut and locked again. Were other women being treated as she had been?

Some time later, to her deep embarrassment, she found herself twice having to empty herself on to the straw. Unable to see, she desperately tried to cover her wastes with clean straw. How shame-making! Had the liquid been a purge of some sort? Was she being cleaned out for some purpose? How horrible! But why?

Hours later, perhaps, she thought, the following morning, she heard the sound of voices outside and of other doors being opened and shut. Finally, she heard her own door being unlocked and then flung open, and what she guessed were several people entering the room. Scared, she cowered in the corner.

Her head was again seized, but this time the blinkers over her eyes were snapped open. She gazed about her, dazzled by the light of a bare electric bulb hanging from the ceiling. She was in what seemed to be a windowless cellar, with bare brick walls and ceiling and a floor of flagstones that sloped away slightly to a drain hole in the wall. The room had a small, solid looking door. It was ajar, and Emma had a glimpse of what seemed to be a corridor.

She trembled as she saw that Sabhu was standing over her, his whip in one hand and a long walking stick in the other. She tried to speak but found she was still gagged. Alongside Sabhu was a large, bald, Japanese-looking man, stripped to the waist. His face was expressionless, inscrutable. A short-handled whip was tucked into his wide leather belt. Horrified, she tried to crawl away but the chain on her collar held her fast, making the Japanese man burst into a cruel laugh.

Then the familiar and dreaded figure of Doctor Anna entered. She was followed by Ursula and Ingrid, who were laughing and talking to each other. With a sinking heart, Emma realised that her Mistress must have ordered her to be treated like this and that it was not just a matter of Sabhu exceeding his authority to get his revenge.

'So?' asked the doctor in her strong German accent. 'Has she performed properly?'

By way of a reply, Sabhu used his walking stick to raise the straw in the corner of the cellar and display two little piles of wastes. Still kneeling on all fours, Emma blushed, and Ursula laughed, as the doctor used Sabhu's stick to prod the two little piles. How could Ursula allow them to humiliate her so?

'Good. But no solid food until I perform the treatment this evening.' She turned to Sabhu and pointed at Emma.

'Kneel up!' ordered Sabhu.

Recognising one of the the standard commands, Emma quickly knelt up, parted her knees, clumsily clasped her heavily gloved hands behind her neck and looked straight ahead.

The doctor bent down and felt Emma's breasts carefully. 'Yes, I think we'll get a very good result.'

'And the nipples?' asked Ursula.

'I think they will respond well,' replied the doctor, rubbing one of them into erection, as Emma moaned softly. Emma was horrified at the way they were casually discussing her as if she were some dumb animal, but with Sabhu's whip only inches from her backside she did not dare to open her mouth in protest.

'That's what we need!' laughed Ingrid. Then she turned to the doctor. 'But how certain are you? Can we really rely on you?'

'Oh yes,' cut in Ursula, 'I've never known Doctor Anna's treatments to fail.' Then she turned to the expressionless Japanese man. 'Well, what do you think of our offering?'

'Very nice,' came the impassive reply in a heavy Japanese accent. 'This one also very suitable.'

Suitable? thought Emma with trepidation. Suitable for what? And what did he mean by 'this one also'? Then she remembered that she had heard the moans of other girls.

155

'Well, you'd better let her rest,' Ursula said to Sabhu as she turned towards the door. 'But make sure the slut can't touch herself. I want her in good form this evening.'

Sabhu bowed. 'With those gloves, Madam, she can't do anything, but in any case –' he pointed at the fat, half-naked Japanese man, '– my colleague and I will be watching her through the spyhole.'

Then they all left the cellar. The door was slammed shut and locked, leaving Emma still kneeling up and the light burning. Emma saw that there was indeed a glass spyhole in the door, through which someone outside could look into the cellar without being seen. The switch for the hanging electric light bulb must be outside the door. There would be no privacy. Emma hated the thought of being supervised like a naughty little girl by these horrible men.

An hour later, the big Japanese man came in with a large pot of yoghurt. Emma was by now feeling very hungry and eyed it eagerly. Silently, his face still expressionless, he threw several spoonfuls of the yoghurt on to the stone floor, as if throwing food to a dog. Then he pulled back the zip fastener over Emma's mouth. 'Eat!' he ordered. Then he turned on his heels and left the cellar.

Dismayed, Emma tried to scoop up some of the yogurt with her hands, but her unwieldy gloves made it impossible. Driven by hunger, she put her head down to the floor and started to lick it up. As she did so, she heard numerous footsteps from beyond the door, and laughter, as if from several men, from behind the spyhole. She was being watched! But by whom? Oh, the humiliation!

The same scene, and the same footsteps and laughter, were repeated several hours later. Oh, how shame-making it was!

It was not until what Emma thought must be late in

the afternoon that the two men came for her. They were now incongruously dressed like highly respectable butlers in black suits and ties. The contrast made Emma feel her own nakedness and collar chain all the more acutely, as she shrank back into the corner of the cellar.

It was the sight, however, of the lead in Sabhu's hands that made her realise that something different was going to happen. This time he pulled off her immobilising gloves and then snapped the lead on to the ring on the front of her collar, before unshackling the heavy chain that kept her fastened to the ring in the corner of the cellar. She held up her head, expecting him to take off her mask, but he paid her no attention. 'Out!' he said simply, and gave her a smart little rap across the buttocks with his whip.

With a little cry, Emma ran out of the little door, tugging at the lead that Sabhu was holding. She found herself in a long whitewashed passageway, along one side of which was a line of small doors, like that of her own cellar. High up on the wall facing the doors, was a line of large metal rings, and from each hung a short length of chain and a pulley.

Emma gasped, for there, each shackled by a lead like her own to one of the rings, were three women. Like Emma herself they were all naked except for leather collars fitted with brass studs and black leather masks that left only their eyes uncovered. Their bodies were slim and curvaceous, just like her own, and each was gazing at her with astonished eyes, just as she was gazing at them.

Emma saw that above each girl's eyes, her mask had been marked with brass studs which formed a letter or a number. She remembered seeing that her own mask had been decorated with the number '4' before Sabhu had slipped it over head whilst she was sitting in the car outside her house.

Sabhu reached up and snapped a padlock hanging

157

from the end of one of the lengths of chain on to the end of her lead. Then he pulled the chain over the pulley and Emma felt herself being drawn up by her collar until she was standing on the tips of her toes.

The two men, chatting to each other in broken English, strode down the passageway to a metal grille which they opened with a key and through which they then disappeared. Emma was now just one of four naked women left standing in the brightly lit corridor, each shackled by her collar to the ring high above her head. Like Emma's the other girl's leads were so taut that they were all kept standing on tip-toe.

Who were these women? Emma wondered. Why were they here? Indeed, why was she here, and anyway, where was 'here'? Emma longed to whisper to them but, remembering the punishment for talking in the cages at Ursula's, was too frightened to start. Anyway, she realised, they were all effectively muzzled.

The women just stood there, their eyes looking worried, each presumably wondering what was going to happen. Although the masks hid their faces, Emma suddenly thought that she recognised the very pretty blue eyes of one of the women. She looked again. The girl turned and looked at her. Their eyes met. The other woman's eyes were sparkling. She nodded her head as if to say she had recognised Emma.

Suddenly, Emma realised that it was Sofia, Ursula's very pretty new girl, whom she had last seen in cage number six. Sure enough, the number on her mask was '6'. Sofia must similarly have recognised Emma from seeing number '4'.

Beneath her mask, Emma smiled at Sofia. How wonderful to have a friend here! Then she looked at the other two women. One seemed slightly older. Were they also from Ursula's stable of young women? To her disappointment, she saw that the older woman's mask was marked with an 'A', and that that of the younger woman was marked with a 'B'. Clearly, wherever they came from, it was not from Ursula's cages.

They must, Emma realised, have been brought by Ingrid. Had each of the two women produced two slavegirls and an overseer? But why and for whom? Was the big Japanese-looking man in charge of the other two women, just as Sabhu was in charge of Sofia and herself? Each looked as frightening as the other, thought Emma with a shiver of fear.

Oh God, how long are we going to be left here? she wondered, as she strained to keep on the tips of her toes.

Had Ursula been lying when she had spoken of a fun weekend? Lying so as to get her keen and excited? Oh, how she hated Ursula. What a horrible and cruel woman she was! Was this Ursula's real revenge for her going off with Henry? If so, then she had to admit that she did deserve to be punished. But just what punishment was in store for her?

21

Strange Preparations

At last, the two men returned. Silently they each unlocked his two women from their rings and, holding
their leads, pointed to the floor. Terrified, the women all
dropped to their hands and knees.

'You lead on, Yamoto!' called out Sabhu.

The Japanese-looking man cracked his whip and the
two women, 'A' and 'B', scuttled along the corridor on
all fours in front of him, tugging at their leads like a pair
of eager whippets. My God, thought Emma, what
horrors had those two women been through to be so
desperate to obey their overseer? And she had always
thought that Sabhu was the cruellest man in the world!

'Yes, you pair of sluts,' grinned Sabhu. 'You lucky
you looked after by nice kind Sabhu and not by
Yamoto! But you crawl like the other two women or
you get Sabhu's whip! Move!'

Scared out of her wits, Emma found herself scuttling
along on all fours, next to Sofia, and tugging at her lead
– just like the other two women had done.

Driven on by their overseers, the women crawled
through the barred iron gateway and on up an inclined
passageway to a doorway that led into what was a large
bathroom, in the middle of which was a big tub filled
with steaming hot water. Along one side of the room
was a line of make-up tables each with its own brightly
lit mirror – rather like those found in a theatrical
dressing room. Goodness, thought Emma, are we

indicating that Emma should rub it all over her face and breasts. Then, whilst the cream hardened into a mask, she showed Emma how to paint her mouth, eyes and nipples in the traditional way, and then how to cover her lips and nipples with a shiny lacquer to make them glisten.

Soon, Emma saw with amazement a strikingly beautiful blonde Geisha girl, with a lustrous white face and breasts, staring back at her, as expressionless as a doll, from her mirror.

Meanwhile, girl 'B' had been brought back by Yamoto from Doctor Anna's attentions and was also making herself up in this strange way. Under Yamoto's approving supervision, she then showed Sofia what to do. Clearly, this was not the first time that Yamoto had ordered Ingrid's girls to make themselves up in the traditional Japanese way.

It was not until about an hour later that Yamoto was finally satisfied with his now very Japanese-looking Western women. Then he made them all stand up and, to Emma's horror, he daubed a large figure '4' on her belly just over the flower painted on her mound. An equally large '6' was then painted on Sofia's tummy and a large 'A' and 'B' respectively on those of the other two women.

He and Sabhu then led them over to a cupboard in which several brightly coloured silken Japanese robes, like kimonos, were hanging, and each girl was made to put one on. These robes were, it seemed, cut to be worn open to the waist, where a broad silken sash then held the edges together. Under these gorgeous kimonos however, the women were stark naked.

Suddenly, an internal telephone rang. Yamoto picked it up and listened. Then, putting it down he turned to Sabhu. 'They are ready for them,' he said.

22

An Unusual Performance – and an Unexpected Ending

The cocktail party was well underway with Yamoto and
Sabhu, still dressed as butlers, passing round trays of
champagne and delicious canapés.

A dozen smiling and bowing Japanese gentlemen,
dressed like successful businessmen in well-cut blue
suits, were courteously chatting to each other and to
Ursula and Ingrid. Ursula was looking very dramatic in
an emerald-green silk suit, whilst Ingrid was wearing a
beautifully cut dark blue cocktail dress.

Periodically, one of the men would go and bow to one
of the four silent European women dressed as Geishas.
Emma was wearing a brilliant peacock-blue embroidered
kimono with a dark green sash, and the others were a
startling rainbow of scarlet, saffron, and turquoise.

The contrast, Emma was thinking, between this
civilised scene and what she had, only minutes earlier,
been experiencing in the communal bathroom could not
have been greater. Had it all really happened? Had the
awful couch and Doctor Anna, and the dreadful dungeon, all been some sort of dream?

Only the feeling of nakedness under her gorgeous
silken robe, the name badge pinned on to her breast
with just '4' written on it, and the leather collar hidden
by her brightly coloured silk scarf, made her realise that
this was indeed really happening to her.

166

Who are these men, Emma wondered, with their cold expressionless eyes and dapper clothes? Were they leading Japanese businessmen here for some sort of convention? Were they members of a cartel coming to check on its progress? Under their veneer of respectability might they even be drug smugglers? She had heard of the international activities of the Yakuza, the Japanese equivalent of the Mafia. Was this a meeting of the heads of some Yakuza gang?

Was she just here as part of the light entertainment that would form the background to their serious discussions? Were these the same men who had been laughing as they had watched her through the spyhole licking up her yoghurt, like an animal, from the floor of her dungeon?

Was the present scene, and the way in which the women had previously been treated, some sort of deliberate oriental cruelty? Were the men perhaps excited by the contrast between the civilised beauty of the women in their opulent costumes, and the way they had looked – naked, degraded and humiliated – when they had been chained up in the cellar?

'Why are you all here?' Emma asked one of them, feeling daring.

The man smiled enigmatically and replied, in a heavily laboured Japanese intonation, 'We are in England to check up on our investments here.'

Investments? Emma had been about to ask him to elaborate when she had caught a furious glance from Ursula and promptly shut up. She knew how Ursula hated curiosity in a girl. 'Curiosity killed the cat – and gets my girls six strokes of the cane!' was a favourite saying of hers.

After a time, Emma saw that Yamoto was discreetly beckoning the girls to a small door. It led into a small service corridor. Sabhu ushered them through the door and shut it behind them.

167

Emma gave a gasp as Yamoto pulled his short-handled whip out from where it had been tucked inside his trousers, and Sabhu, too, produced his long dressage whip. Once again, the contrast between the convivial voices laughing and chatting behind the closed door and the sight of these two threatening whips was overwhelming.

With Sabhu bringing up the rear, Yamoto now preceded the women down the corridor to another door. It led to what seemed to be a small stage. A heavy curtain shut the stage off from what, Emma guessed, must be the auditorium.

'Now you women listen carefully,' said Yamoto, raising his whip menacingly. 'You now practice for nice little show – starting shortly!'

The sound of oriental music filled the room. Still wearing her geisha girl robes, Emma stepped on to the stage and, as she had been made to practise, walked round it with small hesitant steps, tottering on strange Japanese shoes with high wooden heels and soles. They appeared to be specifically designed to make a woman walk in this humiliating way.

She blushed under her thick Japanese make-up as a burst of applause came from the men, who were sitting with Ursula and Ingrid at little tables and enjoying a delicious dinner. Surprised, she noticed that several of the men had cameras with them. She had noticed that Japanese tourists in London always took masses of photographs, but, good God! What on earth were they going to photograph here to take back home as holiday snaps?

One by one the other three girls came on to the stage, all walking with tiny steps in these strange shoes. Each was greeted with applause.

Then suddenly Sabhu stepped on to the stage. He was no longer dressed as a butler but was wearing what

168

Emma though of as his 'circus lion-tamer outfit' – blue coat with black frogging, white breeches, shiny black leather riding boots and a military-style hat. He cracked his whip, making the women jump. Quickly they formed a line, again as they had just been made to practise.

In the Japanese way, the watching men hissed their appreciation of this spectacle.

Sabhu cracked his whip again, and one by one the women slowly unfastened the broad silken belts that had held their embroidered kimonos closed and dropped them to the floor. The whip was cracked a third time and, one at a time, like well-trained performing animals, the women, undulating their hips in time to the music, slowly pulled their kimonos open. As each woman did so, she exposed both her bare belly on to which her number or letter had been prominently painted, and also her smooth and intricately painted mound and beauty lips.

Applause and more hissing greeted this erotic and carefully choreographed scene, with the men evidently discussing the various merits of the numbered or lettered bodies on display.

Yet again the whip was cracked, and the women pulled their kimonos back over their shoulders, baring their breasts and painted nipples.

Yamoto now came on to the stage. Unlike Sabhu, he was still dressed in his black butler's suit, which contrasted vividly with the white nakedness of the women. He went up to each of them in turn, squeezed their naked breasts, and then gave what appeared to be a description in Japanese of their firmness and texture.

Again the whip was cracked and, accompanied by a running commentary from Yamoto, the women began to shake their breasts, turning first to the left and then to the right so that they could be seen from every angle.

The discussions between the men grew more animated. Some of them, Emma noticed, kept pointing at her, and others at the other women. It was as though some sort of selection was being made. Could it be a beauty contest? she wondered innocently. Was she, she wondered proudly, thought to be the prettiest? As they seemed so obsessed with her breasts, she now eagerly shook them and turned her body to show them off.

Then suddenly Doctor Anna appeared at the back of the auditorium and strode up to the stage. Yamoto bowed and, turning to the audience and pointing to the women's breasts, said something in Japanese that produced gasps of delight.

The doctor came up on to the stage and the women stood to attention, holding back their kimonos to display their bellies and breasts. Yamoto called each woman forward in turn by her number or letter. The doctor, meanwhile, had produced a box of pills and, as each woman stepped forward, she thrust several pills into her mouth.

There was more applause, and Doctor Anna bowed and left the room.

What, Emma was thinking desperately, were those pills she had just been made to swallow? Was there some connection between them and whatever it was that the doctor had done to her on the couch in the bathroom? And what had they to do with the apparent preoccupation these awful men seemed to have with the women's breasts? My God! she thought.

The guests were now shouting something to Yamoto. Emma recognised some English words, intermixed with the Japanese ones. Astonished, she realised that they were 'Number Four' and 'Letter B'. Had she and the younger of Ingrid's girls been chosen as the winners of the beauty competition?

She saw Yamoto beckoning her and the other girl down from the stage. Happily, she followed him down some steps. He led them to a pair of strange-looking devices, which looked like a cross between a mediaeval stocks and a pillory. Emma saw that they were mounted on swivels. What had they to do with winning the competition?

Yamoto now motioned to Emma to throw off her kimono. She hesitated to appear completely naked in front of so many men, but with an angry gesture Yamoto drew his whip out from under his coat. With a little cry, Emma hastily let the kimono fall on to the ground. Oh well, she thought, they've already seen most of me anyway, and if it's just a beauty competition, then who cares?

Then suddenly she realised that things were going wrong. This was not a beauty contest at all! Indeed Yamoto suddenly seized her by the nape of her neck and thrust her down on to her hands and knees in front of one of the low pillories. She saw that just below her tummy was a sort of raised cushion. Yamoto pushed her head forward and closed the pillory around her neck. Her navel was now resting on the cushion.

Emma screamed and started to beat the unyielding wood with her fists. This was greeted with laughter and applause, and then Yamoto bent down again, gripped her by the hands, and then locked her wrists into solid clamps on either side of her head. Then he fastened a strap around her waist, tying her down on to the cushion. He turned a handle and she felt her buttocks being raised up until they were higher than her head.

Yamoto then swivelled the stocks around so that she was now facing the audience. She could see the grinning faces of the men and amongst them those of Ingrid and Ursula. They were looking proudly proprietary as they acknowledged the congratulations of the excited men. Oh, how she hated Ursula for allowing this to be done to her, but at the same time she could not stop herself from becoming aroused by being helplessly tied down and displayed.

Someone focused a bright light on to her, half

blinding her. She heard the click of cameras. So they had been saving their film for this!

She was aware that Yamoto was now fastening the naked girl 'B' into the other pillory alongside hers. Soon there were two frightened and anxious little faces peering at the applauding audience from their well-lit stocks. What was going to happen? And what of Sofia and woman 'A' who were still displaying themselves on the stage?

But her thoughts were interrupted by the noise of the door at the end of the room being opened. There was a burst of applause from the audience. Because of the spotlight focused on her, she could not see who had come in, but evidently, whoever they were, they were popular figures.

Suddenly, she was amazed to see two astonishing figures coming down past the tables. They were two hugely fat Japanese Sumo wrestlers, naked except for a twist of silk around their huge waists from which a tassel hung down in front of their manhoods. Their fat bodies glistened with oil.

Open-mouthed, Emma watched as the two wrestlers, their vast bellies quivering, slowly waddled down past the pillories and ponderously climbed up on to the stage.

While everybody had been watching the wrestlers' entrance, Sabhu had busied himself tying the hands of Sofia and woman 'A' behind their backs with the silken belts that they had earlier discarded. He had also clipped their leads on to their collars once again. They now knelt, their beautiful kimonos still pulled back to display their naked bodies and the number or letter painted prominently on their bellies, whilst behind them stood Sabhu holding their leads in one hand and his long dressage whip in the other.

The two kneeling women made an erotic sight as, utterly helpless and seemingly petrified, they watched the two monstrous male figures slowly coming towards them, their hands reaching eagerly out towards them. The women gasped as they saw that, beneath the hugely bloated bellies, two manhoods were beginning to thrust aside the silken tassels that only partially hid them.

The men now stood over the kneeling women, their manhoods jutting towards their painted faces, and their hands gripping their lacquered hair.

'Suck!' cried Sabhu, giving each of the women a sharp tap across the shoulders with his whip.

Except for appreciative hisses from the wrestlers, and the click of cameras, there was now complete silence in the room. The heads of the two women bobbed up and down as, urged on by Sabhu's whip, they strained to prepare the two grotesque men for what was to follow.

Moments later, Sabhu nodded to Yamoto, who now swivelled the two pillories around so that the raised bottoms of Emma and girl 'B' were facing the audience. Emma blushed with shame as she heard both applause and even more cameras clicking.

Then Yamoto swivelled them around again so that the girls were now sideways on to the audience.

The two wrestlers, now satisfactorily aroused by Sofia and her companion, came down to the pillories. The audience hissed as they saw the wrestlers thrust aside the tassels hanging down in front of their manhoods. Each stood behind the cleverly raised body of a girl, and gripped her by the waist. Then they gave a sudden jerk, and the watching men saw the faces of Emma and 'B' suddenly twist with a mixture of pleasurable pain and astonishment as the huge wrestlers penetrated them, their vast bellies resting on the girls' bottoms.

Meanwhile, Sabhu had led the other two women down from the stage and had made them kneel behind the two wrestlers as they thrust in and out.

'Number Six! Lick!' he called out to Sofia, who was kneeling behind the wrestler who had mounted Emma.

173

He emphasised his order with a stroke of his whip across her bottom and, with a little cry, she pressed her face against the huge buttocks in front of her and reached down with her tongue, causing the wrestler to give a little jerk of pleasure.

'Letter A! Lick!' he then ordered, and obediently the older woman reached forward to apply her tongue, too, to the wrestler who had penetrated the slim figure of 'B'.

Emma was horrified to find herself unable to resist responding to the attentions of the brute who had so carelessly mounted her. She heard the audience laugh as she began thrusting back in time with her ravisher's own thrusts into her. Oh, the shame of it! Through the glare of the spotlight she could make out Ursula, licking her lips with excitement. Oh, how could she have arranged all this?

Then she saw Doctor Anna standing at the back and nodding approvingly at the scene. My God, thought Emma, was there a connection between the treatment the doctor had given to her earlier and what was now being done to her?

But her rising excitement made her put such thoughts aside. She could hear the two monsters groaning with increasing pleasure – a sound that raised her own level of arousal, too. Suddenly, she felt the man's warm seed jetting into her and, with a cry, she, too, climaxed.

Seconds later, a similar little cry came from the other pillory.

It was a quarter of an hour later. The audience was now enjoying another course – this time of meringues and strawberries.

On the stage, behind the curtain, Sabhu was putting a mystified Emma into an artificial but very realistic-looking dog skin. It fitted her tightly, just leaving bare her eyes and mouth, her breasts and, to her embarrassment, her intimacies, inside which, to her horror, she could still feel the wrestler's seed.

174

To her delight, however, her collar – the hated collar with the little attachment that had given her all those shocks in her garden – had been removed, and another simple dog collar put on over the dog skin.

Sabhu motioned to her to get down on all fours, and handed the lead attached to her collar to Sofia who, like the other two women, was once again dressed in her gorgeous Japanese kimono.

The leads of two real bitches, lovely Red Setters, were being similarly held by the women 'A' and 'B'.

Emma saw that Doctor Anna was now standing in the wings watching, her black doctor's bag in her hand. Why? What on earth did she have in it? Now what was that awful woman going to do to her?

But then the curtain parted and 'A' and 'B', leading their Red Setter bitches, walked on to the stage as if miming two Japanese ladies taking their dogs for a walk. Then there were gasps from the audience as Sofia led on the crawling Emma, her dog skin closely matching that of those of the real bitches. Her breasts were hanging down prettily below her and her intimacies – now painted an arousing shade of scarlet – glistened with her excitement as Sofia led her around.

The three women now lined up facing the audience, their bitches in front of them. Once again, Emma blushed as she realised the view the audience would now have of her intimacies.

Suddenly, she heard the sound of the doors at the back of the auditorium bursting open. There were cries of delight from the audience. Emma, like the real bitches, turned around to find out what was going on, and was rather surprised to see two eager real Red Setter hounds bounding eagerly down towards the stage.

Then she was astonished to see, gambolling along behind them, a young man, dressed like she was in a realistic, tight-fitting Red Setter dog skin. She also

175

noticed that the youth's pink manhood was thrusting forward through the furry skin that surrounded it.

Emma watched with apprehension as the real dogs and the youth in the dog skin began to come up on to the stage. She longed to break away, but Sofia, herself terrified by the watching figure of Sabhu, standing in the wings with his whip raised, held tightly on to her lead.

Then, suddenly, the auditorium doors flew open again. There were shouts in Japanese, and Emma saw that a group of Japanese men had burst into the room. Several seemed to be carrying guns. They were shouting at the men in the room, who were shouting back – all in incomprehensible Japanese. Within seconds, there was a scene of utter confusion.

Suddenly, she saw Ursula rushing up on to the stage. She snatched Emma's lead from Sofia and shouted at Sabhu and the doctor, 'Quick! Get out of here! This is a rival gang wanting money from our friends! I'll take Emma and the doctor. Sabhu, you take Sofia back to London. Move – before they realise we've left!'

With that, she gripped Emma, pulled her to her feet and hustled her and the panting doctor through the wings of the stage, down a corridor and out into a yard at the back of the house. It was dark outside, but Emma managed to make out Ursula's Mercedes.

Ursula flung open the boot of her car, and pushed Emma into it. 'Don't make a sound!' she warned her, and slammed the boot shut. Seconds later, Emma felt the car shoot forward. It was, she realised, being driven fast – very fast.

After what seemed like hours, the car stopped. Doors were opened and slammed shut again, but she was still left hidden in the boot of the car. At last the boot was flung open. Unsteadily, she got out. It was still dark, but she saw that she was standing back in the drive of her own house.

Ursula got back into the driving seat. 'After this little

escapade,' she said, with a laugh, 'I'm going back off to the Aegean tomorrow, before that other lot of Japanese can try anything on. I'll be taking Sabhu and the girls with me and closing the house, so you won't have to make any reports. And I'm taking Mrs Maunder away with me, too! But don't you get up to anything whilst I'm away. I'll be back when the dust of all this has settled again.'

Emma saw Mrs Maunder coming towards the car, carrying her suitcases. She gasped in astonishment. She was going to be free! Free of Ursula, free of Sabhu and the awful cages, free of Mrs Maunder, and free of her Bikini-belt and of that terrifying collar.

She saw Doctor Anna coming towards her holding out something in her hand.

'Take the doctor's pills and you'll be alright,' said Ursula, with a bitter laugh. 'We'll have to try again another time.'

'What do you mean?' cried Emma, nervously, taking the plastic bottle of pills.

'Never you mind – just take them as directed,' growled Doctor Anna.

'Make sure you do,' laughed Ursula, starting the engine. 'Come on, Doctor! And remember, Emma, be a good little girl!'

23

Emma Meets her New Master

It took Emma a little time to get over the shock of what
had happened at the special event, and the dramatic way
in which it had ended. She could not help wondering
just what it was that they had intended to do to her,
before everything had been interrupted by the raid by
the rival Yakuza gang. In any case, whatever they had
already done must have been counteracted by the Doctor's mysterious pills, and she had felt no ill effects.

But it had made her all the more delighted to be free
of Ursula and all her works – for the time being,
anyway! Longing to talk to someone about it all, she
had rung Henry, who was the only person who knew
about Ursula and the strange hold she had over Emma.
To her dismay, she learnt that he had gone abroad.

John would not be returning from abroad for another
two months, and so she was feeling very lonely and
down in the mouth when, a couple of days later, she
received a letter. The envelope was addressed in handwriting that Emma was sure she recognised. Eagerly, she
opened it, and found out that it was from Paddy, a
racehorse trainer and an old friend of her family in
Ireland. He was inviting her, very pressingly, to come to
a dinner party at a floating restaurant in Westminster.

'Do come,' he wrote, and she could imagine him
saying it in the slight brogue that took her straight back
to her childhood days. 'Just for old times' sake. You'
be doing me a great favour.'

178

They had known each other since they had been children, but she hadn't heard from him recently. Her house was on his route to London from his racing stables, he told her, which meant that he could pick her up and drive her to the party. He had been lent a house in London and could put her up afterwards, if she liked. It would be great to see her again.

A party in London! With Paddy! But did she dare go? Hesitantly, she rang Ursula to check that she really had closed her house and left – only to hear a recorded message saying that Miss de Vere had gone abroad.

'Whoopee!' Emma cried, feeling as excited as a schoolgirl at the end of term, as she ran upstairs to her room to write her acceptance of the invitation. Suddenly, she was over the moon with excitement – and all her thoughts and concerns about Ursula were forgotten.

Driving up to London, they were held up by traffic and were a little late arriving at the restaurant. Paddy dropped her off and went to park his car. Emma walked up the gangplank and was shown to his table and sat down in a vacant chair, feeling a little lost. She recognised several faces from the racing world, but no one she knew well.

She was wearing a black jersey sheath dress, under which her breasts and nipples were clearly defined. Thanks to the absence of knickers and of pubic hair, the dress was flat on her tummy. She was looking, she knew, very good.

Evidently eyeing Emma with approval, her neighbour courteously introduced himself, in an attractive voice with a slight Arabian accent. 'I'm Prince Faisal.'

A Prince! An Arab Prince! Emma glanced up at his strong face, with its deep-set brown eyes and short, pointed beard. He was a virile-looking man in his forties, rather ruthless perhaps. He was dressed as an English gentleman, and only his prominent hooked nose, and perhaps his unusually shaped beard, betrayed his Arab background. Well, she thought, well . . .

179

But just then Paddy arrived. 'Emma!' he cried. 'You're supposed to be sitting over here.' As she repositioned herself, Emma wondered why the other women were looking at her as if she were Exhibit A.

Just then, a striking girl arrived. She had long straight hair and brown eyes and was wearing a red leather mini-skirt with a sleeveless white T-shirt. Her legs were tanned and, as she leant over to greet Paddy, Emma caught a glimpse of the lace tops of her hold-up stockings. Almost immediately she started talking about her recent trip to Israel to see her family.

'Bugger!' hissed Paddy in Emma's ear. 'Oh well, it'll just have to be yourself, me darling, that sorts him out. Thank the Lord I had the sense to ask you along, too, just in case. The fact is that I need his horses.' Apparently, Paddy had flown the international call-girl in from New York specifically for the Prince's pleasure – never thinking to check on the girl's nationality.

He tapped his glass for silence. 'I think you have all met our esteemed guest, Prince Faisal, who, like many other Arab gentlemen, is doing so much for racing over here –' there were murmurs and smiles from around the table '– And now, Ruth, you come and sit here, and Emma, you can tell the Prince all about our stud in Ireland.'

As Emma sat down, her leg brushed against the handsome Prince's thigh. He was wearing a dark grey pinstriped suit, and her imagination flared into an image of him in traditional Arab dress. What would he wear underneath that, she wondered. Trousers, like a vicar's? Or nothing? And was his manhood huge and hooked like his nose? With a laugh, she remembered being told by a girlfriend that you could judge a man's masculinity by the size of his nose.

Perhaps, she fantasised, she would be riding behind him on one of his beautiful stallions. Holding him around the waist, she would feel her way down to a amazingly erect and dominant manhood that filled her with lust . . .

Hastily, she collected herself, as the familiar ache and wetness indicated just what, at that moment, she really desired . . .

Had the faint odour of her arousal also reached the Prince? Blushing, she glanced up at him from lowered eyes. He was smiling. Oh yes, she thought, he knows what I feel.

Indeed, the Prince was clearly delighted that this vivacious blonde English girl was apparently available for his pleasure, and her reactions appealed to his sensuous nature.

It was an hour later, and Emma drank her Dom Perignon champagne with care, noticing, to her surprise, that the Prince was also drinking. 'When in England . . .' she thought. Obviously, he was well used to Western ways, but how much more intriguing it would be to find out how he lived at home. Did this highly civilised, charming and urbane man have a whole harem of Arab girls at his beck and call? Or might some of them in fact be European women? Goodness! Did his perfect manners mask a cruel and despotic nature? Oh, how exciting!

They had discussed the advantages of the early spring grass in County Kilkenny for bringing on foals born in January, and he had told her of his plan to winter his thoroughbred yearlings in his Gulf state of Marfa. If it succeeded, with the Arabian sun improving their development more than would a normal English winter, then he would have an edge over other bloodstock owners and breeders in Britain.

However, he first had to send a trial consignment of four yearlings to his air-conditioned yard, to assess their reaction to the long flight and to the change in climate and nutrition. He also, he added with a smile, wanted to see if his stable lads were up to the job. He would shortly be returning to Marfa to make sure that everything was ready. Later, these first horses would be returned to his new trainer, whom he had not yet chosen, to be sold as potential hurdlers or to run in handicap races. If all went well, then they would be succeeded by more valuable young stock. He was planning to send out the initial consignment in a couple of weeks' time.

The decisive character of the Prince and his seeming willingness to spend what had to be a lot of money on his new project were like an aphrodisiac to Emma. What a man! How could she see more of him? A plan was forming in her mind. Could she perhaps hitch a lift on his plane – officially to help look after the horses? Could she then see something of his lifestyle and then be seduced when she decided to indulge him? Oh, what fun!

What would stuck-up old Henry have to say about that? What a delightful contrast the two men made. Thanks to the Prince's courteous manners and obvious appreciation of the sexually-aware Emma, she would have a marvellous experience – and be able to throw it all back at Henry next time he went too far in humiliating her.

Oh, I wonder, Emma thought, as she flirted with the Prince, can I brush my nipple against him? She let her napkin slip down on to the floor, then, bending down, she turned towards him, her nipple sliding over his knee. The reaction inside Emma was almost explosive. As she straightened up again, her hand came up between her legs and, through her clinging skirt, her fingers felt her beauty bud, sensitive and firm – and ready for more stimulation. She glanced at the Prince and blushed. He had been watching her!

But the Prince needed no more games! He had already made his decision. He would invite her to his palace. How he would then enjoy the conquest of this lovely blonde Irish lady. Indeed, a longer-term plan involving her was already forming in his mind, especially as it seemed that she was a married woman with a husband who was often away abroad. She might well be ideal for his purposes.

The call-girl had been unacceptable because of her nationality, but this ambitious young trainer had been intelligent enough to get rid of her. Yes, Paddy seemed to understand his needs, and was quick to acknowledge an error and remedy it – just the kind of man he liked to have working for him. He would take him on, he decided.

First, however, this delicious trifle of Irish womanhood must be discreetly tested and then, if she proved suitable, persuaded to accept his invitation. His cunning mind started working out the best way to broach the subject.

But it was an unsuspecting Emma who was the first to raise it.

'I'm married, as you know,' she said 'but my husband realises how much I miss not still being involved with horses, especially racehorses. They were such a large part of my childhood. Perhaps I could use my interest in your racing plans as an excuse to travel out with your horses – and help keep an eye on them. He wouldn't object to that, and anyway he's abroad for much of the time. Would you let me?'

She put on the submissive, humble, pleading face that Ursula loved so much, pouting her upper lip and speaking in a wheedling voice, like a child asking for a lollipop.

'With pleasure, my dear,' the Prince said with a laugh, 'You would be very welcome in the guest house of my palace. How long can you spend with us?' Then he paused as if gathering his thoughts. 'You are very beautiful,' he added, 'and I shall enjoy showing you to my harem. My women will be inspired to emulate your charming and well-mannered ways.'

183

'My palace . . . my women . . . my harem.' The words were racing round Emma's brain. Goodness! How exciting!

The Prince, however, was a clever and cruel man, and his subtle mind was already planning the future of this evidently sensuous and submissive young woman. A week in his palace should suffice to bring her to heel. How he would enjoy playing with this trusting little fool, who thought that she knew it all and that she could beguile him with her big blue eyes and prominent nipples – and with her obvious flirtation. She would be in for a shock. But first he must test her, in a subtle way that would enable him to put her harmlessly aside should she not, in the cold light of day, prove likely to meet his requirements.

'Why don't you come to see some of my four year-olds?' he said. 'You'd find it interesting and we could talk about you flying out with them.'

Emma's heart was in her mouth with excitement, but, before she could say a word, the Prince rose, thanked Paddy, and prepared to leave. He beckoned to his private secretary and gave him instructions to call for his chauffeur and to pay the bill. Despite Emma's hovering anxiously for further confirmation of her invitation, he had ignored her until the last possible moment. Then as, if the matter was already settled, he added, 'I'll send my car to pick you up the day after tomorrow, at nine o'clock in the morning.'

And with that he was gone – leaving Emma to watch him depart, her mouth wide open.

Emma's elation overflowed. 'Oh, darling, darling, Paddy,' she enthused, after everyone else had left. 'You are wonderful letting me meet this marvellous man. He's asked me to come out to Marfa with the flight the horses will be on. Oh yes, and he said he thought you'd be an excellent new trainer for him. Big kiss, darling, I do love you!'

Paddy heaved a sigh of relief. The job was in the bag. Bless little Emma! The strain and suspense began to ebb away and his mind was already working out the financial implications. 'Come on, Emma,' he laughed as she joined him in his car. 'You've now got to pay for your supper! I want your best efforts and let's be having a good look at those tits you've been flaunting all evening.'

He put his fingers around them, kneading them deliciously, and then slipped a hand up her skirt. She had always been a hot little number, he thought. He licked his finger as she watched him. 'You always had your honeypot overflowing for me,' he laughed. But Emma was still reacting more to the memory of the Prince's commanding ways.

'Now backwards up the stairs, Emma,' he ordered, when they arrived at the charming little mews house he had been lent. 'Dress up and legs apart, and let me have my share of the honey.'

His tongue was in her, licking away. 'Wow!' thought Emma, as he crawled up the stairs, bending her backward and thrusting his tongue into her little crevice, searching for her juices. 'This is just what I need.'

At the top of the stairs, he unzipped his trousers and thrust his long thin manhood into her. He climaxed almost immediately, collapsing on top of her, but then went back to sucking her so that she came again and again.

But it was the Prince who was still foremost in her mind. Heavens, what fun it had been meeting him. It really had been pretty cheeky of her to jump in and ask him outright for an invitation to his palace like that. Thank God he had been interested in the idea. And what would the visit really entail? But what a fabulous invitation . . .

Emma and Paddy had had a good evening. They slept the same sound slumber of those days in their late teens when, together in the big Irish barn in Kilkenny, they had climbed erotically, in the same way as they had just come up the stairs, up the ladder to the hayloft. But Emma was dreaming of the Prince.

24

Emma Passes her Test

Two days later, on her arrival at the stables, Emma was not, to her great surprise, taken to the line of looseboxes in which the racehorses were kept. Instead, she was led by a young groom into a large indoor riding school.

There the Prince was exercising a succession of hacks and hunters and popping them over a line of small jumps. He was wearing riding breeches and highly polished boots and was carrying a long riding whip. He greeted Emma courteously and she watched, entranced. What a magnificent man this Prince was, she thought, an intelligent, charming and yet excitingly terrifying man.

Before dismounting from each horse, he rode over to her and described it in detail – its character, its temperament, its degree of obedience and the pleasure it gave when being ridden. Emma could not help wondering if he might describe the women in his harem in a similar way. Did he master and control his women as expertly as he so evidently mastered and controlled his horses?

The Prince went on to describe the way in which his stud groom broke in and trained his horses, and kept them enjoyable to ride. Then, tapping his boots with his whip, he looked down at her and smiled. 'A beautiful and high-spirited horse,' he said, 'is a like a beautiful and high-spirited woman. Both need constant supervision and to be looked after with a mixture of care and discipline, so that they become and remain a perfect ride for their master.'

What an expression! Emma gasped and felt herself blushing. Then she pulled herself together. She was an intelligent woman, not some dolly girl that the Prince had picked up somewhere. But the hypnotic voice of the Prince brought her back to reality – to the reality of her own sensuality.

'My servants are patient, but they stand no nonsense. Their aim is simply to bring me a well-trained, perfectly mannered creature.' Was he talking about his horses or about his women? Emma wondered. Or both?

He looked down at her meaningfully. Had he guessed the secret battles that went on in her mind between her desire to be a sophisticated, self-composed woman of the world and her secret longings to be dominated and controlled? Was he testing her in some clever way? Shyly, she lowered her eyes.

'A hot-blooded man may feel tempted to break a beautiful woman to his will, particularly if she is a European woman who does not yet appear to have learned the joy of submitting to a strong-minded man. But his pleasure will be all the greater if he lets her willingly crawl to his bed and then gives her to his servants to train and discipline properly for his greater pleasure.'

'And if she does not want to crawl to his bed?'

'Oh, she will,' he laughed. 'She will!'

Emma's mind was in a whirl. A woman, a free Western woman, crawling to his bed! To the bed of a handsome and dominant Arab prince! And then being trained and disciplined by his servants. It was all too unbelievable, too thrilling. This knocked anything that Ursula and Sabhu had done into a cocked hat!

'Tradition teaches us,' he went on, 'that women were put into the world for the enjoyment of men and that men were made to excel over women. It tells us to enjoy as many of them as we can afford to look after – and I am a rich man.'

He paused. Emma was hanging on to his every word. How she longed at that moment to be enjoyed by him; to be excelled over by him, to be looked after by him. He looked so fierce, so commanding.

'And the women in your harem are all equally –' she began hesitantly.

'An Arab does not discuss the women in his harem with outsiders,' he said reprovingly, 'only with his servants.'

Emma blushed with shame at the snub.

'However,' he went on with a smile, 'if you simply meant to ask whether, if they existed, they would be kept as well-trained and well-disciplined as my horses, then the answer would be yes. My concubines all know they exist only for my pleasure and, denied even the sight of other men, they think only of how to provide that pleasure.'

'Oh!' gasped Emma. It was several seconds before she could pluck up her courage. 'And if, for instance, they were educated, intelligent women? Western women? European women? Women from this country?'

'Then they would be treated in the same way. They would all just be women who find themselves happy to serve a rich and strong man.'

Again, Emma could feel herself flushing. Was it from anger at his incredible male arrogance? Or was it rather from shame at her own excitement and arousal. Certainly the Prince's arrows were striking home alright. Did he know her secret desires?

She looked up at his strong face, at his strong thighs above his highly polished riding boots, at his equally firm hands grasping the reins, and at the whip with which he was controlling his horse. Oh! Oh!

Before she could collect her thoughts and say something sensible, the Prince had dismounted, and had handed the horse to a groom. Then, gripping Emma's arm, he led her into a palatial tack room full of beautifully kept saddles and bridles.

189

Leaving Emma standing, he sat down on a comfortable-looking chair. There did not seem to be anything else to sit on. She had heard that it was considered bad manners in Arabia for a woman to sit down in the presence of a man, but even so she was rather taken aback at her first experience of the way Arabs naturally treated women.

Smiling, the Prince pointed to a tray on a table. On it was a coffee pot and a small cup and saucer. She noticed that there was only one.

'Pour me a cup of coffee,' the Prince ordered nonchalantly, stretching his hands behind his neck. It was, she realised, the first time that she had served him with anything, and, moreover, the first time that he had commanded her to do anything. He had not said 'Please'. He must be very sure of himself, she realised, and a wave of anger momentarily swept over her.

Indignantly, she looked up. He was looking straight at her. She could not meet his gaze. She lowered her eyes. The anger left her.

What was the point of walking out now, she asked herself, just when she was on the point of being invited to stay in a fabulous palace? Anyway, she enjoyed being ordered about. She would do as he said. He was, after all, a very rich man and she had offered, in effect, to enter his employ. What was the technical legal expression? The relationship of master and servant. Master!

Blushing, she turned and poured the coffee. How should she serve it? she wondered. There was no little table near the sofa. How does a mere woman serve an Arab prince in Arabia? Was this some kind of test? A test of her submissiveness? Goodness! Was he deliberately establishing his authority over her?

She turned towards him, the coffee cup and saucer in her hands. Expressionless, he looked her up and down. She was wearing jeans and he had not seen her in them before, she realised, blushing. Did he approve of what he saw? Still he did not say a word. Clearly he felt that he had given his order and that there was no need to say anything more. Again she lowered her eyes.

Suddenly, obeying some instinctive urge deep down inside her, she dropped to her knees and held the coffee up to him. It seemed only right and proper.

'Your Highness,' she murmured.

He smiled down at her. He said nothing. It was as if seeing a young Irishwoman kneeling at his feet was the most natural thing in the world. Then slowly he picked up the cup, leaving Emma holding the saucer with both hands. He sipped the coffee. Emma kept quite still. He put the cup back on the saucer. Then he touched Emma's cheek with his hand. She could not hold back from gently rubbing her face against his strong hand.

It was, Emma felt, a thrilling moment.

Suddenly, greatly daring, she put down the cup and saucer. She grasped his hand. She brought it to her lips. She had been about to kiss it humbly when, again as if obeying some strange primeval instinct, she did what she had never done to a man before: she turned his hand over and gently licked his palm.

It was, she knew, a secret, intimate gesture of subservience to a man whom she hardly knew and in whose service she now was. She looked up at him. She felt that she was in the power of a real man, a cruel and ruthless man, but one who would take care of her. A feeling of complete and utter happiness spread over her.

With his other hand he stroked her hair gently. At that moment, she knew, he could have done anything, absolutely anything with her. Had he any idea what she was feeling?

In fact, however, he knew exactly how she felt and was delighted by her reaction to his test. After a little training in his harem she would be just what he was looking for: an attractive, submissive, well-educated and sophisticated young married woman whose husband was often abroad. His mind was made up.

'One of my cars,' he said decisively, 'will take you home and bring you back here tomorrow morning to discuss with my stud groom the arrangements for the flight. My private secretary will make all the necessary arrangements and give you a cheque for ... what I will call your expenses. The plane is due to leave in a week's time, and I shall expect you to stay on in my palace guest house for a week or so after that. Alright?

Dumbly, Emma nodded, overcome with excitement and anticipation.

'To avoid any silly tittle-tattle I suggest that you do not tell anyone where you are going. You will not, in any case, be seeing any other men there – it would cause great scandal, for we Moslems do not like other men to see our women.' He laughed and then added, 'Nor do we allow our women to see other men. So, if anyone asks where you are off to, just say you are going away to Switzerland for some mountain air.'

He rose to his feet. 'I shall look forward to seeing you out there shortly,' he said, and left the room, leaving Emma still on her knees and emotionally drained. He had, she realised, taken complete charge of her. Where, she wondered jealously, would he be going now? Flying back to his harem? Goodness!

25

In the Palace of the Prince

It was the warmth and a distinctive and exciting smell
that first struck Emma as the doors of the big transport
plane swung open. It was getting dark. Still wearing the
blouse and jeans she had put on to look after the horses
during the flight, she looked out. Her first sight of
Arabia!

The journey had been uneventful. Paddy had arranged for both Emma and his own experienced lad,
who had accompanied the horses, to be taught how to
tranquillise any horse that panicked. However, despite
Paddy's fears and precautions, the horses had all quietly
dozed or munched away at their sweet-smelling horse-
age throughout the long journey.

A smart new Lambourne horsebox drove up to the
plane. Two young Arabs lowered the ramp and the
Prince's head groom introduced himself.

The horses were led down the ramp of the plane and
up into the horsebox. Nothing could have been easier.
Emma fetched her case and, after saying goodbye to
Paddy's lad and the crew of the aeroplane, swung
herself up into the horse box.

Now that the horses had been handed over to the
Prince's Arab grooms, her work was done. What now?
She still had no real idea, except for a note from the
Prince's private secretary saying that she was expected
at the palace guest house. With this was enclosed a
reassuring ticket for a flight back to England in a week's

time, and a substantial cheque – a very substantial cheque – 'for her time'.

A whole week at the palace! Well, Emma had wondered, what was the Prince planning to do with her? Had he cunningly and deliberately not told her, so as to heighten the anticipation, the excitement? If so, he had certainly succeeded. She had been on tenterhooks ever since that dinner on the floating restaurant just over a week ago, and even more so since that extraordinary meeting at his stables.

The horsebox drove from the airport through the darkness and across what seemed to be an expanse of empty desert to the Prince's stud farm. The grooms were chattering amongst themselves. They seemed to speak no English. Emma saw that the well-lit stud buildings were all painted white and beautifully kept. Gorgeous Arab horses grazed in the small high-fenced paddocks surrounding the actual stables. Money seemed to be no object.

She saw that the Prince, now wearing the traditional long white Arab dress with a black, gold-edged *kafiya*, or rope, around the headpiece, was waiting for them. Laughing to herself, she remembered her fantasy in the restaurant about what he would wear under Arab dress. She could not make out any sign of anything. But how strong and handsome he looked!

She was taken aback when the Prince seemed to ignore her presence entirely. Clearly out here men did not speak to women in public.

Instead, a young man led her to a huge, chauffeur-driven, air-conditioned Mercedes car with tinted side and rear windows and a similar opaque window between herself and the chauffeur. Silently, the boy ushered her into the vehicle and then got in himself. The car drove off through the darkness. There seemed to be no sign of any town.

Then the car stopped before some tall gates, set in

194

some very high walls. Emma sat quietly as armed guards flashed torches into the car, before signalling for the gates to be opened so that the car could be driven through them – only to be confronted with another inside gate and more guards. Security was obviously very tight.

Finally, they took a road through what appeared to be a park, and the car was then brought to a stop in front of a pretty white-painted bungalow with iron bars on its windows. Two laughing Filipino servant girls, in long Arab caftans, came down the steps and opened the door of the car. Behind them, Emma saw a hugely fat black man in a white Arab robe, presumably a servant of some sort. His podgy face was impassive. Watched by the man, the two Filipino girls took Emma's baggage and led her into the house. The man closed and locked the door behind them.

The house seemed spacious and was air-conditioned. Emma was shown into a pretty bedroom, furnished in a chintzy English country house style, and with a large bed. Emma was also surprised to see, facing the bed, an illuminated portrait of the Prince in Arab dress, and looking rather severe.

The servants brought her orange juice and then a light supper of delicious morsels of roast lamb, followed by pieces of mango. She ate it all eagerly. Meanwhile, the giggling Filipino girls started to unpack her clothes, showing each item to the silent black man. Embarrassed at having her things seen by a man, Emma tried to wave him away, but one of the girls laughed and whispered to her in simple English, 'Don't you worry. He used to looking after European women.'

What? thought Emma. Did the Prince often bring European women to stay here?

But by now she was too tired to argue. She just wanted to go to bed and sleep. She had to be ready for the Prince in the morning!

As if reading her thoughts, the man went over to a cupboard and produced a gorgeous silken nightdress. He handed it to the girls, saying something to them in a strangely high-pitched voice.

To Emma's horror they started to undress her in front of the man. She began to protest. 'Don't you worry,' whispered the girl again in an encouraging tone, as if talking to a little girl. 'He used to seeing Prince's women naked.'

'Well, he's damned well not seeing this one,' cried Emma, in a sudden fit of temper. Before the big man could say anything, she bundled him out of the room, slammed the door shut and turned, grinning, to the two girls, brushing her hands as if wiping off his taint.

The girls stood there aghast. 'He very important man here,' cried the girl who spoke English. 'He Ali Efendi. He in charge of all Prince's women.'

'Well, he's not in charge of this one,' laughed Emma. She had not shaken off the clutches of Sabhu to fall into those of another foreign overseer.

Shaking their heads fearfully, the murmuring girls helped her into the nightdress. She saw that Arabic writing had been embroidered on the right breast. It looked very similar to the Arabic crest on the horses' travelling rugs. Was it the Prince's name? How exciting!

Tired and emotionally exhausted, Emma got into bed. The maids switched off the light and left the room. But the portrait of the Prince remained lit up. Sleepily, she found herself looking at it again and again. What a man he was! But who were all those women that Ali Efendi man was meant to be in charge of and was used to seeing naked? The Prince's harem girls? A pang of jealousy ran through her.

The next two days passed slowly for Emma in the guest house. She saw only the giggling Filipino maids. She longed to go off for a drive and to see this exciting new country, but every time she asked if she might, she was told that no car was available. There just seemed to be nothing to do. Had the Prince forgotten all about her? she wondered. Was he playing some game of cat and mouse with her? But why? She longed for a stiff drink, but there was only fruit juice.

Photographs and portraits of the Prince dominated every room, making sure that, whether she liked it or not, her thoughts were constantly of him as she lounged about the house. She asked about the Prince, but was told he was busy. Busy in his harem, she thought, with mounting jealousy.

She thought of walking down to the palace gates and going out for a walk, but the Filipino maids were horrified and told her that the guards would never let her out. Was she a prisoner? she asked herself, as she eyed the high, unscalable walls that surrounded the palace grounds. She remembered what the Prince had said about not allowing his women to be seen by other men, or even to see other men.

Then, smilingly, one of the maids handed her a note. It was a polite formal invitation from the Prince to join him for dinner that night. Oh, the joy! Thrilled, she wrote her acceptance and sent it off with the maid.

All day she could think of nothing else but what she would wear and how she would do her hair. Her hair! How she longed for a hairdresser. Then, as if in answer to her silent prayer the maids told her that Hazud, the palace hairdresser, had arrived.

A palace hairdresser! Astonished, Emma went to meet him. He was a dapper young black man. He spoke quite good English, but once again with a high-pitched voice. Anyway, thought Emma, he certainly knew what he was about when it came to arranging women's hair and making up their faces. To her surprise, he had even unlocked a proper little hairdressing salon in the guest house.

After Emma's long hair had been washed and dried and freshly tinted, it shone as beautifully as she had ever seen it shine. But when she asked Hazud to coil it up in a sophisticated style, he just shook his head and brushed it so that it hung down her back like the hair of a much younger girl. 'Master like that,' he explained. Just like Ursula, Emma thought, ruefully.

Then the hairdresser started to make up her eyes in the Arab style. Emma was startled when she saw an Arab *houri* staring back at her in the mirror – a *houri* with huge eyes outlined in heavy black, brightly rouged cheeks and glistening lips and eyelids.

Back in her bedroom, she was astonished to see that the maids had laid out a beautiful cream-coloured silken caftan. 'Ali Efendi send this over. Present from Prince. You wear this tonight.'

Thrilled, Emma lifted up the gorgeous dress. Then she gasped as she saw, embroidered on the right breast, as on her nightdress and as on the saddle cloths of the horses, the insignia of the Prince.

'Hurry!' whispered the Filipino maid, pulling some sheer, self-supporting stockings up over her legs and then lifting up the caftan to slip it over her head. 'Ali Efendi now coming to take you to Prince.'

'But I haven't got any underclothes on,' Emma protested. The thin silken robe would accentuate her every curve – and it was slit up one side.

'Prince's women not wear underclothes,' giggled the girl. Emma had been about to insist when she heard a cough from the doorway. Ali Efendi was watching her. Hastily, she allowed the girl to slip the caftan down to hide her nakedness.

'Come,' beckoned Ali Efendi in his strange high voice. 'Prince waiting.'

Uncomfortably aware of her near-nakedness under the long caftan, Emma followed the big man into a large air-conditioned Mercedes car. Tinted glass hid the chauffeur from Emma's view, reminding her of the Prince's remark about not allowing his women to see other men.

They drove several hundred yards across the palace grounds, and up to a magnificent white-painted house built like an Italian villa, with steps leading up to a doorway surrounded by columns. To one side was another very high wall surrounding a wing of the palace. Over the wall, she had a glimpse of a few barred windows made of frosted glass. Was this the harem? Emma wondered. Was the frosted glass not only to prevent the women from being seen by visiting men, but also, as the Prince had said, to prevent the women from seeing other men? Goodness!

The palace was cool and very luxurious. Emma was led through a large hall and up a marble staircase into a reception room furnished in simple Arab style with low sofas and couches, and little tables with gleaming beaten-copper tops. There, evidently waiting for her, stood the Prince. He was alone.

Astonished, Emma saw that he was wearing a European-style dinner jacket and black tie. The contrast with her own flimsy Arab caftan was marked. She felt very naked and embarrassed. Had he deliberately arranged all this to emphasise his psychological ascendency over her? And if so, could she turn it to her own advantage and use it to seduce him?

But the Prince was charm and courtesy itself, as, smiling, he ushered her to a sofa. She listened spellbound as he began to talk of his successes in the past racing season in England and France and of his hopes for the future. He showed her the latest daily fax from his racing manager reporting on his various horses in training, and on his mares and foals. He clearly knew a great deal about each one of them individually.

Then, ever so subtly, he began to tease her with snippets of information about his harem.

'Oh, it's well known that my concubines are under the strictest supervision in my harem,' he said. 'I have to be seen to uphold ... certain traditions, and to set an example to my people. And in any case,' he continued, 'I've found that the harsher the discipline is in my harem, and the larger the harem is, the happier I am.'

'Oh!' gasped Emma, who was already getting the distinct impression of a dreadful male chauvinist society. And yet a sudden rush of arousal made her wonder if it was not all rather exciting. 'But how,' she asked, finding her words with difficulty, 'would the more traditionally-minded men in your country react if it became known that you had – European women – Christian women – in your harem?'

The Prince laughed. 'Well, of course, it never would become known, anyway not for certain, for Moslem men do not discuss the women in their harems. But if it were rumoured that I did keep some European women locked up in my harem then that would make me all the more more popular with the traditionalists, since they would know any European women would be kept under the strict control and supervision of my black eunuchs.'

'Black eunuchs!' cried Emma in disbelief. 'You mean they still exist in this day and age?'

'Oh yes, I have four of them. You've already met three: Ali Efendi, my chief eunuch, Hazud the harem hairdresser, and young Abdul, who's coming on well. He's developing into a natural strict disciplinarian – just what's needed in a harem. He accompanied you in the car when you travelled to the palace from the stables. Then there's Nagu, an older eunuch who supervises the harem by night.'

Emma sat spellbound, then took a deep breath. The Prince, however, anticipated her question – the obvious question under the circumstances – and forestalled it. 'It's not for me to tell you where I find my eunuchs, though I will say that there is no shortage of men willing to undergo ... the necessary procedures,' he said.

200

'But how dreadful!' commented Emma.

'Not at all,' laughed the Prince, dismissing her concern. 'They have a much better life here, in charge of the women in a rich man's harem, than they ever would have had where they came from, and much more responsibility too. Ali Efendi is as important, when it comes to my women, as my racing manager is to my race horses in England, or as my head groom is to my stud of Arab horses here. That's why he has the title of Efendi, to show off his high rank, and the respect with which he should be treated . . .' He broke off. 'Ah, here he is in person!'

Seated on her sofa, Emma could not help but give a little shiver as the large, fat, black man, dressed as usual in an immaculate white Arab robe, came waddling into the room, bowing humbly to the Prince. Was it a shiver of fear or disgust? Or was it just anger at being interrupted in her hopeful seduction of the Prince?

She saw that in his left hand he was holding, like a wand of office, a long, slender, silver-tipped bamboo cane with a curved handle. In his right hand he held what seemed to be a printed list of names. There were ticks and Arabic writing against each name. Ignoring the presence of Emma, he proudly handed the list to the Prince.

'Ah,' said the Prince to Emma. 'You see, this is his daily report on the state of my concubines – the women in his charge. It's as important, in its way, as the daily report on my valuable horses that we've just been discussing.'

Damn that man and his silly report, thought Emma. She wanted the Prince to be thinking of her, not of his wretched concubines. And anyway, what a shockingly callous way to treat women: to have a daily report brought to him like the report on his racehorses. And how many concubines did he have, for heaven's sake? The list seemed quite long.

Indeed, the Prince was going down the list, nodding and putting the occasional question in Arabic to Ali Efendi. Emma noticed that the Prince was pointing to one name against which a black star had been put. 'Ali Efendi has the authority to award up to six strokes of the cane,' the Prince explained to Emma, 'but he wants to give this girl twelve. She's getting slack – lack of zeal we call it – and getting above herself. He feels that she needs a proper thrashing to shake her up.' He turned back to Ali Efendi and nodded.

Horrified at the casual way in which a woman had been sentenced to be thrashed, Emma found herself looking silently at the long whippy cane in the overseer's strong hand. My God!

'My women all get a good thrashing from time to time,' the Prince nonchalantly informed Emma. 'It makes them adore and respect me all the more.'

Oh, the sheer arrogance of the man! Emma wanted to hit him, but she had to admit there was, going by her own experiences, some truth in what he had said. Her thoughts were then interrupted again by the Prince, who was pointing at half a dozen red ticks against some of the names. 'Please excuse me for a moment,' he said politely, turning back to Emma, 'but I must discuss these recommendations for a shortlist for this evening's selection parade.'

Emma eyes widened. This evening's selection parade? Did the Prince really mean what she thought he meant? She simply could not believe what she was seeing, as the Prince and his chief black eunuch began a detailed discussion in Arabic, both repeatedly pointing to the names against which the red stars had been placed. Then the Prince gave the list back, and the overseer, throwing a curious glance at Emma, again bowed humbly and left the room.

'He always has his favourites,' complained the Prince as Ali Efendi left the room. 'Well, I'll just have to see later . . .'

Emma caught her breath. Was he really talking about a selection parade of his women? And did the shortlist really include European women? She felt a sudden pang of jealousy. What about herself? Why wasn't he interested in her? Or was she just imagining it all? Could this charming, civilized man in his well-cut dinner jacket, who spoke such good English, really have a harem of Arab girls at his beck and call, selected for his pleasure by a black eunuch?

'Now, how about a little dinner?' said the Prince briskly. 'I've ordered some local delicacies especially for you.'

He led her courteously into a beautifully furnished European-style dining room with a small round mahogany Regency table and Regency chairs. The only light came from silver candlesticks on the table and sideboards. How romantic, Emma thought for a moment, just what I need. Then she remembered the earlier scene with Ali Efendi and his damn list. She gave a little of shiver of despair.

Then she was astonished to see that two very good-looking white young men were drawing back chairs for her and the Prince. They were dressed in bright blue European pageboy outfits with buttons going down the front of their tight tunics. On each of their right breasts was the same embroidered insignia that Emma wore on her own breast. Perched at an angle on one side of their heads were little blue pillbox hats, secured in place by fine leather straps going under their chins.

'I copied their uniforms from those of the pageboys in Claridges,' explained the Prince with a laugh as he saw Emma staring at the two young men. 'They're orphans who were only too happy to have the chance to start a new life out here – even if it did, first, mean becoming eunuchs.'

'Eunuchs!' cried Emma as she sat down, looking up at the youths' smooth skins.

'Oh, yes, it's an old custom here in the Middle East for wealthy men to use white eunuchs as their personal attendants or valets, and as confidential clerks – and black eunuchs to supervise and discipline their women. White eunuchs are very different to black ones, but both types have one thing in common: they're both exceptionally loyal to their Masters. Like neutered dogs they don't run away . . .'

The Prince paused and then laughed. 'And with them being eunuchs, I can also safely use these two to attend on me even when I'm enjoying one of my women, particularly a new one – holding her down for me, taking her to the bathroom, and so on.'

Holding her down! Taking her to the bathroom! Emma looked at the two youths with a new respect. They looked so fresh-faced and innocent. 'You mean –' she stammered, 'you have them with you in your bedroom whilst you're –'

'– Making love?' said the Prince, nonchalantly. 'Oh, yes! They can make themselves very useful, particularly with a new girl. And, moreover,' he went on, 'they can also unobtrusively accompany me as my valets when I travel to Europe. People just think that they are rather effeminate personal servants.'

Poor Emma was altogether too stunned, by all that she had seen and heard, to want to make much conversation during dinner, or to do justice to the delicious food. Indeed, she wondered whether the Prince was secretly laughing at her, given that he had succeeded both in shocking and exciting her, and in making her bitterly regret coming out here at all, even though she was also being thrilled out of her mind by what was happening.

All that she could really think about was the fact that somewhere in the palace was a harem, a harem in which women were kept hidden away, purely for the pleasure of this all-powerful man. It was astonishing.

She would have been even more astonished had she known what the Prince was planning for her, as he carefully judged her reaction to what she had heard and seen – what, indeed, he had been planning from the first moment he had seen her.

26

Emma's First Glimpse of the Harem

Suddenly, as if reading her thoughts, the Prince asked Emma: 'Would you like to see inside the harem?'

Then, turning to the two white pageboys, he pointed to a curtain that ran down one side of the room. They pulled it back to reveal what seemed like a window with a long piece of glass – a one-way mirror, Emma realised, and felt intrigued.

The window looked straight into a large room, beautifully decorated in the Arab style, and with brightly coloured mosaics on the walls and ceilings. It was simply furnished, with large, coloured leather cushions.

Emma gasped as she saw that, walking about or sitting talking on the cushions, were a dozen young women. Then she gasped again.

'But they're all European women!' she cried out.

'Indeed!' laughed the Prince. 'I would have thought that you would have realised by now that my tastes in nearly everything tend towards the European way of life. But, of course, I can't spend all my time in the West. So I need a little touch of Europe back here too – and where better to have it than in my harem?'

Emma saw that the women were all dressed in beautifully tailored caftans, just like the one that she herself was wearing. Through the thin material of the caftans, the lines of the women's bodies showed erotically. She remembered what the Filipino maids had said about no underclothes being allowed in the harem. Goodness! Did she look like that in her caftan?

Embroidered on the right breast of each woman's caftan, just as on hers, was the Prince's insignia. Their hair gleamed and hung down their backs, just as Hazud the hairdresser had arranged hers, and their eyes were heavily made up in just the same way as hers were.

Some of them were slender, others were quite plump. 'I like them to be all different shapes and sizes,' she heard the Prince say, 'provided they're beautiful, of course, with good breasts.'

Then she saw that each of them was wearing a shiny metal collar. Something about these collars reminded her of the leather collar that Ursula had locked her into after the special school. Yes, it had the same little box at the back. The Prince must use it to prevent his concubines from escaping from his harem, just as Ursula had used hers to prevent Emma from escaping from her own home. Well, he certainly seems very with it, she thought – and up to date with all the latest electronic gadgets.

Occasionally, the women would look towards the one-way mirror and smile coquettishly, as if they were wondering whether or not they were being watched.

'Yes,' said the Prince, 'they know I often watch them unseen from behind this one-way mirror – and other similar mirrors and wooden screens. I find it fascinating – rather like many people find it fascinating to watch fish in an aquarium! I can happily watch my women for hours, all the while enjoying the feeling of owning such lovely and helpless creatures – now kept purely for my pleasure.'

Helpless creatures! Kept purely for his pleasure! Emma could feel herself becoming aroused.

The Prince saw her flushed face. Yes, she might well do brilliantly in the role he was planning for her – after a spell in his harem so that she could be taught to please him properly.

'But,' said Emma hesitantly, 'there don't seem to be any children in the harem, and I don't see any of the women –'

'In an expectant state?' The Prince completed her question. 'No, these are merely my white concubines, and as such they aren't worthy to be the mothers of my sons. Ali Efendi ensures they don't become pregnant. How he does it I don't enquire – he doubtless has his own methods.'

He laughed. 'No, motherhood is the role of my two high-born wives, the Princesses, who each live with their children in their own house, away from the harem, in the palace grounds. I visit each of them at home one night a week and sometimes take one of them with me to Europe.'

Emma gasped at his arrogance. Then she saw two blonde girls sitting together on a cushion and holding hands. They were dressed in identical caftans and looked remarkably alike. Surely, she thought, they could not be sisters, twin sisters – not here in a harem? They were very pretty with bright blue eyes, pretty ankles and extraordinarily long, slender necks. They were looking at each other and smiling. The Prince pointed to them. 'Twins,' he said, proudly.

Emma looked at him, astonished.

'They're from Poland,' he continued. 'Very sensual – and very valuable, of course.'

Emma smiled to herself. She had often overheard Ursula describing her as valuable, and if the Prince had a taste for valuable girls . . .

'When I acquired them, they were still virgins, straight from a convent. They originally came to the Middle East to teach in a girls' school. Then I made them an offer they couldn't refuse and they found, instead, that they were the ones being given the lessons

208

– by Ali Efendi – in how to give me pleasure, not only together in my bed, but also by performing together, in front of me.'

'Performing together!' repeated Emma. 'You mean – but I imagined . . .'

'That lesbianism is forbidden in a harem? Yes, of course it is, and so is masturbation. I've no real objection to either, but the black eunuchs regard both as infidelity to the Master, almost on a par with adultery, and certainly an insult to them, the guardians of my women's purity. So, if they catch two women alone and not under the supervision of a black eunuch, or alone by themselves, then they always assume the worst – and it's an automatic ten strokes of Ali Efendi's cane in front of this mirror, and their companions have to watch, too.

'Yes!' laughed the Prince cruelly, 'they have to be feeling pretty desperate to risk it, but then, of course, the harem system keeps them feeling pretty desperate. So it's all a game of cat and mouse between the women and the black eunuchs – an amusing game for me to watch. Mind you, the black eunuchs' rules don't stop them teaching the girls to put on a little . . . exhibition for my enjoyment, but they only let them go so far, unless I give my permission for them to continue. Yes, I like watching a woman – or several women – being made to arouse themselves in front of me.'

The Prince paused. How awful, Emma was thinking, it would be to have to play with herself in front of the Prince. How embarrassing. But also, how exciting! Blushing, she heard the Prince continue.

'Of course, it's only natural for the women in a harem, deprived as they are of even the sight of another man, to – what is your English expression? – ah, yes – to form crushes on each other. I don't mind particularly, but the black eunuchs do; they are afraid that if a girl is not kept frustrated, then she will lose her drive to catch my eye. That's why they watch all the women so carefully. They even insist on me paying extra for the old retired black eunuch, Nagu, to patrol the harem dormitory all night – to make sure that all the little creatures remain frustrated in their own little cots, with their hands well in view above the sheets.'

He paused for a moment. 'Yes, I let Ali Effendi have free rein to run the harem as he likes, provided, of course, he produces my women for me, at any time of the day or night, happy, vivacious and eager to please. So, dealing with the women is his responsibility. I don't ask questions about how he does it. Why keep a dog and bark yourself, as you English say.'

The Prince laughed sardonically. 'Yes, to use another English expression, he runs a very tight ship, with lots of petty little rules that the girls have to learn – just what has to be done, where, how and at what time; how they should address him or the other black eunuchs, and so on. The girls all know that any breach of the rules is likely to result in her getting the cane from him. But, as you can see, he certainly doesn't keep them all cowed and sulky. On the contrary, as I'm sure you'll agree, they're a happy-looking batch!'

The Prince paused. 'But, I must confess, I do like to see them treating my chief black eunuch with the respect he deserves. If, as very occasionally happens, he reports a girl to me for impertinence or dumb insolence towards him or young Abdul, then I automatically support his authority by authorising him to give her a full dozen strokes of the cane. And I do the same if any girl is not desperate to please me in my bed – something that Ali Efendi takes as a personal affront to his authority.'

'Yes,' he continued, 'it all works out very well and, I must say, he's certainly turned my Polish girls into an eager and accomplished pair of lovers – and a very beautiful pair at that!'

My God, thought Emma, uncertain as to whether she

was more shocked or more jealous. Memories of the awful Sabhu flooded back. How strange it was, and yet how true, that some women could be wildly happy and yet be subject to the strict discipline of their Master's, or Mistress's, servants – something that both Ursula and the Prince were evidently well aware of.

But, before she could say anything, the Prince had pointed to a beautiful woman, probably in her late thirties, with delicate cheekbones and dark flashing eyes. She was talking to a younger girl of perhaps eighteen. They were smiling happily and were dressed, like the two Polish girls, in identical caftans. But curiously, despite the difference in their ages, there was a strange resemblance between them.

'My hot-blooded Italian mother and daughter!' laughed the Prince. 'They are also very valuable. Pretty mothers and daughters don't grow on trees, you know. The daughter was still a virgin. The mother was a divorcee. She hated it here at first, especially as she was used to having lots of boyfriends. Now, of course, I'm her only boyfriend! Indeed, except perhaps for a distant view of a guard, or a gardener, she hasn't even seen another man, other than my black eunuchs, since she came to my harem ...'

The Prince paused reflectively for a moment. 'Yes,' he went on, 'by not allowing them to see another man, or to know anything of what is going on in the world beyond the very high walls of the harem garden, and by treating them like younger girls, my black eunuchs keep my women both frustrated and fascinatingly innocent at heart – even though they have the skills and desires of very experienced and lustful women.'

The Prince laughed yet again. 'These two resented being trained by Ali Efendi at first, and he had to use his whip a lot before he had them ready for me. But now the daughter is as desperate for a man as the mother – and both are desperate to catch my eye! Of course, they know that I'm only interested in them for my bed if they're both going to concentrate on my pleasure.'

A mother and daughter in a harem, Emma was thinking. Trained to work in tandem to please their Master! Prevented even from seeing other men! European women kept in the harem of a Moslem Prince! A man who outwardly is a highly civilised and erudite man, well known in Europe!

'And,' went on the Prince, 'to make sure that they do regard themselves as a pair and not as individuals, they both get beaten together by Ali Efendi, whenever one of them breaks one of the harem rules, or if I feel that one of them was lacking in eagerness to please me in my bed. It makes each of them very anxious to ensure that the other always behaves properly, smiles happily and never sulks – and the sight of them both nervously bending over for Ali Efendi's whippy little cane can be a very arousing sight, even if I'm feeling a bit jaded.'

'You mean you watch your women being punished by Ali Efendi?' cried Emma in mock horror, secretly thinking how exciting it would be to be punished in front of the handsome Prince.

'Of course! It's one of the principal joys of having a harem. But to return to my beautiful mother and daughter concubines,' continued the Prince, 'I shall never forget that first night, when Ali Efendi proudly brought them both to my bed, and I took the girl's virginity whilst the mother licked me from behind – just as she had been taught to do. And then they had to swap places, both knowing that the one who gave me less pleasure would be getting a thrashing from Ali Efendi in the morning. That really was a memorable occasion.'

'Oh!' exclaimed Emma. How awful for the mother to have to witness the defloration of her daughter. How equally awful for the daughter to have to witness the shaming of her mother. But, she had to admit, how exciting for the Prince.

'So,' asked Emma, after a pause, 'how on earth did you get hold of them?'

'I rarely have a problem finding what I'm looking for,' said the Prince, enigmatically. 'And Ali Efendi, too, usually knows if anything suitably interesting is on offer at any one time. I leave it all to him – provided he keeps within his budget. And to his assistant, whom I was telling you about, young Abdul. He's also developing a good eye for a likely performer.'

He pointed to the young black man standing in the corner of the room. Emma recognised him as the youth who had travelled with her in the car from the stables to the palace. He was dressed just like Ali Efendi, but instead of a cane, he was holding a black leather whip with a short handle. The whites of his bloodshot eyes gleamed as they darted to and fro, whilst he carefully watched the women's every movement.

Emma's head was reeling from all this. White European women in a harem! A budget for paying for them! A young assistant trainer! Developing a good eye for a likely performer! My God! Was the Prince talking about his women or his horses?

'You mean you often acquire new women for your harem?' Emma stammered.

'Oh yes, but I find that about a dozen at any time is a comfortable number to jog along with.'

'My God,' cried Emma, unable to keep her thoughts to herself any longer. 'You're the most arrogant and self-opinionated man I've ever met. You're just the –'

'The most irresistible man you've ever met?' he laughed.

'Oh, you – you –' she cried. Then, seeing the way in which he was laughing at her, she, too, could not help bursting out laughing. 'You're just impossible,' she finished lamely and then added, 'And, anyway, even if what you say is true, what happens to the girls you get rid of?'

'Oh, that's no problem. It's always possible for me to offload women whose services I no longer require. Remember, I get the cream of the crop, and there are plenty of men out there who are happy to settle for less, as it were. And, of course, there is always a good demand for girls who have already been broken in by an experienced chief eunuch.'

Offloading a girl! Broken in! Emma almost gasped aloud. My God! Then, collecting her thoughts, she asked, 'But surely there's the risk that they would talk about you and your harem – and create a scandal.'

'Not really, everyone here knows I have a harem. It's expected of me.'

'Yes, but what if one of these European women should later tell the world press about your harem? Think of the story in the English papers. How would that affect your image in England as a benefactor of the turf?'

'Oh, I think the English racing fraternity would be very surprised if I did not have any women in my life. But anyway these European women here don't even know where they are or who I am, so they could hardly cause much of a stir even if they did try to sell their story to the papers.'

'What!' cried Emma in astonishment. 'You really mean they don't know where they are or in whose harem they are? I can't believe it!'

'Of course they don't. Why should they? Most of them have never seen over the walls of the harem, never mind over the walls of the palace grounds. All they know is that they came to the Middle East, and were subsequently brought here to the palace. To them I am just the Prince, their Master. Otherwise they only see the eunuchs and the occasional servant girl – and my staff are in no doubt as to how severe the penalty would be were they to tell my women who their Master was.'

The Prince paused and looked Emma in the eye. 'And

the same would apply, of course, to anyone else going into the harem temporarily – or leaving it. We Arabs have a long arm. Anyone opening their mouths back in Europe would also find themselves in serious trouble. It's as simple as that!'

Emma caught her breath. Was he giving her a warning? The threat was certainly clear and unmistakable.

'But – but,' she stammered. 'Isn't there a risk of them getting someone to smuggle out a letter to their family back in Europe, or perhaps of them discreetly giving a note of their family's name and address to a visitor?'

'Oh, no, Ali Efendi makes certain that there are no pens or pencils, or other writing materials, in the harem. It's a tradition going back to the days when women were deliberately kept illiterate.'

'But surely they might still tell a visitor their names?' said Emma, wondering if they might, should she ever visit the harem.

'No, no,' laughed the Prince. 'Ali Efendi would first warn them not to talk to the visitor. It's one of the strengths of the harem system that the identity of any woman in one remain completely secret to the outside world.'

Shocked, Emma looked into the harem again and, through the barred windows on the far side of the room, she saw an illuminated formal garden, and beyond that the high palace wall. She noticed that several other rooms led off from this large room. There were no doors, there was no privacy.

Suddenly, she saw the hugely fat figure of Ali Efendi waddling into the main harem room. The youth Abdul clapped his hands. All the women respectfully stood up or stood quite still. Clearly, he had them all well disciplined. Watched by the women, Ali Efendi ponderously made his way to the middle of the room. He pulled the list out of his pocket. The women's eyes were on it, as if waiting eagerly or expectantly.

Slowly Ali Efendi read out some names. As he did so, first one woman and then another would blush with excitement. He finished and put away the list, leaving the other women looking sad and disappointed. He clapped his hands and gave an order. The excited-looking women all ran off to one of the alcoves. Emma saw the twins amongst them, but not the mother and daughter. They and the others all now sat down meekly on the cushions.

Emma could see that the alcove, to which the women had run, had, seemingly, been fitted out like a larger version of the hairdressing salon in the guest house. And, indeed, she then saw Hazud being besieged by the half-dozen eager women.

Then the Prince snapped his fingers, and the curtain was once again drawn over the one-way mirror. 'We'll see them again soon, when Ali Efendi has them ready to be paraded for my final selection for tonight.'

Final selection! Again a wave of jealousy washed through Emma.

'Well then,' she said, getting up from the table with a flash of anger. 'There's not much point in me staying here any longer.'

'Oh, but there is!' laughed the Prince, putting out a strong hand and pulling her back down on to her chair. 'I'm sure you're secretly longing to see what happens next. You might even learn something!'

'What!' she cried. But secretly Emma knew that the Prince was right. She was indeed fascinated by it all, even if she was being driven mad with jealousy over this handsome and astonishingly self-confident man.

The Prince now cleverly started to ask Emma about herself – about her upbringing in Ireland, about her marriage and about her country house. Emma was terrified that he might trick her into talking about Ursula or Henry, but he was far too well-mannered to press her.

Suddenly, a red light started flickering above the curtains covering the one-way mirror. The Prince nodded and the two pages once again drew back the curtain.

Emma gave a gasp of surprise.

27

A Jealous Emma Sees the Prince Select his Bed Companions

Emma now saw that, standing immediately before the the one-way mirror, were the two Polish girls, the twins, looking more lovely and beguiling than ever. They were identically made-up, their hair was beautifully brushed back over their shoulders and they were wearing identical caftans of silken pink gauze.

Behind them stood the frightening and repulsively fat figure of Ali Efendi, his long bamboo cane menacingly gripped in both hands across his chest and bent so that the middle was raised up towards his chin. Behind him could be seen those women who had not been chosen. They were sitting on their leather cushions, and looking bitterly jealous as they watched in silence. But were they, Emma wondered, feeling quite as jealous as she was! Why were they being made to watch? Why, for that matter, was she? For the same reason? To make them try harder to catch the Prince's eye? Goodness!

Then young Abdul and Hazud the hairdresser appeared. Each was carrying a little cane in one hand and a short length of silvery chain in the other. They bowed at the unseen Prince and then each snapped his chains on to a ring at the back of the girls' shiny collars.

The Prince pressed a button on the table. The haunting sound of 'Night and Day' filled the room and the two girls, their collars held by the two eunuchs, began to sway in time to it, their breasts and haunches quivering beneath their silken caftans.

'I like all my women to have a theme tune,' laughed the Prince, 'and I love this one – and it seemed so apt for these twins. I love dancing to it with them both together. I call the one on the left "Night" and the other one "Day".'

Even the shocked Emma could not help giving a little laugh. Perhaps this cruel Master had a sense of humour after all.

Then she noticed that the girls were now wearing a different type of caftan – one which buttoned up the front. The eunuchs gave the girls a tap on the buttocks with their canes and, immediately, they lovingly started to unbutton each other's caftans, kissing each other passionately and baring their full breasts. Emma saw that their nipples had been painted a glistening scarlet to match their lipstick. Then, as the caftans fell to the floor with a rustle of silk, she saw their smooth mounds on to which the Prince's crest had been painted in henna, and their naked beauty lips which had also been painted a gleaming scarlet. What an exciting sight! And all for one man!

The Polish girls swayed against each other to the music, their bodies touching erotically as they strained against their taut collar chains, still being held by the black eunuchs, to play with each other's nipples in what seemed to be a well-rehearsed routine. Soon, they were both clearly becoming aroused, their eyes glazing and their necks reddening.

Frequently, the eunuchs would pull the two girls back by their collar chains, leaving them frustrated but still swaying to the music, their hands outstretched pathetically towards each other. Then, with a sharp stroke of their canes, the eunuchs would drive them forward to touch and stimulate each other once more, only to be pulled back when the men judged that they were getting too aroused again.

The eunuchs, Emma realised, were making the twins put on a very exciting and well-rehearsed exhibition of female sensuality – and one that was clearly being appreciated by the watching Prince. What would it be like to be made to perform like this with another woman in front of the Prince? She wondered.

Then, as the black eunuchs made the girls turn around to display their back views, Emma saw the marks of a recent caning on each of their bottoms. Driven mad by constantly being made to practise arousing each other but denied any relief, had they perhaps been caught desperately trying to play with each other? Or had they simply been insolent to the dreaded Ali Efendi? Either way, it was clear that life in the Prince's harem, under the supervision of Ali Efendi, was no bed of roses.

It was a highly erotic sight, and even the jealously watching Emma could feel herself becoming aroused, too. How, she wondered, could the Prince ever want anybody else, other than these two glorious girls? But then the music died away, and the two girls, moving as one, fell to their knees in humble abeyance, their foreheads touching the floor, their long blonde hair flung forward towards the Prince, and their collar chains held taut by the black eunuchs standing proudly behind them.

Ali Efendi tapped the floor with his cane and, led by the two black eunuchs, the two girls flounced proudly out of sight. Then he gave another signal, and immediately a gorgeous girl, dressed as a belly dancer, sprang into sight. The rhythm of the music changed to a much faster Arab tempo and the girl began to dance the age-old routine.

'She's Mira, a Greek girl, and I saw her belly-dancing in a night club in Istanbul. I arranged for her to be offered a contract she simply could not refuse – to dance in a night club in Cyprus. But somehow she fell asleep in the special plane she thought was taking her there. It was my own plane, of course and, by the time we arrived at the palace I'd, well, talked her into joining my harem.'

Whilst the Prince had been talking, the girl had slipped off her bra top and continued dancing, her heavy breasts jiggling. Emma saw that her nipples, too, had been painted a glistening scarlet to match her lipstick. Moments later, off came the slip of gold cloth that had hidden her more intimate charms. Now, as her naked belly jerked in and out, the henna-coloured crest on her mound and her bare beauty lips, again painted scarlet like those of the Polish girls, started to play an essential part in the whole display.

'You'd never think that when she first jointed us Ali Efendi had a little difficulty in persuading her to dance here for me in a rather more uninhibited way than she was used to doing. But such is the power of the cane that she soon learned to perform wonderfully!

'You can imagine I'm sure just how strong her internal muscles are,' said the Prince as Mira's belly undulated rapidly. 'And I'm also sure you can appreciate that they work in quite a different way to untrained muscles.'

Emma's own internal muscles contracted involuntarily.

'And those same muscles can give me enormous delight too. That is, after all, the whole point of training a girl to belly-dance,' said the Prince.

Moments later the Arab music reached a crescendo, and when it stopped the girl flung herself down on to the shiny parquet floor in front of the mirror, offering herself in a well-trained gesture of utter subservience.

Again, Emma could not help jealously thinking that nothing, not even the two Polish girls, could ever be so erotic.

Then it was the turn of an exquisite half-Chinese girl.

She was dressed in a long, heavy green robe embroidered with red dragons and, accompanied by the music of Chinese gongs and drums, she sang a Chinese song in an appealingly helpless and childlike voice.

'Where did you find her?' whispered Emma.

'Oh,' replied the Prince airily as, now naked, she continued to sing. 'She's just a little perk I got from doing a friend a favour.'

'Who?' asked Emma, but he refused to be drawn any further.

Then there was a pause and a large double wheel, over six feet in diameter, and made of aluminium bars, was rolled in front of the glass window. Strapped inside it by her wrists, and with her ankles free but pressed against another part of the wheel, was a beautiful white girl. She was stark naked except for the gleaming metal collar around her neck.

To the strangely evocative music of the waltz from the *Merry Widow*, she cleverly rolled the wheel to and fro, while smiling entrancingly. One moment she was hanging upside down, with her long blonde hair cascading down below her head, and her legs wide apart displaying her scarlet-painted beauty lips. The next, she was suspended the right way up with her knees chastely drawn up to her navel.

'This is Helga,' said the Prince. 'I found her in a nightclub in Hamburg. Having decided that she'd be better off performing her many acrobatic tricks for me in private, I arranged for her to be brought here. She's settled down very well, all things considered, and has taught some of the other girls to perform tricks for my enjoyment. It's interesting, having a contortionist or two available for one's bed.'

It was the phrase 'available for one's bed' that was racing around Emma's head as the girl struck a succession of highly erotic poses. How could she make the Prince realise that she, too, was available?

Then she noticed some scratches on the girl's face and body.

'I expect she's been fighting again,' said the Prince disparagingly, as if he was talking about a badly behaved pet bitch. 'It often happens in even the best-regulated harems – even normally well-mannered European women get frustrated and jealous of each other, and the atmosphere becomes explosive. It's this sort of thing that makes it all so fascinating to watch from behind the one-way mirrors and screens. The eunuchs are constantly having to step in and separate girls trying to scratch each others' eyes out – and then they have to thrash them so that they don't do it again, at least, not for a day or two.'

Once again, Emma caught her breath. Oh yes, she knew all about the terrifying power of sexual frustration and jealousy. She could believe every word that the Prince was saying. She herself was, even now, feeling . . .

'Come,' said the Prince, interrupting her thoughts and rising from the table. 'Let's have a little dance ourselves!'

Emma slipped into his strong arms and looked adoringly up at him, as they slowly waltzed around. It was, she knew, all utterly incongruous. Here she was, being watched by two white eunuch boys as she slowly and romantically waltzed around to the music of Franz Lehar. Her partner, a cruel and despotic Arab prince, was dressed in a dinner jacket, and one of his European concubines was cavorting, completely naked, on the other side of a mirror, desperately trying to catch his eye. It was all mad. But never mind; at least she was in the Prince's arms!

The music stopped. The curtain was yet again drawn over the one-way mirror. Reluctantly, Emma sat down. The magic spell was broken.

One of the pages handed the Prince an internal telephone.

'Well, which ones should I choose tonight?' he asked the once again furiously jealous Emma.

Then, without waiting for her reply, he said thoughtfully, 'I was very taken by our *Merry Widow* and by 'Night and Day', but I think that for tonight my Eurasian girl and Mira, the belly dancer, will make an interesting pair for me to try out in combination. The Eastern girl is naturally very tight and Mira's muscle control gives the same feeling.'

Emma could feel herself becoming more and more angry and jealous as the Prince continued.

'Yes, I think I'll go firm on those two. Just excuse me a moment, my dear, whilst I tell Ali Efendi to get them both ready.' And with that he gave an order over the phone in Arabic, then handed it back to the page.

'You, you –' cried Emma, unable to believe what she had just heard. Here she was, still aroused from dancing in this gorgeous man's arms and crazy to please him, and all he could do was arrange, in front of her, to take a licentious belly-dancer and a little chit of a half-Chinese girl to bed for the night.

However, the smiling Prince seemed not to have been aware of her jealous outburst. 'Well,' he said briskly, rubbing his hands as though in eager anticipation of the pleasure that the two chosen women would shortly be giving him – and as though Emma were a child he wanted out of the way. 'It's time now for you to say 'goodnight' and for me to send you back to have a good night's sleep in the guest house. My pages will see you back.'

It was with a mixture of fury, jealousy and despair that Emma watched him get up to leave – fury at the cavalier way she was being treated, jealousy at the way he was openly planning to make love to other women and despair at the lack of interest he seemed to be showing in her.

However, at the door, he turned and smiled. 'Oh, and

224

by the way, don't hesitate to let Ali Efendi know if you would like to see what things look like from the other side of the one-way mirror. You're a highly attractive woman and I think you might enjoy it, if you don't mind putting up with a little discipline. All I need is your promise that you'll keep your mouth shut about where we are, and you wouldn't break that, would you?'

And with that he was gone, leaving Emma staring after him, once again open-mouthed.

28

Emma Enters the Harem

For three whole days, Emma was left alone in the guest house, brooding over the astonishing scenes she had witnessed whilst having dinner with the Prince.

Her jealous fury was yet further aroused when, every time she asked to see the Prince, she was told that he was 'engaged in his harem'. Was he making love to that Italian mother and daughter? she wondered. Were the Polish cousins disporting themselves in his bed? Or the German Helga? Or any of the other beautiful women? She could think of nothing else as, lying frustrated in her bed, she kept looking up at the portrait of the Prince on the wall.

His parting words, about telling Ali Efendi if she would like to see what life was like from the other side of the one-way mirror, raced round and round her brain. Was he telling her that she would not see him again unless she joined in a selection parade? My God!

Naked in the bathroom, she looked down at her mound on which a little fuzz was now starting to grow again. She remembered the smooth, painted mounds and beauty lips of the Prince's concubines. Would she again have to lose her body hair and be painted there too?

So, she kept asking herself, should she ask to be put into the selection parade? It sounded crazy that she, a European woman, should ask to be allowed to parade in an erotic competition to give pleasure to an Arab Prince. She must be mad even to consider it. Moreover

226

could she, as the Prince had said, put up with what he had called 'a little discipline'? She remembered the stripes across the bottoms of the two Polish girls.

But was there any real alternative to asking to be allowed to compete for the Prince's favours? She could not just sit here in the guest house, bored out of her mind, for the next few days, being driven mad by thoughts of what the Prince was getting up to in his harem. And anyway the thought of being made to parade half-naked in front of the Prince was terribly exciting. But did the Prince have some secret long-term plan involving her? Goodness!

These thoughts were still occupying her mind when she went back to the bedroom to rest. Unable to avoid looking up at the portrait of the Prince in there, she felt herself becoming moist with desire. What a man!

She turned and looked at herself in a gilt-framed mirror. Slowly, she opened the neck loops of her caftan and lifted out her right breast. Using her thumb and forefinger, she squeezed the nipple so that it became prominent, and felt a thrill deep inside her. She took out the other breast – oh, how exciting it would be if the Prince was doing it to her!

As she twisted both her nipples thus, she was almost overcome by the sensations. Her breasts were looking wonderful and the sight of them made her feel even more sensual. They jutted out high and proud, and the cleavage between them was deep, as though she was wearing a balconied bra. And, oh, how the nipples longed to be sucked and caressed.

Emma picked up her lipstick and painted the brightened glass over each of her nipples in turn. The effect was extremely stimulating – they now looked like two luscious cherries, just like the nipples of the girls who had been paraded before the Prince had done. Oh, now she wished she had her vibrator or, better still, some of Henry's or Ursula's toys.

One hand slid down between her legs whilst the fingers of the other rolled a nipple. Then, alternatively looking up at the portrait and down at her own breasts in the mirror, she let the fingers of the first find her already moist beauty bud. It was tender and enlarged and she could feel the liquid of desire inside her. She could feel it swelling yet more.

She remembered what the Prince had said about enjoying watching a woman playing with herself. She closed her eyes as she felt the first tingles of her approaching orgasm and imagined that she was standing in front of him. Oh, the excitement! Then, whilst her sensations grew, she remembered with a sudden shiver what he had said about what happened to those girls of his who were caught misbehaving. But he had also said that, how in their desperation, they would still run the risk of being thrashed. Oh yes, she too would run the risk. She too was desperate for relief. And, at any second now . . .

'Stop!' came a high-pitched voice.

Horrified, Emma opened her eyes. My God! There, standing in the doorway and watching her reflection in the mirror, was Ali Efendi, his cane of office in his hand and his eyes blazing with anger.

'So you ready now, eh?'

'Ready for what?' asked Emma falteringly, her eyes on the long whippy cane as, blushing, she took her hand away from her beauty bud and shame-facedly adjusted her caftan. She felt just like a naughty little girl, caught stealing sweets. Surely he didn't mean that he was going to beat her for misbehaving? She was the Prince's guest staying in the guest house, not one of his harem concubines – at least not yet.

The big overseer smiled condescendingly, like a man talking to a little child. 'Ready for what you really want,' he said slowly, in broken English. 'To go into harem. To offer yourself at selection parade for my

Master's pleasure. That what you really want, no? Well? Well?'

Emma gasped. How could he have guessed? But now that he knew the truth about her feelings and desires, there was no point in her lying to him about them. 'Yes,' she mumbled. She was still weak from her arousal, from being interrupted just as she was on the point of . . .

As soon as Ali Efendi registered her affirmation, he sprang into action, coming up behind her, and seizing her wrists in his strong grip. She heard a rattle of chains and then found that her hands were cuffed behind her back.

Ali Efendi now came round and faced her. Then, deliberately, he slowly reached forward and slapped her face. 'You being unfaithful to Prince. You disgusting girl,' he said, contemptuously. 'I report you to Master. You get cane. Soon!'

Emma opened her mouth in horror. What was it that the Prince had said was the standard punishment for infidelity? Ten strokes! But she was not one of his harem of concubines, she was staying in the guest house, as an honoured guest. Or was she?

'Oh no!' Emma cried, trying to free her hands. But it was too late. The chains held her helpless.

Ignoring her struggles, Ali Efendi called to one of Filipino maids, who promptly came running into the room. He gave her an order. She ran off out of the room. Then Emma saw that Ali Efendi was now holding a shiny collar in his hand – just like the ones she had seen the women in the harem wearing.

'No, please –' she started to say.

'Silence!' He slapped her face again. 'In harem all women wear collar. You now only speak if spoken to! Other women warned they not allowed to speak to you.'

Her cheeks smarting from his blows, Emma remembered what the Prince had said about his women not being allowed to speak to visitors to the harem. She also remembered what he had said about giving Ali Efendi a free hand to do what he liked in the harem provided his methods made the women ever loving and eager to perform. Was she, too, now utterly in the overseer's hands?

She felt the collar being fitted around her neck. Then she heard the click as it was closed. She gave a little sob, but was not certain whether it was of despair, or of excitement.

The maid returned carrying a long, black, all-enveloping shroud that covered Emma from head to foot. In front of her eyes was a small lace grille. She longed to tear it off but with her hands fastened behind her back was quite unable to do so.

'Follow me!' Ali Efendi ordered.

'But my clothes, my things, my passport, my credit cards, my . . .' cried Emma from behind her shroud.

'They stay here. Not allowed in harem. Now, no more talking. And remember you not talk to other women. Now follow me!'

He led the way out of the guest house, across the spacious palace grounds. Through the lace grille Emma saw that they were passing a group of European men, businessmen in well-cut tropical suits, chatting to some men in traditional white robes, as they made their way back from the main entrance to the palace. They ignored her completely. She was just some local woman being escorted by a black servant. Emma was tempted to cry out to them, but the frightening Ali Efendi gripped her elbow warningly.

'Silence!' he said in a low tone. Veiled as she was by her shroud, no one would ever have guessed that a pretty Irish girl – a married woman, a fellow European – was being taken into the harem.

Waddling, he led her towards a surprisingly high wall. This must be the harem wall, Emma realised. It was far too high to be climbed and on the top she saw what

230

appeared to be electric cables. Goodness, was it electrified? To stop the women from escaping?

Set in the wall was a small door, reinforced by iron bars. The wall was guarded by several men armed with sub-machine guns. They pointed the muzzles at her and then grinned at Ali Efendi, apparently calling out pointed and coarse remarks in Arabic, before, at his request, ponderously unlocking the door.

Were they, Emma wondered, used to seeing women, heavily veiled women, being taken through this door, to be locked up in the Prince's harem? Was it, indeed, the only door from the harem into the outside world? Was that why its hinges sounded so rusty – because the women were so rarely allowed out? She heard the door slam shut behind her. How long, she wondered with a little shudder, would it be before it was opened for her to leave?

Ali Efendi reached up and inserted a small key through a little slit at the back of the shroud behind her head and into the little box at the back of her collar. Then he turned it. He must be switching it on, she realised, remembering how Ursula's rather similar collar had worked. Sure enough, she felt a tingling in her neck that eased as the Prince's chief black eunuch led her away from the wall.

The collar would, she realised, stop her from approaching the wall. The Prince certainly took strict precautions to prevent his women escaping from his harem. Was he nervous about the scandal that might ensue if the world press learned of his two Polish girls, or of the mother and daughter, or of ... herself?

Then she gasped as she looked about her.

29

Emma's First Taste of Harem Life

Emma was standing in a pretty formal garden with little gravel paths that twisted to and fro under the shade of palm trees and between beds of exotic flowers. Under a large awning, she saw a blue, circular swimming pool. A dozen beautiful women were standing in the water, under the shade of the awning, laughingly playing with two large rubber balls. They were naked, their bodies strangely white as if they were never allowed to be exposed to the sun. Amongst them, playing happily like little girls, Emma recognised the Polish twins and the mother and daughter.

Carefully watching the women stood young Abdul, and Emma noticed that he was again holding his short-handled black whip. Looking up, Emma saw a latticed window overlooking the pool. Was this so that the Prince could watch, unseen, as his women played in the water? His morning business meeting over, was he now watching them? Might he be watching her own arrival in his harem?

There was a sudden hush as the women saw Ali Efendi and the shrouded figure of Emma approaching. They stopped playing with the balls and stood still and silent, with their hands at their sides – just as she had seen them do when Ali Efendi had entered the harem during her supper with the Prince. Their scarlet-tipped breasts were rising and falling from the exertion of their play. They were all looking curiously, and rather jealously, at Emma. A new girl!

Emma looked at her new companions. She remembered what the Prince had said about his women being kept on the tightest of reins, never seeing another man or knowing about what was going on outside the harem. She looked at the high walls that completely hid all signs of the outside world.

In his strangely high-pitched voice, Abdul called out something in Arabic to his superior, as if reporting that all was well. Emma saw that Ali Efendi was counting the women. Then, apparently satisfied that they were all there together, he nodded to Abdul. Goodness, Emma thought, did the women all have to be together all the time? Were they constantly being counted by the two black eunuchs, like schoolgirls out for a walk? She remembered what the Prince had said about the black eunuchs not allowing any of the girls to be alone, or two to be alone together.

Emma was led away from the pool and through an iron-barred French window. She recognised the same large harem room into which she had looked with the Prince. It was cool and evidently air-conditioned like the rest of the palace. She looked around and saw a large, innocuous-looking mirror. Was that the one-way mirror in the Prince's own apartment? Was he watching her through it now? Looking around, she saw other similar mirrors. Were they to enable the Prince to look into his harem from different rooms in the palace?

Ali Efendi took her into one of the alcoves off the main room that she had previously noticed. It was the one fitted out as a hairdressing and beauty salon, and standing in it, apparently waiting for her, was the young black eunuch, Hazud, who had come to do her hair in the guest house.

The two eunuchs took off her black shroud. She was now dressed in only a simple caftan. Her wrists were still handcuffed behind her back. Ignoring her protests, he now began to slip the caftan down over her shoulders to

233

her waist. He laughed when he saw her amateurishly-painted nipples. Then he unlocked the handcuffs behind her back, purely to allow him to remove the caftan, and then fastened them again. Emma was now standing in front of him, stark naked except for her shiny metal collar. She blushed with shame – oh, she longed to cover her intimacies and breasts with her hands.

Ali Efendi gestured to Hazud to hold Emma still and then sat down in front of her. He nodded approvingly as he looked her body up and down. Then, to her horror, he reached forward and ran the back of his hand over her mound, on which the hairs were yet again beginning to grow again. She blushed again as he called out some instructions in Arabic to Hazud and then, even worse, parted her beauty lips and felt them up and down. He called out some more instructions and then rose to his feet and left the alcove.

'Prince very strict about hairs,' explained young Hazud with a smile. 'He find one little hair and girl gets beaten. So now we make sure, eh?'

Dumbly, Emma nodded. What else could she do? Hazud pointed to a couch.

'More comfortable for you, if I take off handcuffs,' he said. 'You promise not to try to run away?' Emma remembered the walls, the small guarded door and the activation of her collar. Where on earth was there to run away to? She nodded.

Hazud unfastened the handcuffs. Emma rubbed her wrists in relief and lay down on the couch. She could see Hazud preparing something hot and sticky. Memories of Sabhu doing much the same thing flooded in. Would she never get away from being controlled and dominated? But, then again, she had to ask herself, did she really want to?

Minutes later, the alcove rang to her cries as Hazud expertly tore off the hot wax, leaving Emma's mound as bald and smooth, once again, as an egg. 'That's better,' he laughed. 'You've got to be perfect for your public thrashing in the harem.'

'Oh no!' Emma cried. She had forgotten about that. What a fool she had been to play with herself – even if it was in the guest house.

'Oh, it's not too bad. Only ten strokes of the cane. And Ali Efendi will want the marks to go before too long, or the Prince might be angry.'

Emma did not know what to say, as Hazud then started, delicately and carefully, to paint her nipples and beauty lips with the same glistening waterproof substance that she had seen on the other women. Then, he traced the Prince's crest in henna on her mound and sprayed a waterproof lacquer over it. Next, he let down her hair and brushed it so that it hung down her back, and then, finally, he made up her eyes and face even more heavily and elaborately than he had done before. Glancing in the mirror, Emma again saw an erotically painted Eastern houri, and liked the effect.

Just then, Ali Efendi came back, his cane gripped ominously in one hand. Carefully, he inspected Hazud's handiwork, before nodding his approval. 'Raise hips!' he ordered brusquely.

Emma was obliged to part her legs and bend her knees, and then to raise her body off the couch so that her weight was now supported by her feet and her shoulders. Then Ali Efendi bent down over her, and she realised, blushing, that she was wide open to his inspection. Biting her lips with embarrassment, she glanced around the room, and noticed yet another large mirror set high up in the wall. My God! Was the Prince watching whilst his chief overseer checked her body for him?

She gave a little jump as he found her beauty bud, and was horrified to find herself beginning to respond to his touch. Then she felt his fingers exploring inside her intimacies. Was he checking that she was worthy of the

Prince's attentions? She remembered the list he had presented to the Prince. Would she now be on it? She wondered what Arabic remarks would be written against her name.

Ali Efendi straightened up. He gestured to Emma to get up from the couch. 'Come!' he said, giving her a sharp tap on her bottom with his cane. 'Run to swimming pool. Run!'

Again the cane came down, this time harder. With a little cry Emma sped off, stark naked, across the big harem room and out to the pool. The women, again playing with the large balls, glanced up at her as she stood nervously on the edge. She saw Ali Efendi coming towards her, his cane raised.

'Get in!' he shouted.

Hurriedly, Emma jumped in. The water was lovely and warm and came up to just below her naked breasts. She stood amongst the other women. Ali Efendi called out something to young Abdul and raised one finger. Was he telling him that the number of women, that he would repeatedly have to count, had been increased by one? Was she now just another of the Prince's concubines?

'Catch!' called the pretty Italian daughter, throwing one of the balls to her. Emma caught it clumsily, and was surprised to find that it was rather heavy. Raising her arms over her head, she passed on it to the girl's smiling mother. It was quite an effort and she could feel her breasts tautening as she strained to throw it. Did the eunuchs make the women play with the large, heavy balls every day not merely because they liked treating grown-up women like schoolgirls, but also to keep their breasts firm?

For the next ten minutes, Emma joined in the game, laughing and giggling like the others as they alternatively caught and dropped the heavy balls, and threw them to their companions. She longed to speak to them, but she noticed that none of the other women were talking to each other as they played. Was talking forbidden, or did they just not have a common language? She saw that Abdul, fingering his black whip in a frightening way, was watching her. She remembered Ali Efendi's warning to her not to talk to the other women. She kept quiet.

Suddenly Abdul cracked his whip. He called out something in Arabic and then in English: 'Swim!' The women immediately pushed the balls to one side of the pool, and started to swim around in the shallow water, one behind the other, using breast strokes only. Once again, Emma wondered as she dutifully swam round and round the pool, was this to keep their breasts firm?

Again the boy's whip cracked. He shouted something in Arabic. How humiliating, Emma thought, being controlled by a mere boy. 'Out!' he called in English. 'Run to bathroom!'

The women all rushed to get out of the pool and, still stark naked, ran into another alcove in the big harem room. Swept along by them, and still dripping water on to the tiled floor, Emma found herself in a large bathroom. There was a line of some ten showers along one wall and, along the other, a line of ten Turkish-style loos, each with a little tap beside it.

All of the women were hastily lining up, back to back, in two lines, one of which faced the showers and the other the loos. They were standing to attention, their legs together, their heels touching, their heads up and their hands clasped behind their necks. Then the two Polish girls grabbed Emma by the wrists and pulled her into line between them. She was now facing the showers.

Emma could feel her bottom touching the equally naked bottom of one of the women in the line behind her. It was Helga, the German girl whom the Prince said he had found in a nightclub in Hamburg. How exciting! She was about to put her hand back to stroke it when the Polish girls urgently gestured to her to clasp her hands behind her neck like all the others were doing. Were the girls forbidden to touch each other? she wondered. Or even themselves? Was that why they had to stand with their hands raised and clasped, so that the watching Abdul could see that nothing untoward was going on? Oh, how shame-making!

The Polish girls nodded up towards yet another mirror set high up in the wall. Emma gasped. Did the Prince watch his women even in the bathroom? Might he be watching right now?

The women stood quite still and kept completely silent, each one looking straight ahead of her whilst the water from the swimming pool dripped down from her naked body, and the sodden wet hair hanging down her back, on to the tiled floor. Goodness, thought Emma, discipline seems strict here.

There was a long pause. Suddenly Emma sensed one of Helga's hands being slowly and surreptitiously unclasped from behind her neck, and was then astonished to feel it being slid down her back and in between the cheeks of her bottom. She gave a little gasp and, as she felt it probing excitingly between her legs, she gently parted them. The fingers started to probe more deeply.

'Twelve strokes!' came a whisper, in a German accent. Emma gave a little shiver of fear.

Then, suddenly, the hand was withdrawn. Out of the corner of her eye, she saw Abdul slowly coming towards the entrance to the alcove. Clearly, whilst the women were expected to move at a run in the harem, the eunuchs could just take their time and stroll along at their own pace. For a moment, Abdul stood in the doorway and counted the women, and then he slowly walked down first one line and then the other. It was, thought Emma, just like a general inspecting a guard of honour – except that the guard was composed of unarmed naked women, and the general was a young black eunuch.

When Abdul came to Emma, he stopped. Had this

238

mere lad seen what Helga had been doing? Would he notice Emma's state of arousal? Oh, how humiliating! Terrified, she held her breath. With the stock of his black whip, Abdul tilted her chin higher up, and then slowly looked her up and down. Reaching forward he silently lifted a breast as if weighing it, then let it go and moved on down the line.

The boy stood back. Slowly he pulled out of his robe a whistle hanging from a lanyard around his neck. He blew on it once, loudly, and, out of the corner of her eye, Emma saw the row of women behind her running towards the line of Turkish-style loos. She was about to turn around to see what was happening, when she noticed that the women in her own line were still looking straight ahead, and so she did not dare to move a muscle.

Suddenly, there came a double blast of the whistle, and the Polish girl gave her a push towards the line of showers. Emma found herself running across the bathroom towards them with the rest of her line. She saw that the women all turned on their showers and then stood under them, their hands once again clasped behind their necks.

She also saw that facing her across the bathroom was the other line of women. They were now squatting over the Turkish-style loos, their hands also still clasped behind their necks, their faces strained and their eyes also fixed straight ahead. She saw Abdul strolling, whip in hand, up and down the line, as if checking the women's readiness.

He then stood back and gave a double blast on his whistle. Its significance was, Emma realised, only too humiliatingly obvious – and it was immediately obeyed. Had Sabhu, she wondered, got some of his ideas from a harem – or did this sort of thing just come naturally whenever a man was in charge of subjugated women?

Then she saw Abdul, his whip still in his hand,

walking again up and down the line of blushing women. Once again he blew his whistle, and the women lowered their hands, turned on the little taps and washed themselves. Then, in obedience to yet another blast of the whistle they raised themselves into a standing position, their feet still on the footrests of the Turkish loos and, looking straight ahead, once again clasped their hands behind their neck.

Apparently satisfied, Abdul now came over to Emma and the rest of her line of women, all of whom were standing underneath their showers. He blew his whistle and Emma saw all the women parting their legs and bending their knees. The Polish girl gestured to her to follow suit. Then Abdul took a piece of soap and began to wash each woman in turn all over her body and down in between her parted legs, whilst they stood motionless, their hands still clasped behind their necks.

Emma's eyes almost started from her head when he reached her and began to rub the slippery bar of soap against her now swelling beauty bud. And, when he moved on to the next woman, oh, how she longed to reach down and give herself relief. She had to clench her hands desperately to stop herself. Oh what a clever and experienced swine of a young man this Abdul was! Was it the deliberate policy of the eunuchs to arouse the women in their charge, and yet keep them frustrated, so that they would be all the more eager to catch the Prince's eye? Certainly, she would now do anything – absolutely anything – to feel the Prince's hands on her body.

Abdul had now almost finished washing Emma's line of women. Would it soon be their turn to run over and exchange places with the other line of women, and to have to spend a penny under Abdul's supervision?

Oh, how shame-making it all was! Presumably, however, it was intended to remind these otherwise vivacious and independent-minded women of the extent

240

of the authority of the Prince's black eunuchs – and of how they were subject to their control and supervision even in their most intimate moments.

It also seemed to Emma to be a very slow and drawn-out process, but then, she thought, presumably there was plenty of time in the harem. What else could the women usefully do when not pleasing the Prince or parading in front of him?

Had the Prince invited her into his harem, Emma wondered, just to have her disciplined in this way, and perhaps – she blushed at the thought – in front of him, whilst he watched unseen? Certainly, she now eyed the Prince's cunning overseers with a new-found respect. No wonder he supported them so strongly against his women. What was the standard punishment for being reported to the Prince for impudence or dumb insolence – even towards Abdul? Twelve strokes of the cane!

No wonder, she was thinking, these women were all so obedient, when suddenly there came the harsh jangling of a bell, like a fire bell. The effect on the two lines of docile naked women was electric. They all stood on their toes, looking at young Abdul as if they were waiting to be released. Released to do what?

The bell stopped ringing. There was a long pause. Then, suddenly, Abdul clapped his hands and nodded. The women all hurried to the door in the bathroom alcove, carrying Emma along with them in the rush.

30

Punished, Chosen and Prepared

As she ran into the main room of the harem, Emma saw that a red light was flashing over the big mirror on the wall – the one that she had presumed must the one-way mirror through which she had seen into the harem from the Prince's suite.

There was utter pandemonium amongst the women. Some rushed into an alcove containing a line of numbered cupboards from which they each retrieved a beautifully embroidered caftan. Others rushed into the hairdressing alcove and, under the supervision of a grinning Hazud, began to brush their long hair, and to paint their eyes and lips.

Emma was wondering what to do when she noticed Ali Efendi coming towards her holding a little pair of red chiffon harem trousers and a matching red bolero made of a stiffer material.

'Quickly, put these on,' he ordered, 'and then go and make yourself beautiful for Prince's punishment parade.'

Punishment parade? Who was going to being punished? she wondered. Then she remembered what the Prince had said about girls caught being 'unfaithful' being given ten strokes of the cane in front of the one-way mirror whilst the other women looked on. Was that why they were all so desperately trying to make themselves look beautiful? Taking the chance to try to look irresistible in the hope of catching their Master's eye as he watched another one of them being thrashed? Goodness! But this was also a chance for her to catch the Prince's eye too.

Quickly, she ran into the hairdressing alcove, and put on the skimpy harem outfit. To her embarrassment the trousers were cut away in between her legs at the front leaving her painted mound and beauty lips blatantly exposed. Similarly, the cut of the stiff bolero left her bare, painted nipples peeking provocatively around the edges. She saw that, as usual, the Prince's crest was embroidered on the right hand side of the bolero.

Again, there came a sudden harsh ringing of the loud bell. With little cries of despair, the women abandoned touching up their eyes and faces and ran into the main room. They formed a perfect graduated line across the middle of the room, all facing the mirror, with the tallest girl on the right and the shortest on the left. Each knew her place. Young Abdul pushed Emma into the line next to the beautiful Italian mother. Then he stood back and made her change places with the woman's daughter. Evidently, Emma, too, was now perfectly positioned.

Emma saw that, in front of the larger mirror, a sort of wooden vaulting horse had been been placed. It was mounted on a swivelling platform and had a leather pad on its top surface. It was fitted with rings at the bottom of each of its legs, as though for holding on to. How odd, she thought, innocently, and also wondered why Ali Efendi had dressed her differently to the other women in their long caftans.

Suddenly, the women all stood up straight as the sinister figure of Ali Efendi, his face glistening, approached them. As usual he was carrying his long thin whippy cane. He walked down behind the line of women. Suddenly, Emma felt his hand on her bottom. He stroked it through the thin material of her harem trousers, as if assessing – what, exactly? Surely not its ability to stand up to a thrashing? My God! Was she the

243

one who was going to be punished? For being caught playing with herself by this utter brute? Was that why she was dressed differently? Oh my God!

The large figure of Ali Efendi came to the front of the line. As usual, he counted the women. Then he turned to the mirror and made a gesture, as if presenting the women to their Master.

Then he turned back to them again and, with his finger, silently beckoned Emma forward. Terrified, she obeyed him. With his cane, he pointed to the wooden horse. With her heart in her mouth, she bent over it. Still maintaining his silence, the black eunuch then pointed to the two rings at the base of the legs beneath her head. Obediently, she gripped them, so that her buttocks rose up, and her knees bent slightly. She felt Ali Efendi adjusting the position of her bottom, and, at the same, felt herself becoming wet – as she so shame-makingly always did when she was about to be beaten.

Ali Efendi stepped back and swivelled the platform around so that her bottom was towards the mirror. Then he pulled down her thin little harem trousers, and parted the cheeks of her buttocks as if to show her now soaking wet beauty lips to the Prince, who was no doubt seated comfortably on the other side of the mirror. Oh how shameful! And in front of all these other women, too.

Then he turned the horse around again, so that she was now facing the mirror itself. Was the Prince really watching? she wondered. She gave a little smile towards it, a smile that broke into a scream as Ali Efendi brought his whippy cane down across her bare bottom. It felt like a line of fire had streaked across it. She let go of the rings and her face contorted with the pain of the blow. She was about to straighten up and rub her aching bottom, when the strong fat eunuch gripped her neck and pushed her down over the horse again.

'You not move!' he warned. Desperately, she bit her

lips and gripped the rings again. The Prince, she realised, would be watching her face as she absorbed the pain.

She saw Ali Efendi step back and raise his cane. A second later, and then again a few more seconds later, her screams echoed around the harem room, making the watching women shiver nervously. There but for the Grace of God go I, each of them was thinking, just as she was intended to do.

Then, instead of pushing Emma down across the wooden horse, Ali Efendi pulled her up by her hair and thrust her down on to the shiny marble display area in front of the mirror.

'You disgusting girl!' he cried. 'You tell Master you ashamed of being unfaithful. Go on – speak!'

'Master,' cried Emma, terrified and crawling on her knees in front of the mirror, but unsure as to exactly what she should say. Everything had happened so quickly – and so painfully. 'Master, I'm so sorry.'

'Sorry for what?' cried Ali Efendi angrily, raising his cane. 'You tell Master!'

'For being a naughty girl. For being unfaithful to my Master.'

'You tell Master whether you do it again,' ordered the stern chief eunuch.

'No, Master, no,' cried Emma fervently, and, with her bottom still on fire, she really meant it. 'I promise I'll never do it again. I promise!'

Ali Efendi grunted and then, grasping her once again by her hair, thrust her back over the wooden horse. 'Bend over for next three strokes!'

Obediently, Emma bent down and gripped the rings. Three more strokes! Would that be all? Oh, please God, make it only three more. She could feel herself becoming more and more aroused at the idea of being beaten in front of the Prince, but it was still jolly painful.

Emma's desperate prayer was not to be answered. It

was the full ten strokes that Ali Efendi applied to her soft little rear. The next three were given with her naked bottom facing towards the mirror so that the Prince could enjoy watching each stroke as it was administered. They were then followed by another little scene which again saw Emma grovelling on the floor in front of the mirror and assuring the Prince that she would not be unfaithful to him ever again.

Then came the final four strokes with the wooden horse turned sideways on to the mirror, so that the Prince could enjoy watching her jump, and desperately grip the rings, with each stroke. But, Emma realised, the strokes were no longer being applied very hard. Was the terrifying Ali Efendi now holding back so that she could shortly give more pleasure to the Prince?

Suddenly, it was all over. Rubbing her bottom, and pulling up her harem trousers, Emma tottered back to her position in the line of silent women. Then, suddenly, there came the ringing of a telephone. The women all held their breath as Ali Efendi waddled slowly over to a corner of the room and picked it up.

Emma saw him nod. She remembered how, after the highly erotic selection parade, the Prince had used an internal telephone to give his chief overseer instructions regarding the women he wanted for his bed that night. She also remembered how angry and jealous she had been. Was he now doing the same following a punishment parade? Had that, too, been an erotic and arousing sight for the Prince? But would she be the one to benefit from the pain and humiliation she had suffered?

'You!' called Ali Efendi. 'Step forward!'

Nervously, Emma did so. What now?

'You lucky girl,' he said. 'Master want you now – at once!' He turned to the line of jealously watching women. 'Alone!'

There was a murmur of disappointment along the

line. They had tried so hard to make themselves beautiful and to catch the Prince's eye, and now he had chosen this new girl, this outsider who wasn't even a proper concubine and who had had to be beaten for playing with herself. It was not fair.

'Beds!' ordered Ali Efendi, and the women all ran off to the dormitory with its line of little cot beds. As always when the Prince was enjoying himself with a woman or women, those not chosen would have, frustratingly, to lie on their beds in silence under the supervision of Abdul, and to look up at a picture of the Prince. To heighten the effect a red light would come on beneath the portrait, whilst the Prince was in his bedroom, signifying that he was otherwise engaged.

Lying there in silence, each woman would be jealously imagining just what was going on in the Prince's bedroom. Each would be wishing so much that it had been she who had been chosen, and each would be scheming to make sure that, next time, she was indeed selected.

Meanwhile, a half-naked Emma, the stripes of her thrashing gleaming through her transparent trousers, was led by Ali Efendi up a little spiral staircase in the corner of the room to a large door with an electronic lock controlled by a pad of numbered push-buttons. He pressed the required combination and the door swung open.

Emma found herself in a large darkened bedroom. It was dominated by a huge bed covered in a black satin sheet. On one wall was the inevitable one-way mirror, this time looking down into the dormitory where the other women were lying frustrated on their beds. On the facing wall heavy curtains covered a window.

Lying on the black satin sheet was a large silken bolster. With his cane, Ali Efendi motioned to her to get up on to the bed and to lie on her back with the bolster raising her thighs high in the air. She felt him chain her ankles wide apart and then fasten her wrists to more chains at the head of the bed. She was now stretched back and her body formed an arc with her beauty lips, exposed by the cutaway in the trousers, at its highest point.

Then he slipped a strange-looking black leather head collar on to her. Attached to a wide leather strap that fastened at the back of her neck, was a rubber ball which filled her mouth. To keep this gag firmly in place, it was secured to more straps, ran up over her crown and down under her chin where they were tightly fastened.

Ali Efendi stood up and looked down at the silent, helpless creature lying on the bed, positioned ready to be taken. She made an erotic sight. He would much have preferred to have had the time to break her in, slowly and properly, in the harem so that, finally, crawling to the foot of the bed, she would have offered herself to her Master. But time did not permit this and the Master, aroused by seeing her being thrashed in the harem, had wanted her here and now.

As usual, he had left the details to Ali Efendi, who had now ensured that, whilst again making for an arousing sight, she would not be able to struggle whilst the Prince took her, and certainly not to scratch or bite, nor curse or protest.

He reached down and parted the helplessly proffered beauty lips, and smiled as he felt the moistness of her arousal. Then, taking a little pot from a pocket in his gown, he rubbed a little scented grease up inside her – it would give the Prince greater pleasure.

He laughed as he saw Emma's eyes almost starting from her head and heard little moans coming from behind the gag. Finally, he placed a small dog whip on the bed beside her for the Prince's use, and then turned and left the room, closing the electronically-locked door behind him.

This was not at all the romantic seduction scene Emma had imagined. But, even so, she could feel her excitement mounting as she lay there still and silent in the half darkness.

Suddenly she heard footsteps approaching the chamber.

31

The Prince's Plaything

With his two white eunuch pageboys standing dutifully
on either side of him, Prince Faisal looked down on the
arousing sight of the skimpily clad Emma, gagged and
chained back over the large bolster.

He could feel his manhood stirring beneath his heavily embroidered robe. It was all that he was wearing for,
following the erotic spectacle of Emma's punishment
and his decision to send for her now, the pageboys had
helped him to undress and shower.

The girl's white body, only partially covered by her
diaphanous harem outfit, contrasted pleasingly with the
jet-black satin sheet on which she was so delightfully
displayed. It was a contrast made all the more stark by
the way in which her long, soft, honey-coloured hair lay
spread around her on the shiny sheet.

The Prince glanced at the two pageboys standing with
an innocent air in attendance on him, long ostrich
feathers in their hands. He laughed at the cruel thought
that they would not be feeling any arousal.

Emma's carefully painted, and well displayed, beauty
lips looked entrancingly inviting. Except for the quick
glimpse he had had of them from behind, whilst watching Emma being thrashed by Ali Efendi a few minutes
earlier, it was the first time he had seen them – and he
found that he approved of what he saw.

Yes, he thought, this creature could well serve as a
suitable and socially acceptable companion during his

periodical visits to England to see how his racehorses were performing. Used to indulging himself freely with his harem of gorgeous incarcerated European women whilst in Arabia, he missed, when in England, the services of a submissive female.

His position, and the risk of scandal, had prevented him from using call girls or from chasing the wives or girlfriends of other men. He needed someone from the right social set, who would be undemanding, and yet who could be be available whenever she was required. This beautiful and vivacious young woman, with her clear liking for strong and dominant men, and a complaisant husband, might well, with her Irish racing background, provide just the combination of discreet availability and submissiveness that he demanded from a woman.

Bringing her here to his palace had been a necessary part of his plan. His intention had been to frighten her, even to degrade her, and yet to make her both thrilled by it all and besotted with him. And he had certainly succeeded on those counts. He had also had to bear in mind that, while she might prove to be completely submissive in this strange foreign environment, she might nevertheless consider herself to be a free woman when in England and behave accordingly. He had to make sure she realised that he was not a man to be trifled with – and for that she had had to be subjected to a little of the – how should he put it? – care with which, on his behalf, Ali Efendi treated his women.

She had had to see something of his harem and to experience a little of the discipline with which it was run. Ali Efendi had cleverly arranged this without running the risk of allowing her the opportunity to talk to any of his European concubines.

Certainly having her thrashed by Ali Efendi, in front of him and of his other women, had clearly been psychologically important in imposing his authority on her. It had been an experience that she would not forget in a hurry! The pain might soon wear off, but not the memory – nor, more importantly, the fear of being summoned, or even brought, back here for a repetition.

It had all been a test which so far she had come through well, but now came the most crucial test of all. How much pleasure would he actually derive from her luscious, helpless body?

She had chosen to join his harem and had therefore, by implication, agreed to submit, completely and utterly to his will, a fact of which she was well aware. What a shrewd and understanding servant Ali Efendi was. He had seen to it that Emma would not now be able to change her mind about being offered for his pleasure. Bound and gagged, she would be unable to fight him off, or beg him to release her. Ultimately, of course, she had chosen for this to happen, but now she was being absolved of all reponsibility for her actions and responses.

Her eyes were fixed on him, either from terror, or desire – or, more likely as his experience of European women had taught him, through a mixture of both. He turned and nodded to one of the pages who obediently went round to the other side of the bed and began to stroke Emma's gleaming wet beauty lips gently with his long ostrich feather.

Oh the shame, thought Emma, of being aroused in front of the Prince by this young man. She tried to fight it, but his technique was far too accomplished, and soon the Prince was able to see that her eyes were almost starting from her head, as she strained and wriggled against her chains, helpless to prevent herself from becoming increasingly aroused. Little moans were coming from behind the broad black leather gag strapped over her mouth.

The Prince now gestured to the other pageboy who joined his companion on the other side of the bed and

then, pulling Emma's stiff bolero slightly open, began to
tickle her nipples with his long feather. Again a feeling
of helpless shame swept over Emma. It was one thing to
be aroused by one's lover, but quite another to be
aroused for him by two fresh-faced servants. But once
again, she simply could not help herself and the Prince
smiled as the girl's desperate writhing and muffled cries
redoubled.

Then he waved the pageboy away from the bed.
Emma gave a sudden jump as he lowered his hand and
rubbed a now firm nipple between his fingers. She
jumped again as, parting her beauty lips, he fingered her
hard little beauty bud. Soon she was writhing under his
hands as violently as she had under the pageboys'
ostrich feathers.

Oh, what a delightful little creature she is, thought the
Prince, summoning his pageboys to attend to him.

Silently, they unfastened the front of his robe and
then held it open as he lay down on top of the chained
figure. He could feel his manhood straining as he
gripped the helpless girl round the waist and felt her soft
skin against his own. He looked down at her face and
saw that her eyes were again fixed on his. He was
grateful to Ali Efendi for having had the sense to have
gagged the girl: words at this stage would only have
spoilt the ecstasy. Her nipples looked ripe and tempting
and, when he took first one then, in turn, the other into
his mouth and sucked on them, more little moans of
delight emanated from behind the gag.

Moments later, he was kneeling up between Emma's
chained and outstretched legs. Raised by the large
bolster, her parted thighs were just inches in front of his
powerfully erect manhood. She wanted to cry out as one
of the pageboys reached down and separated her beauty
lips for the Prince, and then the other expertly guided
his Master's stiff manhood between them. The Prince
gave a sudden jerk and was inside her. Once again, he

gripped her waist as she began to buck a little, at first in protest at the eunuch's interference, and then, as he drove slowly in and out, with helpless pleasure.

The Prince then nodded to the pageboys who then swiftly and deftly slipped the gag from Emma's mouth. Quickly, without giving her a chance to say a word, he put his lips to hers. They were soft and yielding. He thrust his tongue into her mouth. It was sweet and enticing.

He raised his head and looked down at her, commandingly. He smiled as he heard her first words. 'Master! Oh Master!'

Then he withdrew from her and the pageboys again held the skirts of his robe apart as he knelt over her face. 'Reach up and lick!' he ordered and seconds later felt a thrill run right through his body as Emma's small wet pointed tongue began to stroke and rub him. Oh, the ecstasy! As he had suspected, this girl was already well trained in the art of giving pleasure. There would be no need for her to take lessons from Ali Efendi.

Again he nodded at the pageboys and they resumed tickling Emma's beauty lips with their feathers, which made her wriggle her tongue even more excitingly.

'Now listen,' he said. 'You're going to be my mistress back in England – waiting to be summoned to give me pleasure. Do you understand?'

'Oh, yes, Master,' she said. 'Oh yes, please!'

With a little grunt of pleasure at having so decisively won her over, the Prince rose up a little higher on his knees.

'Then take this as a sign of your acceptance and submission.' He thrust his manhood into her little mouth. 'Suck it and lick it,' he ordered. 'Worship it humbly and dutifully.'

He thrilled to the sensation of her little tongue running over the tip of his manhood. He thrust past it and exploded. 'Take it!' he breathed. 'Take it all! Swallow your Master's seed, like the obedient little slave girl that you are, that you enjoy being. Take it . . . take it all . . . as a sign of your new servitude.'

Moments later the pageboys unchained Emma and slid the large bolster out from beneath her hips. The Prince lifted her up and held her to him. She was crying with helpless delight. 'Master, Master. I just want to be your helpless slave – forever.'

'And so you shall be, my dear,' he laughed. 'But I think that you being the hot little number you are I shall have to take precautions so that you do not go offering yourself all over London to other men – or women.'

'You mean you're going to keep me locked into a chastity belt when you're away?' murmured Emma excitedly.

Well, she's certainly accepted her new role, thought the Prince. It was time to take certain steps. 'Not quite,' he laughed. 'But you'll soon see!'

'Oh, anything,' breathed Emma. 'Whatever it takes.'

At this, one of the pageboys handed her a glass of something cool and refreshing. Eagerly she drank it and within seconds she was fast asleep.

Light was streaming through the windows when Emma awoke. Quickly she pulled the bedclothes over herself. Memories, wonderful memories, slowly came back to her. Oh, the Prince! What a man he was. Oh, the excitement he had caused her. She blushed with shame as she remembered how he had used his pageboys to arouse her, and how they had guided his manhood up inside her. Oh, how could she ever look these boys in the face again?

The fact that she herself had not had any relief did not seem to matter. Her satisfaction had been derived from pleasing him. She remembered his decision to keep her available as his lover in England. Oh, how exciting! Would she be rich and famous? She remembered that he had earlier said that he sometimes took his pageboys with him to Europe. Would he always have them with him in his bedroom when he took her? Oh how awful – but how expert they were!

Was she still in the Prince's bed? Or was she locked up in the harem dormitory? She raised her head above the bedclothes and looked around. To her astonishment, she found that she was back in her room in the guest house.

She glanced at the clock. She must have been asleep for a whole day. She remembered the strange drink. Had she been drugged and brought back here? But why? She saw that she was now wearing her nightdress again – the one with the Prince's crest embroidered over the right breast.

She looked up longingly at the portrait of the Prince on the wall. With a laugh, she remembered the similar one in the harem – and the red flashing light. Jealously, she wondered whether the Prince had enjoyed other women whilst she had been lying fast asleep. His concubines were all so beautiful, so irresistible.

But, she laughed, she was now going to be Number One when the Prince came to England!

Then she noticed a strange feeling in between her legs. She put her hand down – and felt a line of little rings. And there was something else! With a cry of surprise, she pushed back the bedclothes, jumped out of bed and stood in front of the long mirror. Immediately she noticed that the gleaming metal collar had gone. Instead, around her neck were three strands of pearls with a lozenge-shaped diamond clasp. It had two large yellow stones in the centre and she thought that she had never seen anything so beautiful.

Then again came that strange feeling between her legs. She lifted up her nightdress. Yes, gleaming against her hairless beauty lips, and half-hidden by them, was a line of little golden rings. But that was not all, for threaded through them, and kept in place by a tiny padlock that hung between her legs, was a little curved golden bar that was also half-hidden by the lips themselves.

Astonished and now slightly appalled, she looked down and examined them. Ten tiny rings had been threaded through each of her beauty lips, between the front of them, near her mound, and the back. And the long thin curved golden bar had in turn been carefully threaded through each of them, keeping the lips tightly closed. No strange manhood, she realised, could penetrate her now. Nor, she found, could she herself properly reach her little beauty bud.

Panicking, she tried to pull out the little golden bar. But the padlock at the bottom was just too big to pass through the rings. The bar could not be removed. She tried instead to pull it down through the rings, but a wide flat flange at the top of the bar stopped her from doing so. It was also too large to pass through the little rings. The flat flange, too, she saw, was raised so that it covered her beauty bud. It was this that made it almost impossible for her to play with herself.

She tried walking up and down. She hardly felt the rings, provided she took only small, ladylike steps. The pull on her beauty lips, however, made it uncomfortable if she tried to part her legs wide. Yet, she realised, it would not prevent her from spending a penny.

She could not help admiring the ingenuity and unobtrusiveness of it. Was it the Prince's idea – or that clever Ali Efendi's? Or was it just an age-old harem trick?

She saw a note by her bedside. It was from the Prince. *Your plane leaves shortly*, she read. Goodness, was the week really up already? Oh, how sad. She still hadn't seen anything of the country. Was this the Prince's deliberate plan? To keep her hidden away in his palace compound and then to fly her discreetly back to England?

My car will take you to the airport, she read on. *I shall be coming to London in a week's time and my secretary will contact you with instructions as to where to meet me. You are to keep yourself entirely free for me for ten days. He will also give you an advance on the substantial allowance you will now be receiving. I enclose the address and telephone number of a leading Arab doctor in London. He is a friend of mine and has one key to the padlock hanging between your legs. I have another. You may ask him to remove it at any time you wish, but in that case I do not promise to go on paying your allowance. Whilst the padlock is in place, you are my paid servant – a very well paid servant, but with the rights only of a slave. I look forward to continuing our little bedroom scene in a week's time.*

Emma's head was reeling. To be the pampered Mistress of one of the richest men in the world! Oh, how exciting! And, how equally exciting to have her sensuality locked up behind those rings and that gold bar. She put her hand up to touch the pearls around her neck. Would they be the first of many such gifts? Goodness!

Again, she read on.

'*But remember, too, that Ali Efendi also has a copy of the key and that, if necessary, I shall have no hesitation in flying you back here for a little refresher training in obedience.*'

So that was why the Prince had shown her his harem and had had her beaten by his chief black eunuch. To impress upon her his power and authority, so that she would behave properly, even when she was back in England. Well, he had certainly succeeded in that – her bottom was still sore from her thrashing.

Oh yes, by bringing her out here, he had now cleverly subjected her to his power and authority, all right. And that was not all. She also remembered what he had said

258

about Arabs having a long arm and that anyone who opened their mouth about his harem would be sure to regret it. She gave a little shudder of fear. She would certainly never dare mention it to anyone. She was indeed in his power now. How terrifying, but also how exciting. Thank heavens she did not know the identity of any of the women she had seen.

But what should she say to Ursula when she came back to London again? She would explode with rage if she were to learn the truth – or if she ever saw the rings and the bar. And what about Henry? He had been very broad-minded in the past, but what would he say about the Prince? And how was she going to fend off Paddy, now that they were both working for the Prince? Of course, were she to ask the Arab doctor to remove the bar, then she would lose the Prince altogether – and he was so wonderfully dominating, madly exciting in bed, and very rich.

And then there was the problem of John. He was not due back for several months, but after his return she would have to go back to his bed at some time. Would he accept being fobbed off again?

Oh dear, what shall I do, she wondered, as, hastily, she packed.

The same thoughts weighed heavily on her mind as the car taking her to the airport slowly drove past the high walls of the harem. Who would ever have guessed what went on behind those walls?

Then the car turned and passed the front of the palace itself. There standing on the steps was the Prince! Her heart was in her mouth as she saw him smile. Oh, how she longed to fling herself into his arms. She hammered at the darkened window separating her from the chauffeur, to tell him to stop the car. She must say goodbye – or, at least, *au-revoir*. But it was all to no avail. The chauffeur paid no attention and the car drove slowly on, with Emma desperately looking back at the Prince out of the rear window. How sad! But Moslem men, she remembered, do not embrace, or even acknowledge women in public.

Then suddenly the car passed Ali Efendi, his dreaded cane in his hand. Was that terrifying sight, she wondered, intended to be her last memory of the Prince's palace?

On the way back to the airport, and indeed throughout the entire journey back to London, she could feel those little rings. She could think of nothing but the Prince, her new Master, of the key, and of when she going to meet him again.

Oh, how exciting life was, she thought. But also how complicated!

NEXUS NEW BOOKS

To be published in October 2004:

LACING LISBETH
Yolanda Celbridge

Blonde Lisbeth Lache, together with her partner Sabrina Bossi, own a worldwide chain of hedonistic resort hotels. Lisbeth relishes her role as a predatory lesbian boss of innocent secretaries, to Sabrina's secret jealousy.

At Sabrina's suggestion, Lisbeth goes to investigate the possible acquisition of Rum Hole, a secluded, ultra-luxurious pleasure-palace in the Bahamas. Champagne and studs await her, but so does a bizarre heirarchy of man- and maidservants, spanking, and hunting and fishing with girls as quarry. Will Lisbeth escape her predicament? And will she want to?

£6.99   0 352 33912 8

LOVE JUICE
Donna Exeter

This novel charts the career of a fictitious professional dominatrix, but is rooted in reality. Donna thinks of herself as a sexual therapist, and offers love, correction and domination to powerful men in need of relief.

But when the realities of her business close in and a group of gangsters attempt to take it over, Donna finds she must enlist the help of her perverted friends, and pursue an unusual, and erotic, solution.

£6.99   0 352 33913 6

THE BLACK ROOM
Lisette Ashton

The submissive trainees at the Pentagon Agency derive pleasure from even the most demeaning tasks. Their lives are dedicated to sexual servitude; they enjoy pain and humiliation on a daily basis. There is only one punishment they try to avoid: the black room. When private investigator Jo Valentine is assigned to infiltrate the Pentagon Agency, she is prepared to do anything to get results – but nothing can prepare her for what lies in the black room. The more she discovers about the agency, the more she learns of her passion for dark and bizarre sexual games that go beyond anything she has experienced before.

£6.99   0 352 33914 4

If you would like more information about Nexus titles, please visit our website at www.nexus-books.co.uk, or send a stamped addressed envelope to:

  Nexus, Thames Wharf Studios,
  Rainville Road, London W6 9HA